A KISS

like

THIS

SARA NEY

Second Edition: April 2017
Library of Congress Cataloging-in-Publication Data
A Kiss Like This
ISBN-13:978-1544944555
ISBN-10: 1544944551

Thank you, Internet, for providing the inspiration for the dating quotes at the beginning of each chapter. They're all based on *real* conversa-tions, pickup lines, come-ons, and texts between actual people.

For more information about Sara Ney and her books, visit:
https://www.facebook.com/saraneyauthor/

Verity

A KISS
like
THIS

A KISS ON THE
lipa = 😊
- smooch

Suzy

Dedication

Abby

Somewhere out there is a guy who will make you blush for all the right reasons, and for once, you will stare at him for more than 3 seconds before looking away. You're brilliant and clever, and I'm so glad to know you and call you my friend.

This book is for you.

*I*t all started innocently enough on a Friday just like any other, with classes and a coffee run, then straight to strategic planning for the evening ahead.

Now, normally, I'm not the first person to volunteer for a night out, even on the weekends. The simple truth is, I would much rather stay home, rent movies, read a book, and eat snacks on my couch—one hundred percent of the time, hands down, no debate.

However, tonight is different. Tonight, my cousin, Tyler Darlington the Third—when I was younger, I used to call him Tyler Darlington *the Turd*—became an officer of his fraternity, and in his mind, *that* is something to celebrate.

I also want to point out that Tyler becoming an officer of *anything* is kind of a big deal—to both his parents and mine. Believe me when I say, the whole entire Darlington clan is in a *tizzy* over the fact that Tyler has been admitted to a Big 10 school. Not only that, but he's managed not to flunk out of that same Big 10 school or cause any property damage to or burn down his fraternity house.

Naturally, these things alone are cause for celebration (that was sarcasm) and my parental units are practically *forcing* me to attend his celebratory frat party.

Okay, maybe forcing is a strong word, but they did have to promise me a fifty-dollar pre-paid Visa gift card if I went.

To put it bluntly: Tyler is kind of a moron.

And by moron, I mean pothead.

So, despite my usual penchant for staying in on the weekends like a hermit, there is definitely something to be said for the simple act of getting ready to go out with friends that is *more* fun than the actual act of going out.

For example:

1. Cramming multiple young women into *one* bathroom, then crowding around the only mirror in the apartment—unless of course you count the cheap mirror hanging behind your bedroom door, which you do *not*.

2. Borrowing clothes that never seem to look as cute on you as they do on your friend or roommate. Damn her.

3. Getting sprayed/blinded by the hairspray because you were standing too closely behind your friend wielding the can, which we all know is inevitable. Someone always get sprayed in the eyes.

4. Smudging your eyeliner because you get elbowed by your friend every time you lean over the counter to draw a more precise line. We call this irony.

Sounds like funsies, right?

That's because it is…for the most part.

There's always tons of wild laughter, annoyed grumbling, and in the end, everyone looks stunning and ready to take on the town—or in this case, a house party.

Tonight is no exception.

It's a short walk to the fraternity house from our crappy rental house, and even though the air is a tad too chilly for my liking, we chose to walk the short distance rather than drive, despite the heels most of us are wearing.

Having already decided it's going to be an early night, we spend the remainder of the evening huddled together in the corner of my cousin's fraternity house, not because we're wallflowers, or party poopers, or stuck up. No. We're huddled together because the house is dirty and falling apart, and the crowd it draws isn't exactly my "scene".

My scene is the library. A quaint coffee shop with an acoustic guitar player, smelling of rich coffee grounds. The campus study center with its overstuffed couches. My small but tidy bedroom in my off-campus rental.

This crowd…this crowd is collegians on academic probation. Drunks. Potheads. Girls with loose morals and even looser panties.

I brave the party with my friends in the corner I've forced us to occupy, where we laugh, my friends drink, and we lose track of time.

Before I know it, my friends have disappeared and my cousin is at my side, half-baked (as usual) but in protection mode. Tyler actually convinces me to be responsible and *not* to walk home alone in the dark, even though the last place I want to be is here, in this fraternity house, alone without my friends.

Before the party thins and the crowd downstairs disperses, I'm upstairs in Ty's room, door locked, throwing clothes and books off his queen-sized bed, grateful that it's not a twin or a simple mattress on the floor, and flinging myself on top of it in a tired heap.

The one beer my friends Tabitha and Maria persuaded me to drink is the sleep aid I need to close my eyes and shut out the racket below me.

Abby

When it comes to shimmying down a metal gutter pipe, it's probably not a good idea to get much dignity involved. Don't get me wrong, a lot of hard work goes into the task, but in order to be successful, you have to let go of your pride—as in, have none. Of course, that isn't saying much, particularly if you're wearing a skirt—which, thank god, I am not.

I glance back into the bedroom from my spot in the window at a slumbering Tyler Darlington, who is spread out on his queen-sized mattress, snoring peacefully. His unkempt brown hair sticks out in a million places, matted in some spots from tossing and turning, and an unsavory dark puddle of drool wets the area where his gaping mouth and pillow meet.

Ugh, gross. If only the ladies could see this *ladies' man* now…

Before sticking my first booted foot out the second-story window, I nervously twist the gold ring on my right hand and take one last look at Tyler, whose eyes are slowly blinking open. He looks around the room and catches sight of me, resting his chin on his elbow, and watches me with an amused look on his arrogant face.

My stomach twists into a knot.

"Are you sure you don't want to exit out the, oh, I don't know, perfectly good door?" His head jerks toward his sturdy, solid door with perfectly functioning hinges on the opposite side of the room.

"Um, yeah, I think I'll pass. *They* are still out there... waiting. No freaking way am I getting caught up in that... that..." I wave my hand around airily, at a loss for words. "I can't face them. It's humiliating; I couldn't bear it."

I will not go out in that hallway—no matter how badly I have to pee.

I'm too reserved. Most people, especially those who don't know me well, might even call me shy, and I'm sometimes so easily embarrassed, it borders on absurd.

My ears perk up, and I can still hear the chanting from my spot in the narrow window frame, the loud, boisterous voices filling the small space that is my cousin's bedroom. Somewhere within the long corridor, another door opens and closes, setting off a chorus of cheering, laughing, and shouting.

"Those guys are such fucking morons," Tyler says as he rolls his eyes, checking the clock on his nightstand and sitting up straighter to fish for his glasses.

"Yeah, and those morons are your fraternity brothers," I mutter, staring out the window, nervously plotting my best course of action. "You *choose* to live with them. On purpose."

"I'll just stick my head out the door and tell them not to shout at you."

I shake my head vigorously. "And you think they're going to listen to you? Please. Those guys have zero boundaries." I glance down at the gutter, mentally calculating its distance from Tyler's window, estimating it to be approximately three feet away—close enough that I could make it, and, if I can safely grab the awning, I just might be able to drop down without breaking my neck. "Listen, don't think for one second they won't sing that song to me. In fact, they'd have a field day if they knew it was me in here with you."

"Abby, stop being so damn dramatic." Tyler sits up and shrugs into a ratty t-shirt randomly plucked from the ground. "It's just a song. It hardly means anything."

I stare at him, my mouth agape. "Just a song? Ugh, have you heard the lyrics? They're foul. Why any girl with self-respect would purposely set foot in that hall is beyond me. No, I like my chances out here better."

I would rather change my name, appearance, and join the witness protection than walk out into that hallway.

"It beats going out the fucking window." He stands in his boxers and stretches. "Whatever, man, just hurry up. I'm starving and need to take a leak."

I shoot him a few daggers. "Wow. Are you this charming with all the ladies?"

"No. Usually I tell them to grab their shit and get out of my room," he says with a laugh.

Raucous laughter from the hallway fills the room, and someone begins banging on Tyler's door. "Darlington, get your boney ass out here. Two skanks just came out of Ackermann's suite."

My lip curls and I brace myself for the lyrics. Loud singing fills the corridor outside my cousin's room, and I shake my head, giving him the *See? I told you so* look.

The girl was fair who went upstairs with her fav-o-rite KOC.

She knocked around and came back down, and now she takes the walk!

The walk of shame, she's not to blame! Who could resist the KOC?

The walk of shame, she found her fame, and now she takes the walk!

Wow. Aren't they charming?

After the brothers of Kappa Omega Chi are done shouting at what I assume are innocent, albeit slutty collegians, Tyler looks at me and shrugs his shoulders. "What? *We* didn't write it. It's from the movie *Sorority Boys.*"

I hold out one of the hands I had been using to brace myself to stop him from talking. "Please. There's no need to explain, but that was all the motivation I needed. Tell Aunt Monica I say hello."

And with that, I ease myself out his window.

Caleb

If you thought that at seven o'clock in the morning on a Saturday, I would have peace and quiet while sitting outside on the front porch of my house, you would be absolutely correct—on any other Saturday, in fact, except this one.

This isn't just any other Saturday.

Other than the chick trying to shimmy out a second-story window next door, then yeah, it's been a relatively uneventful morning.

Just as I'm about to take the first sip of iced orange juice from the perspiring water bottle in my large hand, a slight movement catches my eye from an upper window of the crumbling piece-of-shit fraternity house next door. My ears perk up immediately, and my head tilts with interest when the first leg emerges. All of my senses are instantly on high alert.

I watch, wide-eyed and mesmerized as a single slim leg slips out of the window at the same time a sheer white curtain billows out into the open air and momentarily wraps itself around the face of the leg's owner. I can hear her spitting at it as she pulls it out of her mouth, slapping it away. Meanwhile, her boot-covered toe begins feeling around blindly in the air to gain footing underneath the windowsill.

My trim torso inches forward on the swing, bottle of orange juiced poised just at the tip of my parched lips. The ice clanks together and a few beads of perspiration fall from the bottle onto my shirt when I jiggle it.

I shake my head in disbelief.

"What the fuck..." I can't stop the curse from escaping, muttering out loud when the second leg appears, straightens, then strains toward the gutter guard. "That crazy bitch is gonna get herself killed."

Still, I remain seated, eyes riveted to what is guaranteed to be an entertaining, albeit dangerous show. Swaying back and forth on the white wooden swing, I can't help but wonder what it is about that place next door that has girls scurrying to escape like panicked rats in a flood, weekend after weekend.

I mean, yes, it's a fraternity house. That in itself automatically draws girls to it—not just on the weekends, sometimes even during the week—but it isn't a house where I'd want my kid hanging out if I were a parent. The house is dirty, inside and out, in disrepair, and looks like a Halloween haunted house 365 days a year. It even has an old, rickety wrought-iron fence in the front yard.

Haunted house, rape house—take your pick.

Not to mention, the guys who live there are slobs. Fat, drunken, pothead slobs. All right, fine…to be fair, maybe I'm generalizing, but it's still definitely not a top-tier frat. Word on campus is if you have breath in your lungs and beer in your gut, you're Kappa material.

The house is everything fathers warn their daughters about, and if you need more proof than that, just take note of the crazy chick trying to escape via the upstairs window.

Yeah, exactly.

I angle my head in thought, mentally calculating the distance from the upstairs window to the concrete ground below. "Shit." There is no way in hell she's going to make it down that pipe without hurting herself, and the last thing the university needs is yet another story in the news about some moron hurting themselves at an off-campus party.

Besides, I'm a decent person—I can't just sit her watch her break her neck.

Sighing loudly to no one, I stand and stretch, set down my orange juice bottle, adjust my ball cap so it's riding down over my eyes, and pull up the hood of my baggy sweatshirt. Arms extended, I crack my knuckles a few times before sticking both hands inside the kangaroo pocket of my hoodie and begrudgingly shuffling down the steps to the side of the house.

It only takes me a few moments to reach the side yard of the common shared driveway, and when I do, my mouth sets into a grim line. Tipping my head back, I immediately receive an eyeful of the girl's denim-clad posterior.

I'm impressed. At this point, she's managed to grab hold of the gutter guard and shimmy one foot onto the metal strap securing the pipe to the siding of the house. Those metal straps, by the way, are flat, two inches wide, and extremely flimsy. Attached with a flimsy nail and flush with the siding, the straps are in no way secure enough for a person to rest their foot on.

Or in this case, their black-heeled boot.

I clear my throat. "Hey, what the fuck are you doing?" My voice comes out harsh and unrelenting. "Do you have a death wish or something?"

Abby

I'm hanging.

I'm hanging, losing my hold, and am probably going to die.

It's a veritable struggle-fest, and I'm in the center of it all. My stupid boot slips precariously from the metal thingy I've been perching it on, and I can hear the definitive creaking sound the gutter is making as it slowly releases itself from the side of the building.

Translation: it's going to fall off, taking *me* along with it.

I tighten my grasp on the metal, one hand still on the windowsill. This does me no good whatsoever because of the awkward positioning of my feet, and with both arms overextended like a Teenage Mutant Ninja Turtle stretch toy, there is no way I can crane my neck to look around for help.

Dear Lord, please forgive me. This was a horrible mistake…although, Lord, I would rather be hanging here than facing the humiliation in the hallway upstairs—no I wouldn't. Yes, I would. Guh! Those boys are terrible. Help! Please send help.

"T-Tyler," I croak desperately in the direction of the open window.

The only response is that damn curtain in his window, wafting up and down, lilting airily from the breeze inside the room.

"Shoot, shoot, shoot," I mutter, anxiety deeply rooting itself into every cell in my body. What the heck made me think this would work? Why didn't my stupid cousin stop me? "Okay, Abby. Think." I bite my lip and squint my eyes shut, but no ideas pop into my brain—a brain that, at one point, I thought was filled with brilliant ideas, until the part where that brain decided it should convince me to dangle from the side of a dirty, dilapidated fraternity house.

"Hey, what the fuck are you doing?" From somewhere below, an angry voice booms up at me. "Do you have a death wish or something?" I loll my head, trying to determine the direction the voice is actually coming from. From my left? From my right?

Oh, thank you. Thank you, God. I knew you were listening.

"Let go of the gutter and I'll catch you," the voice demands.

Um, on second thought…

I shake my head. "Nuh-uh. No. N-no way am I letting go of this gutter. Are you nuts?" My tearful voice is high pitched and frantic with worry.

"Hey, man, I'm not the one dangling from a window, so maybe you shouldn't be arguing with me. Drop to the ground before you fall and get hurt. I'm strong. Promise I'll catch you."

My grip quickly becomes sweaty, and the thin metal gutter guard creaks again, this time shifting under my weight.

I gulp, fighting back the tears burning my eyes.

"Come on, come on, come on, be quick about it. I give you two minutes before the gutter gives out and you land on the concrete, probably splitting your head open," the angry voice charitably points out. "But don't take my word for it—it's just a guess."

"Would you shush? Please," I plead down over my shoulder, polite to the core even as I dangle from the side of a house.

"Okay, it's your funeral," I hear the guy grumble. "Literally."

Suddenly panicky, not wanting my lifeline to walk away, I gasp when the wooden siding creaks again. "Wait!" I shout with a tremble. "Okay, okay. I'm sorry! Just please, tell me what to do."

"All right, calm down. I'm going to come stand underneath you, and when I do, let your hands slide from the window ledge and I'll catch you." I can hear his feet kicking up the wobbly concrete somewhere beneath me.

"Oh, sweet Jesus," I whine. "I can't do this."

I would rather shrivel up and die, then have my dead, lifeless body shrivel up and die again. I cannot do this.

"Yes you can. Stop being a little pansy. Ready? On my count of three, release your hands. Ready?"

No! No! No!

"One…twooo…"

At his count, I squeeze my eyes shut, release my hands from the side of the building, and fall faster than I can blink. I'm plummeting, dropping, landing with a thud. I think I'm tumbling to the ground, but I'm not. I-I'm lying on a huge, hulky, solid, warm-blooded male form.

A solid male form that's now sprawled out on the pavement beneath me, spread eagle and muttering a curse. "What the everloving fuck was that? I said on the count of *three*!"

It takes me a few seconds to acclimate myself, and I lie there on top of this new source of warmth. My head goes down, and with the wind still knocked out of me, I rest my cheek on the stranger's comfy sweatshirt, nuzzling the padded torso without thinking twice.

So, so comfy.

Like a big, comfy bear. Like the big, comfy teddy bears at Costco. Mmmm. Aren't they only fifty dollars? I want one of those.

I hear a heart beating erratically, likely from the traumatic force of being knocked on one's ass, and exhale the breath I didn't realize I was holding.

A low, displeased rumble emits from deep within the stranger's chest.

It's enough to rouse me from my shell-shocked stupor. Lifting my drooping head from the broad, muscular body I'm lying limply on top of, my out-of-focus gaze searches out the face of the guy who could very well have just saved my life.

We lock eyes and I manage to blink.

Sweet Jesus is he scary.

And he's glaring up at me.

Caleb

The girl and I lock eyes, but I finally manage to blink.

"Can you get off me?" I mutter, trying to pull myself up on my elbows—no easy task with this chick bedding down on top of me. She's clearly delirious.

"Can you please get off me," I repeat, giving her a nudge. "No offense, but you're no lightweight."

It's a lie, but I want her off me, like, yesterday. She's getting way too comfortable, feels way too soft and warm and pliant, and I'm beginning not to mind.

"I...*excuse* me. Oh my god." The brunette stumbles over her words, a furious blush reddening her face. I suppress a laugh at how hastily she goes from snuggling on top of me in what's obviously a confused, concussed haze to pushing back on my chest—briefly cutting off my air supply, I might add—and rising to her feet, all within seconds.

She stumbles a bit then rights herself.

"Aren't you going to help me up?" I challenge her with an arched brow, glaring up from under the brim of my hat, a whole catalog of first impressions imprinting themselves on my brain now that I'm getting a look at her.

First of all, she is adorable. Flushed. Embarrassed.

Pretty.

Her thick, dark coffee-colored hair, which had obviously been piled haphazardly on the top of her head at one point, is now in a messy rat's nest. Huge chunks of soft waves have escaped the knot to rest lightly upon her slight shoulders and cascade loosely down her back.

Straight nose. Full mouth with a slightly pouty bottom lip.

Her complexion is clear and radiates a blush, either from her recent fall from the second story, or from being ashamed—probably a bit of both.

Large, expressive blue eyes stare down at me from under perfectly arched eyebrows, and I quickly avoid her scrutiny by glancing up to the window from whence she emerged. For a moment, I'm envious of the Kappa Omega Chi fucktard who just spent the night with her, although quite frankly, she looks far too wholesome to be a quick lay.

Naïve. Innocent. No freaking way could she have been in that house having her brains screwed out all night.

I squash the thought back because facts are facts, and the indisputable proof stares down at me as I continue my appraisal.

Second, she's not short.

Even from down on the ground, I can tell that when I stand, I might tower over her with my six-foot-three frame, but it won't be by much. Her short-sleeved, fitted black t-shirt is tucked into belted skinny jeans, elongating a pair of long, athletic legs. Her tight, dark jeans are neatly tucked into a pair of the tall, shiny equestrian boots all the girls are wearing these days.

She begins tapping the toe of those black boots nervously on the paved driveway, regarding me warily, an internal debate making her mouth turn down in a frown and her perfect eyebrows crease. It's obvious she wants to bolt and leave me lying here in a heap but is too polite to actually *do* it.

I mean, I probably just saved her careless neck, and she damn well knows it.

Taking a deep breath of courage before exhaling, her full pink lips emit a long *pppuh* of air before she cautiously bends toward me with her palm extended.

She's shaking.

I stare blankly at that unsteady hand a few seconds before grasping it, wrapping my large fingers around her slender ones, resisting the urge to squeeze—or pull her back down on top of me.

Her bones are delicate, petite, and feel fragile compared to my rough mammoth palms. I'm overly conscientious of the scraps and callouses marring my battered skin.

The unnamed brunette tugs on my arm, heavy and lifeless, unable to budge me. Biting her quivering lower lip, she yanks at me again before extending a leg and planting her booted heel in the ground to gain better leverage.

She heaves and puffs, inhaling a loud gulp of air, holds it, lets out a out a huff, and eyes me skeptically. "Do you even *need* my help?"

Withholding a grin, I shake her hand off and lift myself to my feet in one easy motion, unassisted. "Nope."

All her timid restraint flies out the window in that moment. Crossing her arms and glaring, the brunette purses her rosy-pink lips for the second time. "You! Y-you made me go through all that trouble when you could have gotten up yourself? You are a…a jerk."

Can't deny that.

I snort, amused. "Whoa, a *jerk*? Trust me, I've been called worse." Jamming my hands inside my hoodie, I shrug. "Besides. You had to at least try to help me up…" *since I just saved your ass.*

The implication hangs between us, unspoken.

"I already said thank you. What more do you require?"

"What more do I *require*?" Seriously, who talks like that? "And actually, no, you didn't say thank you."

"I—" She opens her mouth to argue, then clamps it shut. Her almond-shaped eyes go wide for a few seconds, and she takes another calming breath to steady her breathing. I can see her pretty brain counting to ten. "Thank you."

Behind us, vulgar voices float from inside the house as my friends stir to life from within. Pretty soon guys are going to start filtering out to leave for work or time on the ice.

"Listen, I'd *love* to stand here and chat with you, but…" My sarcastic remark trails off as I dust off my gray athletic pants, glancing around to survey the street, which is mostly void of any parked vehicles. I scowl. "Wait, do you have a car around here?"

She waves a hand and bites her lower lip. "No, but I don't live far. I can walk."

"Ah, I'll call you Walk of Shame. It suits you."

The brunette gasps, dismayed, and pleads, wide eyes darting to the Kappa O house. "*Please* don't call me that." She takes another deep, calming breath. "For your information, the room I climbed out of was my cousin's."

"Seriously? That was your cousin's room? Wow, that makes the story even better. So very…backwoods Appalachia of you."

"Backwoods Appalachia! That's... We're not... Are you implying what I think you are...?" She pauses expectantly.

"Caleb."

"Your name is *Caleb*?" she blurts out in surprise, changing the subject.

I accidentally chuckle, the sound coming out in a rich timbre and sounding foreign. "Yeah, why?"

"Nothing. It's just...you don't *look* like a Caleb."

"Wow, thanks. I'll let my mom know," I drawl out slowly.

"Sorry, I don't mean to be rude. It's just. You look more like a..." She clamps her pouty lips shut.

I tip my head, curiously waiting for her response, and prod her on. "More like a...?"

"I don't know. Like a...like a..." Her hand twirls around in the air aimlessly, her cheeks burning up with fire. "Biff."

I almost let out a bark of laughter.

Almost.

"My friends call me Showtime," I supply, growing uncomfortable with the intimate direction our conversation is taking. I don't want to know anything about her, and I don't want her knowing shit about me. Pretty soon we'll be sharing childhood tales and favorite colors.

"Showtime?" She rolls her eyes, mumbling to herself with a feminine snort. "Guys are such idiots. Why would he let anyone call him that?"

"Because I'm *such* a fucking idiot."

"How about you watch your mouth!"

Instinctually, I go on defense. "How about this instead: why don't you tell me why you were climbing out your 'cousin's' window at seven in the morning rather than taking the front door?" Yeah, I use air quotes when I mock the word *cousin's*, sounding suitably repulsed.

"How about you mind your own darn business?"

Darn business? Jesus, doesn't this chick ever swear?

"I *was* minding my own darn business, sweetheart, only you were too busy sticking your ass out your boyfriend's second-story window to notice. Oh wait, I'm sorry, did you *want* me to let you kill yourself?"

"I told you, he's—ugh!" Pausing to shoot me a look of contempt, she starts stomping her feet across the grass and heads for the sidewalk, calling over her shoulder, "I don't have to stand there and listen to you belittle me like I'm full of—"

"Shit? Or were you going with…poopy?" I snicker at her retreating form.

She halts abruptly on the lawn, spinning to face me with her hands planted on her hips. "You know what, *Showtime*?" She spits out my nickname with such disgust I'm surprised saliva isn't dripping out of her mouth. "You have *some* nerve making assumptions about *me* when you stand there looking like a…l-like a common *thug* who rolled off of his mattress just so he could rob the place."

Ouch.

I take a few menacing steps toward her. "Oh, you think I look like a thug because I'm wearing a hoodie and Adidas track pants? Honey, clearly you wouldn't know a thug if he passed out between your thighs. Hurry back to your dorm and bitch about the STD you undoubtedly contracted last night."

The brunette lets out another gasp, visibly mortified, and angrily flounces to the other side of the street. She's so pissed I can hear the heels of her boots thrashing the concrete from here, one angry clomp after the next.

Snarling, I turn toward the massive white house behind me, reaching under my ball cap to run a hand through my shaggy hair. Tugging the hat back into place, I only give pause when a glimmer of something shiny catches my eye. A pit of horror forms in my stomach, and, taking a few steps to my right, I bend down, hooking my index finger through a gleaming gold ring abandoned on the concrete driveway.

More specifically, on the driveway underneath the window of a particular second-story Kappa Omega Chi window…

Shit.

It's a simple band with a small blue sapphire chip mounted on top, and I study it closely in the rising morning sun. I hold it closer to my face for examination, turning it this way and that, and make out the inscription Love Mom & Dad on the inside; it's been rubbed out from wear, and is barely legible.

My head snaps up, and I scan the perimeter for the brunette. Unfortunately, the only sight is an empty sidewalk, and a dog chasing a squirrel around the yard of the house across the street.

I groan.

Shit.

Abby

By the time I get back to my off-campus apartment, I am fuming, breathing so deeply it sounds like I just returned from the Color Run. After flinging my door open so hard it hits the wall, I slam it shut behind me before stalking over and throwing myself on the bed.

Muttering a curse, I let out a frustrated scream. "Who the frick does he think he is?" I ask to no one. "Off all the nerve."

Of course, he *did* kind of save me…kind of.

Whatever! The jackhole.

Caleb.

Caleb, Caleb, stupid Caleb.

Ugh!

I close my eyes, forcing the image of him stowed in my memory to materialize in my mind. It does, so vividly it's like he's here, glowering down at me.

Tall. Broody. Muscular. Of course, the muscles could

have all been an illusion created by his bulky sweatshirt and slouchy Adidas athletic pants. The thick, heavy eyebrows, which peered at me from under a navy blue Flying W ball cap, were creased into a permanent scowl.

With solemn, serious, full lips set in an unyielding expression, he's hardly the man of a girl's dreams.

But that doesn't stop me from wondering about that mass of hair hidden under that well-worn ball cap and the obscurity of his hooded sweatshirt. My thoughts stray to the five o'clock stubble casting a rugged shadow over his angry, chiseled jaw and cheekbones, all of which added to his severe expression.

Believe me, I'm not waxing poetic about Caleb because I'm attracted to the Neanderthal (puh-lease, I'm not that desperate). Nope. I'm simply wondering where he came from, because you have to admit, he did just kind of appear out of nowhere to help me…

My chintzy, hollow bedroom door flies open, smashing against the wall behind it with a thud, and I glance up from under my pillow to see my two roommates in the doorway, both eyeing me with shocked expressions. There's Jenna, who I inherited as a roommate by default, and Meg, who I've been living with since sophomore year.

Jenna is the first one to speak. Her curious green gaze—which has been artfully lined with bright aqua eyeliner—scans my bedroom suspiciously until it lands on the curtains. "We heard a loud bang. What the hell is going on in here? Are you okay?"

I toss a pillow and roll to my back, staring at the ceiling to avoid her watchful gaze, measuring my words carefully. "Nothing. I was just upset before." I give them a glance. "Jenna, you can stop staring at my curtains like a guy is going to jump out from behind 'em?"

She wishes.

Meg, our other, more laidback roommate, shrugs her shoulders and wanders into the room, plopping herself on the edge of my double bed. Unlike Jenna, Meg is still in pajamas—the fuzzy, footie kind we wore as kids. "It's Saturday morning. What on earth could you possibly be pissed off about?" Meg looks down at the vintage silver watch on her wrist that she is never without. "It's barely nine."

"I'll give you one guess," I mutter.

Jenna saunters leisurely to the window, trailing a yellow fingernail along the curtains, none-too-subtly sneaking a peek behind them. Her ever-changing hair is piled in a messy mop on the top of her head, and the lavender and blonde strands wisp around her face when she turns to give me a onceover.

"Hmm. My first guess would be parent-related, but… since you're obviously still wearing the same clothes you had on last night…" Her pert nose wrinkles with distaste and one skillfully plucked eyebrow arches into her hairline. "I'd say you just stumbled in."

Meg flops onto her back next to me, giving Jenna a *duh* look. "Nice detective work, Einstein."

Jenna ignores her. "Please tell us you *finally* gave it up to someone last night."

Meg's mouth falls open and she props herself up on an elbow. "Do you have to go there? Immediately? Why is everything always about sex with you?"

"Because it's always about sex with me." Jenna rolls her eyes. "And because she's twenty years old and hasn't done it with a guy? Abby is still a virgin. I'm trying to *help* her."

My cheeks flush as they continue talking about me like I'm not in the room.

Meg sighs. "Spare me. Not all of us lose our virginity when we're fourteen, okay, hooker?"

"I never said there was anything wrong with being a virgin, just that she was one. Sheesh! And for the record, I lost mine when I was seventeen, and I was in love with the guy, but nice try."

Jenna plops down in my desk chair, her large metal earrings jingling merrily around her face as she gives the chair a swivel. "Let's try not to get off topic here." She gives me a pointed look. "So? What's the deal? Slamming and banging doors is so unlike you."

Meg immediately turns her attention back to me, absentmindedly giving a loose string on her monkey pajamas a few tugs. She snaps it free and lets it fall to my carpet.

"And it's pretty obvious you didn't come home last night, which is also very unlike you."

Under her breath, Jenna mutters, "Unfortunately," as Meg continues. "The only place you ever stay over at these days is Cece's, and she's too far away. You obviously couldn't have gone there."

Cece is my best friend, and she just moved back to the Midwest from California. Her boyfriend, Matthew, is a professional hockey player, and he was just traded to the Chicago Blackhawks. That is great, because now, instead of being nineteen hundred miles away, Cece is only an hour car ride away. Even though we rarely see each other, we text each other every day.

I scoff at Meg's judgment of my evening. "Be serious. I would never have stayed at Cece's in Chicago and made it home by now, you guys. On a Friday night? Not happening." I cross my arms and stretch out on my bed next to Meg.

"Fine. Then the real question is, who was he?"

I roll my eyes, feigning ignorance. "Who was who?"

Both my roommates stare at me, waiting and determined to pry an explanation out of me.

I grab the pillow from under my head, sit up, and rest my back against the wall next to my bed. "You guys, it's not a big deal. Remember how I popped in at the Kappa O party last night? I went with Maddie, Tabitha, and Maria, not because I wanted to, but because my parents paid me to. Anyway, they left before I did, and you know my rule about walking anywhere alone at night. Long story short, I crashed in Tyler's room." I shrug as casually as my churning stomach will allow. "The end."

Snidely, Jenna asks, "Wait, those bitches left you there? Alone? Typical."

"You should have texted one of us," Meg scolds. "I would have walked over to get you."

"Yeah, but then *you* would have been alone in the dark," Jenna points out.

"It was fine," I interrupt before they start squabbling again. "I holed up in Tyler's room. It was gross, but I survived."

Jenna, who's far more astute than people give her credit for, eyes me skeptically. "Right, okay...so what's with all the loud crashing and door slamming? What could your moron cousin *possibly* have done to annoy you this early in the morning? Did lover-boy hog the covers?" She snickers and spins the chair around.

Worse. He drools.

"Yeah, real funny," I grit out, crossing my arms and hugging a stuffed penguin to my chest. "For your information, Tyler didn't do anything but drool all over himself." I bite my lip. "I wasn't pissed off until—"

I stop mid-sentence, causing both my friends to lean forward, waiting for me to continue.

"Until...?" Meg probes, giving me a nudge with her leg. "Until? Until?"

"Until your cousin touched you with his morning wood?" Jenna supplies optimistically.

Even Meg is horrified by that visual. "Oh my god, stop."

"Well, out with it already. We don't have all day," Jenna intones, getting irritated. "Actually, *I* don't have all day, but Meg does," she jokes. "It's only the three of us here. We promise not to tell anyone."

I hesitate, so Jenna tries again, sweet-talking. "Look, we all know something upset you, and if it wasn't Tyler's weiner, then it was someone else's. So tell us who it was. You know you want to. And also, sorry I said weiner. I meant dick."

As crude as Jenna is, she's right; I *am* dying to tell them, not because I want them to be all up in my business, but I am curious to know if they know who Caleb is.

I lean back against the wall. "Do you remember the song they sing at the Kappa house when a girl tries to sneak out in the morning?"

Both my roommates nod.

"Well, this morning I could hear them chanting it, and obviously I wasn't about to be humiliated by walking out into the hall—*especially* since I was in Tyler's room. I mean, can you imagine?"

"You didn't want them to think you were banging your cousin." Jenna stifles a laugh.

"That is so not funny," Meg admonishes. "It's disgusting."

"Come on, lighten up. That's what she was thinking."

She's right; I was.

"Do you want to hear this or not?" I grumble, shifting to get more comfortable. "Anyway, the guys are all singing their plagiarized 'walk of shame' chant, and the words are just awful. Why girls put up with that escapes me."

My roommates exchange glances questionably as I continue.

"Anyway, Tyler's room is only on the second floor, and there's this overhang near his window…"

"Stop." Jenna holds a palm in the air, halting my account of this morning's events. "Stop right there. Do *not* tell me you climbed out his window."

"…so I climbed out the window…"

Jenna and Meg both groan, but they lean closer still.

"…and *just* as I'm about to lose my grip on the gutter guard, this huge, angry guy starts yelling at me to let go. Like, he was really annoyed. Long story short, I fell and he caught me."

Meg puts her hands up. "Whoa, whoa, whoa—back the truck up. Rewind!"

"That's insane!" Jenna shouts excitedly as she loudly slaps her hand on my desk and bounces up and down on my desk chair. "Who was it? Who was it?"

"See, that's the part I'm not sure about. He wasn't someone I recognized, but I think he'd been at the old Omega house. I think. I mean, I thought he walked back to their yard after…"

Jenna rolls her eyes skyward. "How the hell would you know? You were dangling from a roof."

"True. He could have been walking home and just passing by," Meg points out diplomatically.

Jenna rolls her eyes again. "Yeah, right. I'm *sooo* sure he was just out for a brisk morning stroll on a *Saturday* at seven o'clock."

"Some people jog, Jenna," Meg bites back.

I clear my throat and continue. "After I stormed off, I *might* have watched him from across the street, from behind a bush."

"All right, all right, let's assume he was at the Omega house. Are you sure you didn't recognize him from somewhere?"

"No, and trust me, I would have remembered him if I did." I clamp a hand over my mouth.

"Oh *really?*" Jenna's eyebrows shoot up into her dip-dyed hairline. "Made an impression on you, did he?"

"Did you catch his name?" Meg asks.

"Was he hot?"

I hesitate. "Yes, I caught his name." Was he hot? *Was* he?

They both stare at me, waiting.

"Well? Freaking tell us!" Jenna prompts, losing patience and staring at me like I'm dumb as a box of rocks. Oddly enough, even as my roommates stare at me expectantly, I just can't do it. I can't tell them his name.

Or won't.

Same thing.

Deep down, a part of me wants to keep him a secret…a strange, exciting secret.

Nothing exciting ever happens to me—like, ever. I'm just not *that* girl. I'm too boring, too predictable, too quiet, too…everything.

Don't get me wrong—I'm not without my charms. I even possess a myriad of fascinating skills. I'm an amazing painter, for example. I can read a novel in a day if I'm not swamped with studying, and I'm shockingly good at darts.

Not exactly man-bait.

Plus, I'm don't let it all hang out like most girls do to attract attention from guys. My boobs don't pop out of my clothes. In fact, there isn't a single thing in my entire closet that exposes too much skin. I'd much rather use my brain to fascinate the opposite sex, and no guy wants to be fascinated mentally during a house party, or at a bar—nope, he wants to be fondled.

Guys just don't go for girls like me, girls who wear tucked-in, collared button-down shirts to the bar, girls who would rather read on a Friday night than go out. Guys don't go for girls who chastise them for swearing. Guys don't rescue girls like me when they climb out and fall from two-story windows.

But today…today, I *was* that girl.

And a guy did.

And maybe it wasn't just the fall that took my breath away.

Caleb

To clarify, the Omega house is *not* a fraternity house.

It used to be, until the fraternity—Omega Gamma Rho, Omega for short—that resided here for the past fifty years got their chapter removed from campus—dirty rushing, hazing, too many reported cases of alcohol poisoning by parents of pledges—and the house was sold.

To my parents.

And now I live there with my teammates. We still call it the Omega house, even though technically it would be considered the hockey house.

The whole house received a facelift when my parents bought it. The Greek letters have long since been taken down and painted over. Although they don't expect me to single-handedly maintain the joint, I do feel a certain level of responsibility to keep it in decent shape.

Speaking of decent shape…

With a purposeful stride, I cross our bright green, manicured lawn, which is mowed weekly, over to the over-grown, dead, weed-infested Kappa yard. Climbing the dilapidated porch, I open the screen door and proceed to unceremoniously pound my huge flattened palm on the front door.

I push the screen back into place and stand back, waiting.

And wait some more.

It takes a few moments, but eventually the door creaks loudly, shudders a groan, and swings open, hanging precariously on its rusty hinges. I look down at a skinny, dark-haired kid who is staring back at me.

"Sup?" His red, half-hooded eyes make him look stoned, but he gives a quick flick of the chin in greeting.

I cut to the chase. "I need to talk to the guy living in the corner room upstairs. Is he here?"

"Say again?" Unconcerned, the kid eyes me warily, scratching his dry elbow. "Can you be more specific?"

I barely manage to contain my eye roll. "Why yes, yes I can be more specific." I speak slowly so he understands. "Go. And get. The prick. Living in. The corner. Room. Upstairs. *Or*…my fist is going to come through this lousy excuse for a door and beat the shit out of you."

Okay, so maybe I'm behaving a tad like a psycho, but he's making me talk and I don't like it.

The kid gulps, his Adam's apple bobbing in his scrawny neck.

"Hold on a minute." The door slams closed in my face, and a deadbolt slides into the lock.

Smart kid.

A few minutes later, the door creaks open and the "cousin" appears. Standing in ripped mesh basketball shorts that are too long, a sleeveless Nike tank top, and white ankle socks, I know it's him because, believe it or not, he resembles the brunette. Tall with a shaggy mop of wavy brown hair and bright blue eyes, the douche also looks like he just rolled out of bed.

Or smoked a joint.

He arches his back in a yawn, unfazed by the sight of me. "What."

"I need to get ahold of the chick that climbed out your window this morning." How's that for blunt?

"What for?" he asks, rotating his torso this way and that, stretching like he's warming up for an athletic event.

"I have something I think belongs to her."

"So? Just give it to me. She's my cousin."

"I don't have it *with* me," I lie, palming the ring nestled inside the pocket of my slouchy gray athletic pants and rolling it around in my fingers. It's warm from my body heat and solid in my hand, and I'm not offering it over to him—not yet, anyway.

The cousin scratches his balls and yawns again. "Why don't you go *get* it and bring it *back*?"

Okay, now he's starting to piss me off.

"Why don't you just give me her fucking cell phone number and you can go back to jerking off?"

"Why don't *you* fuck *you*, dude. Do I look dumb enough to turn you lose on Abby? You're acting like a psychopath. My parents would kill me."

Abby.

I turn this new revelation around in my head a few times, testing her name out and deciding I like it.

It fits.

I take a deep, calming breath and count to three. "Look, this isn't a pissing match. My parents own the Omega house next door." I point my thumb toward it. "And I was outside when Abby climbed out your window this morning. Trust me, I don't want to hurt her. I just want to see if she's okay, because she fell, and I have something to return to her."

It's more words than I normally string together, and quite frankly, it's making me uncomfortable.

A shout from inside the frat house rings out, something I can't quite discern, and the cousin turns for a second to yell back into the house. "Shit, hold on for one goddamn second." The door slams in my face again, and Abby's cousin disappears into the dark recesses of the house.

I rock back on my heels while I wait, tipping my head back to study the building, which looks like it could collapse any day now. The boards are warped from water damage and haven't been sealed or stained in years. Rusty nails are popping out all over the place, and wires hang dangerously out of the outdated light socket that should've been replaced ages ago.

How girls voluntarily step foot inside this death trap is beyond me.

Shaking my head in disgust, I let out a gust of air, mentally counting to ten so I don't flip my shit. Then the door finally reopens.

"Sorry about that," he apologizes, not looking the least bit sorry. Instead, he narrows his dark eyes and gives me another onceover, and honest to God, he's the first guy I've ever seen purse his lips. "What did you say your name was?"

"I didn't."

He nods his head before shrugging, his disheveled hair falling into his eyes. "Fine. You can have her cell, but you can't tell her I gave it you, and if I find out you fucked with her, I'll kick the shit out of you."

I almost laugh at his pronouncement. Kick *my* ass?

Whatever, dude.

Incredulously, I watch as he programs Abby's cell phone number into my phone before slamming the half-hinged door in my scowling face.

Abby

The text notification comes through just before midnight.

Just as I'm closing my e-reader and taking off the tortoiseshell reading glasses perched on the bridge of my nose, the soft ping of my phone fills the quiet void in my bedroom. I've always considered the gentle sound a reminder that somewhere, someone out there is thinking of me at that *exact* moment.

Regardless of the sentiment, my arm wearily stretches out across my body, grappling for my phone on the bedside table, and I mumble to the empty room, "I swear, if this is Meg, I'm going to freaking kill her…"

I hold the phone up to my face, the light of the small screen blinding me, and swipe the screen with my forefinger to open my messages. I give a small yip of delight. It's Cecelia, and I haven't texted her in a few hours.

Propping myself up on an elbow, I flip a bedside light on so I'm not blinded by the glow of my phone, and I smile when I click open her text.

Cecelia: *HEY SLACKER! You must have been busy to-day. You never sent me a note and now I miss you even more!!!*

Me: *I'm so sorry. You wouldn't believe the day I had. Why are you up so late?*

Cecelia: *Waiting for Matthew to get home. He had a dinner meeting with his agent and I'm up waiting so I can eat his leftovers. He promised me steak. What's your excuse? Why are you up?*

Me: *Reading and NOT waiting to eat my boyfriend's table scraps.*

Cecelia: *Like I'm going to pass up steak niblets. Don't roll your eyes at me.*

Me: *I wouldn't dare ;)*

Cecelia: *Everything is situated in the new condo, and all is well in Chicago. When are you going to come down and visit?? Or should I come up?*

Me: *Maybe we should plan an overnight somewhere during my break. Not ALL of us are done with college, Ms. Master's Degree showoff.*

Cecelia: *Break would be a good time to come up in the fall. Matthew has a bye week soon and I know he'd love to see everyone, so maybe early first semester?*

Me: *Okay. But I also really want to see your new condo. Before we get to all that tho...I have a confession to make. I did something stupid.*

Cecelia: *You???? Abby and 'I did something stupid' do*

NOT belong in the same sentence. MATTHEW and some-thing stupid, on the other hand, or Jenna and something stupid, but never Abby.

Me: *Well, then aren't YOU in for a treat. Are you sitting down? This one is a doozy....*

***

As I move around my bedroom, piecing together my outfit and getting ready for class, I stop to pause in the mirror, studying my reflection with renewed interest.

I've already thrown on jeans, a navy fleece, a fleece vest, and navy Bean Duck boots. My long brown hair is in a loose ponytail, and since it's both cold *and* rainy, I toss on a ball cap for good measure.

Shifting to my dresser, I watch myself in the mirror as I insert small gold hoops into both ears and clasp a thin gold necklace around my neck. Like I do every single morning, my hand reaches robotically into the jewelry bowl for the ring my parents gave me for high school graduation. Dismayed, my fingers touch the cold white ceramic and feebly feel around, but they turn up...nothing.

My mouth turns down, perplexed. Huh. That's odd.

I crouch down a tad and get eye level with my old oak dresser, eyeballing the surface and moving a few things around. I lift my jewelry bowl, looking under a few note-books and a blinged out coffee mug. *I could have* sworn *I put it back in the bowl...*

I stand in front of the dresser, staring at its surface, chewing on my lip and racking my brain. *Where the heck is that ring?*

Getting down on my hands and knees, I peer under the wooden dresser, next to it, and under the bed, feeling my way around the thin, threadbare carpet. I grab my phone and open the flashlight app, shining the bright beam under all my furniture.

No luck.

Frustrated, I stalk over to the bed, yank back my quilt and sheets, flapping them up and down like a parachute, and search for any trace of the gold band I've worn every day for the past three and a half years.

"Ugh!" Why do I even take it off? I'll tell you why: I can't smear moisturizing lotion all over my hands when I'm wearing it without getting cream in all the intricate crevasses and gooping up the small vintage stone.

But still, I've never misplaced it before. Never, not once.

I continue my crusade for a few more minutes until I run out of time and have to leave for campus, missing breakfast and the opportunity to put together a snack for later in the day.

Sighing, I grab my laptop, notebook, and messenger bag, abandoning the rescue mission for now and heading out the door.

Caleb

alancing my six-foot-three frame up on a chintzy six-foot ladder, I lean precariously to the side, brace my forearm against the wall, and grasp the bucket of plaster in another.

Having already patched the large, gaping hole in the foyer, I carefully spread the paste on the old wall over the patching tape, using the putty knife to smooth the edges before the plaster begins to dry.

Some putz on the hockey team named Cubby Billings thought it would be a fantastic idea to take the NCAA National Hockey Championship trophy that's normally displayed in the dining room of the Omega house and hoist it up in the air.

All thirty pounds of it.

At some point this weekend, Cubby stumbled through the door with it after a hockey victory party, lurched to the side—thanks to the five consecutive Jager bombs he'd consumed—narrowly avoided the porcelain Omega vase resting on an antique cherrywood table, and crashed into the wall instead.

Oh, wait.

I forgot the part where a sorority girl named Claudia was riding Cubby's shoulders, and *she* was the one who actually smashed the trophy into the wall—you know, in case you were wondering why I'd need a ladder to repair the fucking hole...which was *eight* feet up off the ground.

So here I am.

Patching the wall.

I lean back, satisfied that the new drywall is even and flush to the wall, and climb down off the ladder to assess it from the floor. My head bobs once approvingly, and I flip my ball cap around so the brim is back in the front, fold up the ladder, and start hauling everything back into the basement of the house.

"You gonna be at the rink tonight?" one of my roommates, Weston McGrath, asks from his position in the kitchen. He's standing at the counter, making a giant sandwich as I pound up the back staircase in my heavy work boots. He licks mustard off his thumb as he watches me close the basement door then lock it behind me.

"Yeah, probably, but first I have to run back to the store and grab some sandpaper. I need to get that spackled hole in the foyer smooth before I can paint it." I walk past him to the fridge and retrieve a bottle of water, twist the cap, and swallow half of it before turning back to face him.

Casually, I lean against the counter, surveying the mess he's made as he slaps a giant blob of mayonnaise on two thick slices of bread, followed by cheddar cheese, tomato, lettuce, and chicken.

A few pickle slices, more lettuce, and some jalapeños.

Ham.

Condiments are all over the counter, and a head of lettuce has been wacked in half with a butcher knife I didn't even know we had in the house.

He's made a giant fucking mess, considering it's just *one* sandwich.

And did I mention he's only wearing underwear?

Weston lovingly holds up the sandwich like it's the Stanley Cup, crushes it between his two palms so it will fit in his mouth, and then takes a huge bite. Slowly he chews, making both moaning and groaning sounds as he does it.

It sounds like he's on the receiving end of one fantastic blowjob.

"Dude." I can't help but laugh, stepping forward to snag a piece of ham. "Sandwich can't be *that* good."

He wipes his mouth on his arm and grins. "No, but it's pretty damn close." Lettuce falls onto his bare chest.

"If Molly heard you moaning, she'd be jealous."

"Nah, my girl doesn't get jealous. She knows she's got this shit locked down," he jokes, jamming the sandwich back into his face. He literally has to crush it against his mouth to take a bite.

I'm not really sure how to respond to that, so I cross my arms and wait for him to swallow. "What time you going tonight?"

He swallows before responding. "Around six, I think. I can't be out late. I have an exam tomorrow." Weston shrugs. "We have that damn exposition game against Michigan on Thursday, and I need more time on the ice than I've gotten in practice."

"Yeah, all right. I can meet you there if you want me in the box."

"You know…" His voice trails off and he clears his throat uncomfortably. "Coach was asking about you yesterday." Weston watches me from the corner of his eye as he takes the second half of his giant sandwich off the white dinner plate.

I nod slowly. Hesitantly. "Yeah? What did he say?"

"He just asked where your head was at, and if you're ready for the season to start, because you seem so…out of it during practice. He brought me into his office to do it, so you know it wasn't just him being polite."

No. Coach isn't polite. He's a colossal asshole.

I don't respond, instead nodding again, bowing my head a little, and removing my ball cap briefly to run my fingers through my hair.

Wes shifts uneasily. "I'm not telling you this to pressure you. I just wanted to let you know that we're all pumped for the new season to start, and we can't afford to have you benched. Haggerty is a piece-of-shit goaltender, even for a second stringer, and everyone knows it."

Yeah, I've noticed.

Zack Haggerty, the rookie goalie who subs my spot in the event of an injury, killed the team's stats the one time last season I was out with mono, and I still can't help feeling responsible.

"You know I've been busting my ass in practice. Of course I'm fucking ready for the season to start." I shake my head, irritated. Just because I'm not like my obnoxiously extroverted teammates does *not* mean my head isn't in the game. "Six tonight, you said?"

He confirms with a nod, his shaggy brown hair falling in his eyes. Dude needs a haircut.

"All right. Yeah, I'll be in the net for you."

"Sweet, thanks, Showtime." He stuffs another hunk of bread in his gullet and swallows, extending the sandwich toward me. With a face full of mayonnaise and meat hanging from his mouth, he asks, "You want a bite?"

Shaking my head, I walk over and smack him on the back with a grin. "No way, man. I'll catch you later, though."

Abby

Why is it that every time you run into a store like Walmart for something simple, you always end up finding *way* more stuff than you actually need?

You know what I'm talking about. Walking in to buy something—say milk, shampoo, or paper towels—but end up spending fifty dollars on random crap that you had no need for and no intention of buying. For example, a new magazine, tank top, or that tube of onyx mascara you only bought because it's never on sale and you finally get to save forty whole cents.

Yeah.

Balancing the pile of such random merchandise I've accumulated because I didn't grab a cart on my way in, my frugality kicks in and, like the spendthrift I am, I begin putting things back on the shelves.

Since I'm technically only here for tampons, I put back the microwave popcorn, fuzzy socks, silver nail polish I will never actually wear, and Blu-ray of *The Longest Ride*.

Actually, no. I *do* want *The Longest Ride*.

I add it back to my pile.

Meandering dutifully back to the feminine products like I had intended to do in the first place, I grab a hot-pink box of regular absorbency, scanning the tampon aisle one more time just in case I missed anything exciting and new.

I round the corner and start down the main drag, retracing my steps past the cosmetics, perfume, and the pharmacy, idly checking over every endcap and eyeing any packaging with metallic sheen that catches my attention—after all, that's what the displays were designed to do, right? Entice me.

Well played, marketing people, well played.

Like a sucker, I stand there scrutinizing everything like it's my job, not because I need any more crap, but because I'm bored and in no hurry to return home to an empty house.

Standing in checkout lane *numero tres*, I study a display of candy, eyeballing a bag of assorted Tootsie Rolls and deciding that if I were to buy the whole bag (hypothetically, of course), I would eat all the blue-wrapped vanilla ones first. I'd definitely toss out the lemon ones—I mean, *who* eats the lemon ones? Who?

Lemon Tootsie Rolls? Come on now.

Get real.

Sighing, I mentally purchase half the chocolate candy bars on the metal shelves, a snack-size bag of Funyuns, and a roll of Mentos. It's a rough life, but I'm muddling through.

Tapping the box of tampons clutched in my left hand listlessly against my thigh, I count the number of items the woman in front of me has stacked up on the counter. Let me tell you, it's a lot of shit, which is annoying, since this is the express ten-items-or-less lane—or at least it's *supposed* to be.

By my estimation, the cheater has at least twenty-five items.

The cover of US Weekly catches my eye, and since I have nothing to do but stand here and wait, I grab the current issue and begin thumbing through page after page, ignorant to the looming figure that has walked up to stand behind me.

Intently, I study page thirty-four. Sheesh, when did Brad Pitt get so dang old? My mom loves him. Seriously, have you ever seen the column *Stars: They're Just like Us*? Um, yeah, what America needs are photos of Luke Bryan pushing an entire shopping cart of French baguettes and beer in the Whole Foods parking lot—and the photo of Theo James filling his car tank with gasoline? I mean, please, do they really expect us to believe Beyoncé buys her own toothpaste?

Apparently.

I shake my head in disgust but continue flipping through it anyway. Then, over the top right-hand corner of the magazine, a pair of light brown Timberland work boots shuffle, appearing in my line of vision and catching my attention.

Not wanting to be rude, I inch closer toward the conveyer belt so I'm not hogging up all the valuable aisle space, turning to shove the magazine back into the metal rack on the endcap.

Finally! The woman in front of me begins digging through her purse for her payment and hands a credit card to the cashier.

Halle-freaking-lujah.

With a jaunty flick of my wrist, I toss my movie and box of tampons onto the conveyer belt, adding a last-minute pack of Hubba Bubba Bubble Gum that I'm suddenly in the mood to chew.

"That seems like an impulse buy. Are you sure you need that?" a deep baritone asks from behind me, and I flinch, startled.

I wince, recognizing the voice without even having to turn around, and my body tenses up.

Cringing and wishing the ground would swallow me whole, I pivot slowly on the heels of my brown calfskin ankle boots and paste a tight-lipped smile on my face that I'm sure looks as fake as it feels.

"Tampons are *not* an impulse buy," I smart with authority as heat singes my face. "They're a necessity."

"I meant the bubble gum," Caleb deadpans in a deep voice.

Shoot. Me. *Now.*

As I face him, doing my best not to recoil like a wuss, a hundred impressions assault me: his height, his brooding expression, his rugged appearance.

His nearness.

Forging on, since we're obviously hostage to this dead-end conversation, I ignore the apprehension rolling inside my stomach. "So, how's it going, *Showtime*?" I use air quotes when I say his nickname, then immediately regret it.

His face remains expressionless.

"Why, it's going splendid, *Walk of Shame*. Thanks for asking." I have a feeling he'd use air quotes too, but his hands are full.

Since mine aren't, I narrow my eyes and boldly plant both hands on my hips. Then I remove them but let them hang clenched at my sides. "Please don't call me that."

Caleb just shrugs his broad shoulders and studies me from under the brim of his ball cap, his dark eyes scanning my figure before they dart to the conveyer belt, where my neon box of tampons rolls gradually…excruciatingly slowly…toward the scanner.

In a time warp.

At a snail's pace.

In slow motion.

It's the slowest conveyer belt in the history of express lane checkouts. Slap some glitter, lipstick, and a spotlight on that box, and we'd have our own Broadway play called, *Hello, cruel world! Abby has her period!*

I draw in a breath and blurt out, "Are you stalking me?"

His hardened expression doesn't waver. "Yup, and later I'm making a lampshade out of your skin." His lips curve into a barely perceptible sneer, and he holds up several packages of heavy-duty sanding paper and a half-gallon of paint primer that he's been clutching in his bear-like paws.

I twist my face into a grimace and roll my eyes. "Ha ha, very funny."

When it's finally my turn, the gray-haired woman behind the counter greets me, her hawk-like gaze shifting back and forth between Caleb and me, a smile playing at her wrinkly lips. "You find everything okay, hun?" She smacks her gum.

"Yes, ma'am. Thank you." I tensely shoot another frown at Caleb, who continues to regard me intensely, and swipe my debit card nervously through the digital card reader. Uncomfortable, I shake my head. *What is* with *this guy?*

"Do you want your receipt with you or in the bag?" the woman asks, extending the white slip of paper.

"Oh, I don't think she'll be returning *those*." Caleb smirks, the muscles beneath his unshaven jaw lifting his full lips into the slightest hint of a smile. As if abruptly re-membering his faux pas, that phantom smile is wiped from his face, replaced by another scowl.

Now, that ghost smile may have disappeared, but not quickly enough, for in the middle of that unhappy mouth, below the flawlessly indented cupid's bow of those full, rich lips, are a set of straight, snowy-white teeth. And among that set of straight, snowy-white teeth?

A gap.

A gap, set in the center of those very wolfish teeth, making its debut for a fleeting moment. I wonder if I only imagined it. Because, *guh!* A gap.

And I caught a glimpse of it.

Dear…Lord….

A *gap.*

I freeze in place, holding the bag of feminine products and candy suspended midair, transfixed—*struck dumb*—by the sight of Caleb's mouth.

He openly stares back at me, and the amused air of his expression grows surly in an *instant*, his mouth snapping shut like an angry crocodile's. I actually hear his teeth lock down.

Even so, I continue my trancelike perusal of him, recognizing with horrifying clarity that I'm no better than any other warm-blooded female who's ever lusted after our male counterparts solely based on physical attributes.

Attributes that will forever make me go weak in the knees…say stupid crap…stammer and stutter…agonize over my words.

Stare. Gawk. Daydream.

I have some friends who go absolutely mental for a set of washboard abs, while others can't resist straight white teeth and an infectious, toothy smile or dimples. Then there are the girls who cannot get enough broad shoulders and rippling biceps—or better yet, rippling biceps with tattoos.

I didn't know until this very moment that I had a weakness of my own. Apparently, it's gaps in a guy's teeth.

Imperfectly…*perfect.*

Swoon.

Caleb

She's staring—staring *hard.*

At my mouth.

Shit.

My cheeky grin falters, and without thinking, my tongue darts out of its own accord, running along the crude edges of the gap in my teeth that a hockey puck put there a few years ago. The exact moment and time I can't recall, but I do remember this: it hurt like a motherfucker.

I watch her studying me, her face getting more flushed by the second. A bright pink rash appears from inside the collar of her pretty cream sweater, rising up her neck, past her cheeks, and all the way to her hairline.

Self-consciously, I pull my lips back down over my teeth, where they belong.

Abby slowly pulls her gaze from my mouth, our eyes meet, and for a few brief seconds, all we do is wordlessly continue to stare each other down.

Stare each other down fucking *hard*, until the cashier clears her throat.

"I-I should… I have to g-go," Abby stutters, accidentally dropping her plastic shopping bag of tampons and gum on the ground, quickly bending to snatch it up and turning to flee, leaving a trail of muttered *Oh my god*s in her wake as she speed-walks toward the exit doors.

The cashier's eyebrows shoot up into her gray curly mop. "That didn't go very well." She chortles wryly, throat scratchy from too many cigarettes, as she scans my sandpaper and primer. "You better work on your flirting technique—unless, of course, you *wanted* to scare the poor girl off."

"Uh…"

"See there? Horrible technique. What is it with you young people? No courting anymore. It's just wham-bamthank-you-ma'am these days." She shakes her head at me. "Your total is nineteen eleven."

I pull out a twenty, careful not to pull out the gold ring mixed in with my loose change, hand it to the old bag, and stare off toward the automatic doors.

***

Abby: *What's the most awkward thing I've ever done?*

Cecelia: *I'm going to need you to give me a minute. There are way too many choices.*

Abby: *Remember that time in middle school, at Kassie Bauer's party, when I got caught on camera digging my wet swimsuit out of my crotch?*

Cecelia: *So what you're about to tell me is WORSE than pulling a suit out of your crotch AND climbing out a second-story window????? I find this VERY hard to believe.*

Abby: *Okay, okay, fine. Maybe not as bad as THOSE. But picture this: me + Walmart + Caleb + one box of tampons*

Cecelia: *(eyes huge) This is me hanging on your every word!!! Start talking, and don't leave anything out. On second thought, I'm calling you. 5 minutes. ANSWER YOUR PHONE!!!!*

Abby

"...and I couldn't even get a copy of the practice test. I mean, I was hardly ten minutes late." Jenna, who's sitting cross-legged next to me on our ratty old couch, finally stops talking. "Hey, are you even listening?" She nudges me in the ribs.

"Huh?"

She rears back a little so she can look me in the face. "What's your deal? You haven't heard anything I've said in the last half hour." She reaches over and snatches the bag of pretzels off the coffee table, grabbing a handful and chomping on one.

"Sorry, I'm just..."

But Jenna isn't a fool, and even though I can tell she wants to say something, she stays quiet instead. It goes without saying that she's totally addicted to those crime-drama shows and has learned from watching them religiously that the most effective way to interrogate a suspect is *silence*.

Silence.

"I'm just…preoccupied."

More silence.

"For your information, I was listening…for the most part."

Again, she says nothing.

"Would you knock it off," I grumble.

She cocks her head and gives me a patronizing, toothy grin with her pearly whites, the contrast against her deep burgundy lips creating a wide, Cheshire Cat-like visual as she mutely watches me.

Dang it. I fall for it every time.

"Remember that guy? The one I fell on top of when I climbed out of Tyler's window?" I ask hesitantly.

"Oh, you mean the guy whose name you refuse to tell us?"

Undeterred and suddenly in the mood to discuss it, I ramble on. "I ran into him today at Wally World while I was buying tampons." I shudder at this memory and then sigh when I continue. "That wasn't the worst part. Oh, no. The worst part was when I couldn't stop looking at him. Like, I was totally checking him out." I cover my face with the palms of my hands in mortification. "My god, Jenna. I was so embarrassed. He must think I'm an utter idiot."

Utter? *Ugh.*

"Uh, Abby? Hasn't anyone ever told you that guys *like* being checked out?" She gives me a *sometimes I wonder about you* look before chewing on another pretzel. "They totally love it. They think you're undressing them in your mind. It's a turn-on."

"I was not undressing him in my mind, I swear, but I was studying him like a science fair project."

"Jeez, you are so adorable when you get all flustered." Jenna pats my leg.

"I'm five foot seven—that's not adorable. Petite—*that's* adorable. *You're* adorable. *Puppies* are adorable. "

"Aww, schucks, you think I'm adorable?" My roommate clutches her heart and bats her long false lashes. "You're so sweet."

I let out a long sigh. "So, here's the thing: he has a *gap* in his teeth. A freaking gap. It's apparentl my kryptonite." I run my fingers through my long hair distractedly, and frown. "He seemed kind of insecure about it, but I couldn't stop staring, like really, *really* staring. It was so…endearing, but then *he* started blushing, and I was already blushing, and ugh, it was horrible."

Jenna stops chewing. "Well, shit, a gap. And sooo much blushing."

I ignore her sarcasm. "Yeah. So then he made a wisecrack about my tampons, I died of mortification, and I exited stage left."

Her green eyes get wide with interest. "What kind of a wisecrack?"

"The cashier asked if I wanted a receipt, and he said I probably wouldn't be returning them…because, you know…tampons."

"That. Is. *Awesome.* I already freaking like this guy." She stuffs another pretzel in her mouth and leans toward me. "Tell me more about this gap."

I close my eyes to conjure up a mental picture of Caleb. I need to remember the details so I can recount them to Jenna, details like him standing in the checkout aisle in his faded, low-slung jeans, beat-up brown construction boots, black Badgers Hockey track hoodie, and baseball hat pulled down over his forehead. The dark, day-old stubble surrounding his strong sculpted jaw, an angry scar marring the upper corner of his eyebrow.

He looked angry, awkward, and about as embarrassed as I felt.

"I only caught a peek of it. He doesn't really seem like the sunshine-and-rainbows kind of guy."

"There you go again with the blushing," Jenna teases. "And you've barely even said anything. I hate to break it to you, but guys totally dig the blushing, virginal look, and you've got it in spades." She glances down at my white cashmere sweater and boyfriend jeans, and raises her eyebrows knowingly.

"Screw you."

"Yes!" Excited, Jenna begins bouncing on the couch cushions. "See! *Screwing!* Now that's the spirit we're looking for!"

She's so obnoxious. "Remind me again why I let you live here?"

"Because I had just transferred to Madison, and Molly already had a roommate, so even though all we do is argue, you were so desperate for a sublessee you had to overlook my domineering personality and our penchant for fighting?"

"Yup, that about sums it up." I fiddle with my hands, nervously twisting the middle finger where my gold ring should be. "Shoot! Crappers!"

"What?"

"My ring. I forgot to look for it. What if I sucked it up when I vacuumed yesterday?"

"Wait, the house gets vacuumed?" She lets out a titter. "Kidding. But you *do* know that if you sucked up a ring with the vacuum, it would sound like this." Jenna begins making loud slurping sounds, complete with *VVVvvvv* suction noises, while she bangs an empty Coke can on the coffee table. When she's done making a spectacle, she nonchalantly asks, "Want me to help you look for it?"

"Er, no. I've looked everywhere. I'm sure it will turn up eventually…"

"And you can't remember the last time you had it?"

I stare blankly at the television screen for a few seconds, zoning out, then snap my fingers. "Tyler's!"

Abby

I don't always go crawling around on the grass outside decrepit frat houses, but when I do, I look like a homeless person scavenging for spare change.

Down on my hands and knees, my palms swipe at the grass in between the Omega and Kappa houses, my head bent so far down at one point, my nose skims the ground, and can I just add—for the sake of details—that *grass* actually went up my nostrils and I sneezed a few times?

Carefully, determinedly, and without pause, I slowly eyeball what I hope is every square inch under Tyler's window, biting my lower lip in concentration. I look inside the basement window wells, finger through the crunchy gravel, and scout under the countless dead scrubs and inside the hose wheel.

I stand.

I crawl.

I sit.

I pick up some random garbage strewn on the lawn, and only stop scrounging around like a hobo when I feel like someone watching me…because someone *is* watching me.

I can feel it.

Raising my head, I do a quick scan of the perimeter, glancing across the street and into both side yards from my vantage point on my hands and knees.

I raise myself up on my haunches, resting my palms flat on my knees, and continue my perusal of the landscape. The super-fine baby hairs on the back of my neck tingle, causing me to shiver.

Narrowing my eyes, I give one more cautious stare into the hedgerow before returning to my hands and knees to continue my search.

"You really shouldn't let your guard down so soon," Caleb's deep voice says from somewhere above me, and I hear a wooden, hollow shuffle. "Now would be the perfect time for you to get assaulted."

He's standing on the porch of the Omega house, leaning against the heavy white balustrade, hands stuffed in the pockets of black Adidas track pants, shoulders slouched. The hood of his light gray sweatshirt is up, but I can see that he's not wearing his baseball cap.

Black.

His hair is jet black.

"I'm not going to get assaulted, unless it's by you. Besides, it's broad daylight." Self-consciously, still kneeling, I look up at him from the ground.

"See, *that's* the kind of rationale that gets girls in trouble." He draws the sentence out slowly, his dark eyes boring into mine.

I emit a scoff. "Do you make it a habit to creep up on people from the shadows?"

He wordlessly continues surveying me from the porch and crosses his arms.

It's driving me crazy. Pushing myself up off the ground, I get to my feet, swipe the loose gravel off the knees of my navy leggings, and pull down the hemline of my running top so it covers my rear end.

"Why do you hardly talk?" I exclaim somewhat rudely to break the unbearable silence, propping my fisted hands on my narrow hips.

Caleb considers this and lifts one shoulder in a shrug. "I don't know." Pause. "Why does everything embarrass you?"

My mouth falls open. "I-I…" I stutter, but nothing more comes out. I take a deep breath and gather my thoughts, and just as I'm about to squeak out an unapologetic quip in reply, another figure emerges from under the overhang of the large covered veranda.

I close my jaw.

Slightly shorter than Caleb but just as large, he's wearing plaid pajama bottoms and stretching, his green t-shirt riding up and revealing a taut, tan six-pack. He yawns, staring down at me with keen interest as I loiter in their side yard.

He's glancing back and forth between Caleb and me,

and I can tell he's trying to assess the situation but coming up short. "Well, well, well—who are *you*?"

I give pause. "Who are *you*?"

The blond guy laughs. "I'm Blaze. What's a pretty little thing like you doing down in the yard? You should be up here, getting to know me better."

How charming.

"Oh, brother," I deadpan, rolling my eyes and crossing my arms. "Does that line usually work for you?"

"I don't know, does it?" Blaze laughs again, his white teeth gleaming in the morning sun against a tan face. Jeez Louise, he's really freaking cute—so much so that his flirting is actually overwhelming me.

Wow, do I suck at this.

He's friendlier, and more welcoming, and *safer* than gloomy Caleb, so I relax a little.

"Maybe you're just having an off day," I hypothesize, giving them both a shy grin before I can stop myself. "I'm sure you'll have much better luck catching the *next* girl who wanders through the yard."

"I sure hope so." Blaze rubs his chin, brainstorming, and then snaps his fingers. "Maybe if I cast an actual net I would catch one?"

I titter. "Excellent idea."

Blaze folds his arms, his heavily tattooed biceps bulging. I catch him dart a sidelong glance at Caleb before giving him a hard nudge from behind with his elbow. Caleb loses his footing and staggers forward, shooting Blaze a dirty look over his shoulder and loudly mumbling, "Would you knock that shit off?"

"Only if you stop being such a cock-guzzler and go talk to her."

"Why are you pushing this?" Caleb hisses.

"Because you're being a little bitch-ass."

"Fuck you."

"No, fuck you."

What. Is. Happening.

Amused, I watch them feverishly taunting each other in hushed whispers. Their vulgar bickering actually makes me choke back an entertained laugh.

Curiously, I brazenly advance a few feet and cock my head to the side. "Does everyone around here have a terrible nickname, or is it just the two of you?"

"Terrible nicknames?" Blaze grins down at me. "Are you trying to say that Blaze is a terrible nickname? We earned those nicknames on the ice, sweetheart."

"Ah, and here I thought they were just sex references."

"Honey, if that were the case, they'd call me Hung Like a Stallion, not Blaze."

I blush a crimson red, embarrassed to even have asked. And yet… "Well, what does your nickname mean, anyway?" My eyes dart to Caleb, who is intently watching my exchange with his friend.

He hasn't moved an inch of what I assume are solid muscles.

"I'm fast, and I score—a goddamn blaze of glory! My buddy Showtime here"—Blaze jerks his thumb at Caleb—"well he's the best damn goaltender in the entire NCAA. Did you know that? We used to call him the Lockhart Show when he was a rookie. You should see him work his stick." He lets out a low whistle, and I hear Caleb let out a horrified groan at the innuendo. My brows only raise a fraction as he continues. "We shortened it to Showtime, right, buddy?"

The Lockhart Show.

Lockhart.

Caleb Lockhart.

God, even his name is schmexy.

My gaze shifts and our eyes meet as Blaze continues to ramble on obliviously, and I force myself not to stare at the grass. "Showtime here could show you moves you've never seen." He winks at me and slaps his hand down on Caleb's shoulder, rotating his hips like he's got a hula-hoop around his waist. "Hockey players are notorious for giving good swivel action."

Caleb shrugs his hand off, agitated, causing the hood covering his head to shift and giving me a better view of his dark, unruly hair.

It falls into his dark, brooding eyes, shaggy and thick, before he reaches up to brush it back under his hood. I swallow at the sight of it, guiltily looking toward the detached garage in between the two houses to avoid his intense gaze.

Bashful now, I clasp and unclasp my hands, glancing back up at the porch. "Well, I didn't find what I was looking for, so…I'll just…you know, be going. Home."

I try stuffing my hands into a pocket of my short shirt before awkwardly remembering this shirt doesn't have one. Self-conscious of the fact that my rear end is on full display, I descend down the driveway, tennis shoes crunching on the loose concrete.

I risk a glimpse over my shoulder and find Caleb glaring after me, then quickly scurry down the driveway.

Caleb

"**B**ro, you should get on that," Bryan "Blaze" Wallace announces beside me, giving me another hard nudge. He stares off into the yard at Abby's retreating form, both of us appreciating the view of her tight navy yoga capris as they showcase her firm runner's ass.

Abby looks back over her shoulder, long chestnut ponytail swinging, before her hands fumble around her aqua-blue top, seeming to search for a pocket but failing to find one.

"For fuck's sake, dude. Don't just stand here, go say something."

I'm rooted to the spot.

"Jesus Christ, Showtime, she's going to be halfway down the goddamn street before you pull your head outta your ass."

Blaze shoves me again, aggressively, toward the stairs. This time, instead of resisting, I go. I go because I want to. I go because my feet are on autopilot, forgetting that chasing girls across my yard isn't something I would normally ever do.

Bounding down the stairs, I cross the yard and make toward the sidewalk.

"Atta boy!" Blaze shouts obscenely loudly from the porch, and I shake my head skyward, making a mental note to sack him in the nuts when I get back.

I jog down the sidewalk, bounding around the corner, and falter momentarily in my tracks when I catch sight of Abby leaning against the stop-n-go light on the corner, forehead pressed to the pole and arms hanging limply at her side.

I quicken my pace. "Abby?" My voice comes out slightly panicked. "Are you okay?" I ask as I approach, jamming my hands back into my pockets.

"Oh my god, Caleb." Abby's head flies up, and her posture straightens as she clutches a hand to her chest. "You can't sneak up on people like that. You scared the crap out of me."

"I'm six foot three. It's virtually impossible for me to sneak anywhere," I point out sardonically. "Are you okay?" I ask again. "Why were you leaning against the pole? Did something happen?"

"Can't a girl take a breather?" Abby ignores my question, looking both ways before hopping down from the curb and crossing the street, leaving me no choice but to trail after her.

I hesitate before gracelessly catching up.

"Yes, but you…"

When I don't finish my sentence, she stops abruptly in the middle of the sidewalk and turns to face me. "But what?"

You scared the shit out of me. Of course, I don't admit that out loud, so I just go with a casual shrug.

"I'm…sorry. I don't mean to be rude." My eyebrows go up as Abby emits a sigh. "I'm just frustrated. I was at the house looking for a ring." She bites her lower lip. "It was a gift from my parents."

Yeah, I know.

"They gave it to me when I graduated from high school"—*I figured*—"and I lost it. I thought maybe it would be outside Tyler's window, but…" She looks down at the sidewalk under our feet, her shoulders hunched in defeat.

I feel like the world's biggest asshole.

"Have you searched his bedroom?" I casually suggest, trying to school my features so I don't look like such a lying bastard.

"I asked him to look. I'd rather not have to go back up there; it's pretty gross. I'm sure he would have mentioned finding it." She doesn't look very confident as she chews on her thumbnail.

We continue walking side by side until we come to an old blue house with a small crooked porch that sags in the middle. Quickly assessing it, I determine it could use new siding, new windows, and new gutters. Abby stops at the end of its gravel driveway, gesturing over her shoulder.

"This is me."

"This is where you live?"

I glance down the street, counting houses, making a mental catalog of the distance.

Two blocks away.

"Yup. This is where I live," she says, smiling. "Home, sweet dilapidated home."

"It's very majestic," I say with a poker face, glancing over at her off-campus rental.

Her amused snicker carries in the wind. "For a dump?"

"I was going to go with shithole," I tease, my lips almost tipping into a smile.

Almost.

Abby laughs a light, airy laugh that hums like a twinkle and causes my insides to flutter involuntarily. Then she smiles, her pale pink lips curving slowly, causing her eyes to crinkle at the corners, and I forget all about the flutters and instead focus on her face. She observes me under long, black, mascara-less lashes, and I allow myself to think that she looks damn pretty without it. Pretty without makeup, that is. Just pretty.

A smile for me, of all people.

I draw in a breath, enchanted, and stop daydreaming like a goddamn girl, when she says, "Okay, so…thanks, for, um…walking me home, I guess. At least it wasn't very far." She's babbling.

I shuffle my feet uncomfortably as Abby turns her back to me, toward the house.

"See ya." She gives a small wave over her shoulder, glancing back shyly at me like she did in my front yard. It's a questioning glance that I'm not quite sure how to interpret. I've always been total shit at these kinds of things—one of the many reasons I tend to stay away from girls.

"See ya."

But Abby doesn't hear my reply, nor does she see my hand raised in a retreating wave.

Because she's already in the house.

Because I waited too long.

Because I'm a fucking idiot.

***

Cecelia: *The suspense is killing me. Got any updates?*

Abby: *Sort of. I went to the Omega house, which is now the hockey house, and was caught crawling around on my hands and knees.*

Cecelia: *Guys LOVE that sort of thing! Just ask Jenna (wink!)*

Abby: *Could you be serious for one minute?*

Cecelia: *I can only promise that I'll try…*

Caleb

I hate house parties.

Fucking hate them. They never end well.

What they *do* end with is me fixing shit up—patching dry wall, repairing or replacing furniture, nailing, taping, or gluing something back together, and generally monitoring the landscape to keep the place in one solid piece so it doesn't end up looking like the frat house next door.

House parties also occasionally end with me getting pissed off and holing up in my suite to spare myself the pain of socializing with my peers.

I should have pummeled Cubby when he started inviting people to the house, knowing it was going to get out of hand, but as usual, I don't want anyone thinking that because my parents own the joint, I'm going to police everything that happens here.

Not my job…well, not technically.

Retreating to the front porch, both to escape the crush

inside and to grab a beer, I ignore the freshman rookie posted at the door. I open a large red cooler, snatch out an ice-cold bottle of beer, twist off the cap, and take a long, refreshing pull. I debate whether or not I should return to the house—privacy versus responsibility, solitude versus socializing. Responsibility wins, and I grab one more beer, double-fisting it before ambling back inside.

The house is already filling with people and buzzing with excitement; the Omega house is known for loud, entertaining parties that last all night and rarely get busted.

Florida Georgia Line blasts out of the stereo, and the last MLB game replays on the giant high-def TV mounted above the fireplace in the spacious living room. Elbowing my way through the throng, I head toward the kitchen and, relieved to find it empty, set one beer down on the counter and lean my hip against the solid oak table.

My solitude lasts for all of three whopping seconds.

"Thought I'd find you in here," Weston says, coming through the door and walking to the pantry, where I can hear him rooting around noisily, like a squirrel digging for a nut—or a bear digging through a metal garbage can.

Emerging with a bag of tortilla chips, he rips it open, stuffs a few in his mouth, and directs his attention back to me. "You aren't in here hiding, are you? Cause that would be silly."

I roll my eyes and take a swig of beer.

"Molly's out there, and she brought a few friends she expects you to meet. That chick Abby that Blaze said you chased down the street is out in the living room."

I choke on my beer and narrow my eyes.

Fucking. Blaze.

"What the hell were you doing chasing her down? Jeez, man, she's best friends with Cece Carter—you know, Matt Wakefield's girlfriend?"

Clenching my jaw, I grit out, "I did *not* chase her down the damn street."

Weston gives me a patronizing look, like I'm some cuckoo cat lady and he has to talk slow so he doesn't unleash the crazy. "All I'm saying is you can't stay in here all night. You have to get out there and make nice. It's your house; that makes you the host by default."

I grunt and shoot him a dark glower.

"Now what are you getting all pissed about? Abby's hot...you know, in a *cute* kind of way." Weston snickers and stuffs more chips into his stupid fat face. As he mutters, "You're too sensitive, bro," chip pieces fly out of his mouth and drop to the floor. "Oophfs."

Grabbing the second beer off the counter, I straighten to my full height and stalk into the crowded living room.

Abby

The longer I stand here, the wetter I get.

Wait, that didn't come out right...

Sighing, the cup in my hand is jostled yet again as someone drunk bumps/dances/falls into me, creating another oh-so-attractive wet spot on the front of my shirt, and I cringe, afraid the shirt is going to be ruined by the end of this torturous night.

The shirt I was required to borrow.

Ambushed while trying to sneak out of my bedroom

unnoticed, my roommates waylaid my escape with a different shirt then forced me to sit in the bathroom while Jenna curled and styled my hair. According to Jenna, and I quote: *"Abby, if you're trying to walk out of here dressed like a librarian, it's working, but if you want Caleb to notice you, let me amp up the sexy-cute. Nothing trashy, just a boost. Trust in the Jenna System."*

By the way, in case you're wondering, sexy-cute is an actual term Cecelia and I made up.

Definition:

Sexy-cute

/ˈseksē/kyüt/

Adjective

Too cute to be sexy, but too sexy to be innocent and boring.

Example: *Oh my gosh! Did you see Margaret? I thought she was such a prude, but that outfit she's wearing is actually super sexy-cute.*

So, yeah. Sexy-cute. Get to know it.

Since I own too many basic cotton t-shirts, I was given (by Jenna) something (of hers) to wear before being plunked down in Jenna's famous chair of torture and dolled up by the experts (Jenna).

Are you sensing a pattern here? She's a tyrant.

Fortunately, my roommate took my wishes to heart, and I was still recognizable when I gazed back at my reflection in the mirror: long hair down and flat-ironed straight, black liquid liner on my top lids with a hint of onyx mascara, shiny lip gloss with a hint of coral. Jenna has me trussed up in dark skinny-jean capris, a skin-hugging baby blue wrap shirt with a deep V-neck, and a thin blue belt cinching it closed and emphasizing my waist.

It could have been considered sexy-demure had it not been covered in wet spots. Now it's downright *wet t-shirt contest.*

Thank god for padded bras.

Molly looks down at the front of my borrowed shirt—the one now plastered to my chest—and raises her eyebrows. "You're not going to want to hear this, but that's actually a really good look for you."

Jenna leans over and inspects the damage. "I'd say it's an improvement."

"Shut Up and Dance" by Walk the Moon comes blasting out loudly over the speakers, and Jenna bounces on her heels, shaking her wild hair as she shouts, "I freaking love this song!" and sings along. "*I said you're holding back, she said shut up and dance with me!*"

My roommate grabs my wrist, trying to get me to dance, but I'm wet and not in the mood, considering we've only been here for, what? Half an hour? Playfully slapping Jenna's hands off my arm, I quickly gulp down what's left of the warm beer in my plastic red cup, sputtering a little from the putrid taste of it.

Ugh, so gross. I hate beer.

So why am I drinking it?

Easy. It doesn't take a genius to figure out I'm drinking because we're *here*, in Caleb's *house.*

The moment I realized where we were headed tonight, I stood transfixed in the yard of the Omega house. While Molly, Jenna, and a few of our other friends busted through its door, I stayed there, debating. I so badly did not want to come. Even on a Friday night, I would have preferred to stay home and bury my head in a textbook rather than come here…or finish season two of *Game of Thrones*.

I'm petrified.

It took every ounce of courage I had to put one high-heeled foot in front of the other, climb the stairs to the Omega house, and push through the heavy front door.

Every. Single. Ounce. Of. Courage.

I didn't see him at first.

For the first half hour, he was completely missing in action. Then, I watched as Jenna whispered to Molly, who leaned over and whispered to her boyfriend Weston, who then walked off and disappeared into some back room. Suddenly, I became overly conscious of everyone whispering to everyone but me.

Conscious of the fact that I'm a little too sober.

Conscious of the fact that Caleb is somewhere in this house.

I take a deep breath and run a finger through my long hair, giving it a gentle toss so it rests over my left shoulder, then give the front of my pale blue shirt a tug. A lot tighter than I would normally wear, it was sticking to my chest before we even got here. Now that it's covered in beer, it's like a second skin. Add in the fact that, like a fool, I let Jenna talk me into a padded push-up bra—well, I look like the kind of girl who does the walk of shame on regular basis and stars in one of those *Girls Who Show Their Boobs on Spring Break* videos.

Groaning, I look back up and find Molly watching me with a smirk on her face. "Need another drink?" she asks smugly, extending another cup toward me. "Here, take this. Weston went to get me another one."

I eye her above the brim of the cup and take a sip.

"I would take a bigger drink if I were you," she says, eyeing the door behind me and leaning forward. "Weston told me about your little run-in with Caleb Lockhart."

"What? How? I don't get it…"

She waves her hand around aimlessly. "Blaze told him and he told me. Better watch out, he gossips like a flipping girl."

"Who? Blaze or Weston?" I ask dryly, unamused.

"Both." Molly laughs and reaches over to tip the cup toward my mouth, silently urging me to take another drink. "I don't want to pry or anything, but…"

"But you're going to anyway?"

"Yeah, pretty much. Don't worry, I haven't told anyone else what Weston told me, so Jenna is still clueless enough to leave you alone—besides the mini makeover. Better steer clear though, because once she hears you were on your hands and knees in his yard"—Molly shrugs causally and sighs—"you're screwed."

"Well, then I'm so excited to be standing here in this damp shirt with half the room knowing my business. I look like I'm about to enter a wet t-shirt contest, for crying out loud."

Molly looks me up and down then smiles wickedly. "You want my opinion?"

"No."

"That damp shirt looks hot. I'm sorry, but he's gonna lay those big angry eyes on you and not know where to look. I almost feel bad for the poor guy." She giggles.

"He's so awkward."

"Shut up, Molly," I whine, taking yet another sip of beer. At this rate, I need all the courage—liquid or not—that I can get.

"Whoa, Nelly, bring it down a notch," Molly lectures. "Pace yourself." She looks up and across the room, her eyes going wide. "On second thought, drink up."

My thoughts exactly.

Caleb

"Pace yourself, bro, or we're going to be dragging your Yeti-sized ass up the stairs before bar time," Stephan Randolph, one of my teammates, complains, giving me a disgruntled sidelong glance. "What's your problem tonight, anyway?

"There's a girl here he's trying to avoid," Blaze responds helpfully into his vodka glass, nudging me with his elbow. He lifts his free hand and points across the room. "See? She's in the tight blue shirt."

I slap his hand and scowl. "Put your fucking hand down."

Stephan raises one drunken eyebrow and squints over in Abby's direction. "Whoa, she's pretty damn cute. What's her name?"

"None of your damn business."

"Huh. That's a weird name. Terrible, in fact." Stephan sways slightly, slapping me on the back and laughing directly into my ear. "I take it you haven't introduced her to

Showtime *Junior* yet?"

Flexing my free hand, I stuff it in the pocket of my jeans so I don't accidentally put my fist through the shit-dick's face.

Blaze notices and steps in. "Whoa, Steve-O, watch it. Showtime here isn't amused."

I glance over to where Abby stands surrounded by her friends, so pretty and seemingly unfazed by all the bullshit surrounding her. See, here's the thing: sometimes being in the spotlight—even on a smaller scale, like on a college campus—is exhausting. Guys pretend to be our friends. Some want to drink with us on those rare occasions we throw a rager. Strangers invite us to their parties, begging us to come to increase their social status. Girls stalk us in various ways, vying for our attention, just to say they dated us—or flirted with, screwed, or blew us.

Take your damn pick.

I glance around the room and notice my teammates getting pawed, hung on, petted, and groped.

Granted, not many guys in their twenties actually *mind* getting their cocks grabbed, but…still.

Lay off mine.

I watch a few girls hang on members of the baseball team while others flirt outlandishly with my teammates, all of them overzealously competing for attention.

It's actually painful to watch.

Abby, on the other hand, looks like she'd rather be anywhere but here, which is…refreshing. Encouraging. Definitely different.

I guzzle the rest of what's left in my beer bottle and

nod above the crowd toward the freshman rookie managing the door. He instantly disappears outside but is back in record time with another bottle for me in a short few, top twisted off and ready to go.

I tip it back and chug.

Someone snickers. "Hey, Showtime, you think if you drink enough of those you'll grow some balls and go over there?"

Not likely.

Abby

"This is getting ridiculous," the voice mutters beside me. I can barely hear her because the music is so loud, but Jenna is loud enough that I recognize the tone when she's complaining. "What is he doing just standing there?"

My slight buzz has me craning my neck to look around the room. "What are you bitching about?" I curse. My eyes widen and I clamp a hand over my potty mouth, apologizing through my fingers. "Sorry. It's the three beers talking. Absolutely *no one* should be letting me drink."

Jenna rolls her eyes. "Keep it up, trucker mouth, and you'll be useless by the end of the night. Sheesh. Get it together." She's teasing, but it sobers me up and I straighten my posture, mindful not to stick my damp boobs out.

Molly taps her chin thoughtfully and loops her arm through Jenna's. "I think we should mingle, don't you ladies? This corner is getting boring. Let's go chat with the guys." She jerks her head, indicating the group of guys Weston is standing in the middle of, holding court.

I can see him gesturing wildly from here, animated,

obviously in the middle of a story, and a funny one, too, if the laughter surrounding him is any indication.

Before I know it, I'm being pulled through the crowd by my two determined friends, toward a crowd of boys with whom I'm hardly familiar, let alone comfortable (besides Weston). It's all I can do to *not* dig my heels into the carpet to stop myself from being propelled forward by my wobbly arms, strong-armed against my will by both Jenna and Molly.

I want to stomp my feet like a baby and run out of this house.

I make a mental list of things I could be doing right now if I weren't being dragged in a struggle cuddle toward Caleb, whose broad back is facing me, and I recite them in my head:

1. Study for my midterms, which are in a few short weeks.
2. Clean the bathroom toilet.
3. Watch *Game of Thrones* on demand. Again. For the twelfth time.
4. Hide under my covers.
5. Hide under my covers.

I don't know about you, but I'm quite partial to numbers four and five.

Caleb

"Incoming!" Blaze announces at the top of his voice, hands cupped around his mouth to create a megaphone.

"Girlfriend rapidly approaching," he says to Weston.

"And she's dragging None of Your Damn Business behind her," Stephan jokes. "Showtime, your lover looks like she's about to barf. Maybe you should take her upstairs and introduce her to your big, cold, empty bed."

Luckily, I've already tossed back about five beers; combined with my large six-foot-three frame, that hasn't made me drunk, but it has given me a decent buzz and taken the edge off.

I ignore Stephan.

Feigning indifference to his barb, I reach up and readjust my ball cap, turning the brim so it faces the back of my head, and hold the brim in my palms, squeezing it to reshape the bill. I lower my hands at the same time a warm body is shoved, stumbling, into our circle. Molly and the girl with the purple hair tactlessly propel Abby so she's standing directly in front of me.

Someone else gives her a gentle push until she's faltering, tripping into my personal space. Instinctively, my palms shoot out to stop her from falling, settling on her slim waist to steady her.

Shit.

I jerk my hands back, body stiffening from the invasion of my boundaries. Then I look down into the crown of Abby's long, straight, rich brown hair; it's shiny and silky, and I kind of want to touch it.

Goddamn beer.

She turns her entire body to face me, mere inches away, tilting her head and biting her lip, mortified. Her hands flutter about her helplessly, fingertips accidentally brushing my chest. Once. Twice.

"I am so s-sorry. This is so embarrassing. My friends are…they…"

"Are assholes?" I have to bend down so she can hear me, practically whispering in her ear. "Mine are too. Clearly."

Her body shivers and she nods, biting her lip before whipping her head toward the group, the action kicking up a subtle flowery scent.

My nostrils flare.

Shit. I can smell her damn hair.

I don't know if it's the five beers I've had, or the music, or the amount of people crammed into the place, but it's fucking with my common sense—so much so that I give myself permission to lean forward and deeply inhale her loose strands.

It must have been a long, loud whiff, because Abby turns to confront me. "Did you just smell my *hair*?" Her eyes are wide with disbelief, and I can tell by her dilated pupils that she's had a few too many drinks herself.

"Uh…" I hesitate a heartbeat too long and consider lying. "Yes?"

As if it were possible, her clear blue eyes widen farther, her glossy mouth forming a surprised O—she obviously wasn't expecting me to be honest.

Abby self-consciously reaches up to smooth her hair down. "I… Oh."

Oh. That little word—spoken *that way*—makes my stomach flip.

She blushes prettily and we both stand there, neither of us knowing what the hell to do next.

Obviously.

Abby

"I… Oh." I fumble, embarrassed.

I knew he was sniffing my hair, but I didn't think he'd actually admit it.

He casts his gaze down between our bodies, and my eyes follow the trail. We're inches apart, and all it would take is one…little…*push* for our bodies to collide.

I wish for it at the same time I will more space in between us.

Eyes downcast, I study his hands, one thumb hooked through the belt loop of his low-slung jeans, the other clutching an amber beer bottle. I glance at his untucked slub cotton t-shirt, its frayed hem hanging limply over his waistband.

Caleb stands frozen in place, his rock-hard body not moving an inch—kind of like the proverbial deer in headlights. He allows my probing eyes to explore every inch of his toned upper body, grazing over the well-defined pec muscles, gloriously emphasized by the tight gray t-shirt, his nipples hard under the soft fabric. Up, up my gaze goes, up to his firm broad shoulders.

I gulp as the cords in the thick column of his neck twitch, the only indication he's still breathing, while I rake my blue eyes over his freshly shaven, square jaw. The dark black hair peeking out from his ball cap wisps around his ears, his heavy eyebrows forced into a severe line.

I want to touch it—his *hair* I mean.

Oh my god.

"Smile," I softly implore, attempting to lighten the mood.

He jerks his head side to side. *No.*

"No? But…why?" Balancing in my strappy corkscrew wedge sandals is a challenge, but I make it to my tippy toes, my lips grazing the outer column of his bright pink ear. My nose touches his neck, and emboldened by my beer-fueled haze, I give his neck a nuzzle before pressing my body against his. Returning his earlier favor, I inhale and—sweet Jesus—his freshly showered, soap-and-musk smell is so heavenly, my eyes flutter shut. They flutter. Shut. "Why won't you smile?" I whisper.

"Uh…"

"I want to see it," I whisper. "Please." Later, I'll blame this all on alcohol.

"See *what*?" he croaks, eyes going wide and tilting his head to the side when I nudge it with the tip of my nose. I sniff him again, the skin under his ear soft against my lips, and *feel* him groan, a deep rumble vibrating against my chest. It takes every ounce of willpower I possess not to wiggle against him.

Maybe I *am* sexy.

The thought gives me courage.

"The gap in your teeth." *Sheesh, what has gotten into me?* "I haven't stopped thinking about it since you smiled at me the other day."

"Really?" he asks, pulling his head back in surprise. "You're shitting me, right?" He eyes me suspiciously, and out of habit, his tongue does that thing where it runs along the edge of his upper teeth.

That action alone has me looking away and biting my

lip.

"How many beers have you had?" Caleb asks with a raised eyebrow, lifting his beer to take a drag. "And when did I smile at you?"

"At Walmart," I say matter-of-factly, powered by alcohol. "You know—when I was buying *tampons.*"

He spits out some of his beer, the spray of alcohol hitting my face and the front of my already damp shirt, and his shocked gaze roams the front of my chest. He jerks his wide, horrified expression away from the cleavage created by Jenna's push-up bra. "Shit, Abby, I am so sorry."

I cock my head to the side and plant a hand on my hip, gesturing to my shirt. "I don't know if you've noticed, but I'm already wet."

I swear to you, I didn't mean for it to sound dirty; it just came out that way.

I swipe away the beer dripping down my left cheek.

Caleb removes his hand from his belt loop and runs it down the front of his flaming-red face. "Do you want to at least try to clean off a little in the bathroom?"

Caleb

As I put my hand on Abby's lower back to steer her toward the bathroom, the group behind us hoots and hollers like a bunch of jackasses, and I shoot a heated look over my shoulder. "Go give her the old poke check, Showtime!" shouts Cubby at the same time Stephan yells, "Bag it and tag it!"

"And here I thought *my* friends were bad." Abby chuckles over her shoulder—or at least that's what I *think* she's saying. It's pretty damn loud in here and hard to hear with the music pumping.

I guide her to the first-floor bathroom, which is off the kitchen near the pantry, but when we get there, there's a line about seven girls deep.

Abby takes a spot at the end of the line, and I lean against the wall next to her as she faces straight ahead, fiddling with her hands. The bathroom door eventually opens, and four girls file out while another two stumble in.

Jesus Christ, it's like Grand Central Station during rush

hour.

Realizing this could take all night, I rationalize that it's not my job to stand here keeping Abby company while she waits to clean off her wet shirt, even if I did spit beer in her face.

I can leave her here and return to our friends.

On one hand, girls are used to waiting in lines at parties, right? Aren't the lines for the ladies' bathrooms always twice as long as those for the guys' bathrooms?

On the other hand...

A blonde in a purple camisole—or whatever you call those silky-looking pajama tank top things—stops in front of me, red lips parting as she devours me with her eyes. "You're Caleb Lockhart, aren't you?" Her smile is one I've seen before: smug, assured, self-confident, and meant to have me eating out of the palm of her hand.

Coldly, I gaze silently back at her, my eyes flicking briefly to Abby, who's taken a sudden interest in counting flowers on the wallpaper.

"Cat got your tongue?" the girl flirts, her bare arm reaching for the sleeve of my shirt and giving it a playful tug with her long fingertips.

"Don't," I mutter, the unfriendly tone reaching my eyes.

The blonde assesses me, not ready to give up the chase, and titters at me. "God. You're even better looking up close." She leans in, and just as she's about to press her perky tits against the front of my shirt, one word crosses my lips.

"Abby."

"Um, no." The blonde gives her head a shake with a frown. "My name is Francesca."

"Not you. *Her.*" After debating, I make a decision. Side-stepping the pretty co-ed, I give Abby a curt nod and demand, "Follow me."

We move through the crush with classmates, team-mates, and strangers greeting us as we make our way back through the living room, some of them sizing up Abby with open interest. Bodies are everywhere with little room to easily navigate, but it's my damn house and I throw a few elbows as we weave our way through.

Just as I round the living room and charge into the foyer, I feel fingers graze the palm hanging at my hip and pause briefly to gape down as Abby slides her delicate hand into it mine.

"Is this okay?" she yells. "I just don't want to lose you in the crowd."

Pleased, I give her delicate hand a squeeze. Latching onto the final post at the bottom of the stairs, I give Abby a tug, pulling her tight against my side and propelling my-self up the staircase.

"Move!" I thunder, paving a path for us to ease our way up, step by step, to the second story.

I stop in front of my bedroom, which is the master and the last room on the right, punch in the combination for my lock, and pull her through the door, flipping on the light switch before locking the door behind us. I point to the door in the far corner of the suite. "Bathroom's over there."

Real suave, I know.

Abby nods, her keen eyes taking in her surroundings: the dark forest green walls that my parents painstakingly painted, the pennants and hockey posters, the large oak desk and computer, the science-fiction book collection methodically arranged by height on a built-in bookshelf.

She pauses before the bathroom door, biting her lip. "I'll only be a minute." Abby taps the doorframe twice then walks through, shutting the door.

Abby

Bracing myself against the counter in Caleb's bathroom, which is the master suite if the double vanity sinks, ginormous jetted bathtub, and spacious walk-in closet are any indication. Masculinity assaults my senses. The entire room smells like guy—aftershave or cologne or whatever guys use to smell amazing permeates the air, and a few bottles of Polo sit on the countertop.

I reach over and carefully pick up a blue bottle of cologne, lift the cap off, and close my eyes, inhaling its musky, outdoorsy scent. Very gingerly, so it doesn't make a clanking sound, I replace the cap and set the cologne back in its rightful place.

Resting my hands on either side of the sink, I exhale and stare back at my reflection.

I'll admit, I don't exactly look terrible.

In fact, the alcohol-induced courage has added some much-needed luminosity to my skin and my eyes are glowing vibrantly. Running my fingers through my hair, I fluff it a bit, tossing it over my shoulders.

A stack of clean green washcloths sits neatly arranged on a shelf, and I grab one, turning on the cold water to dampen it. I wring out the excess water, blotting the washcloth against my sticky skin, down my neck, and into my décolletage.

You never really understand how sticky beer is until it gets spilled—or spit—directly on your skin and left there to dry. Well, I understand it now, and it's freaking gross.

Studying myself in the mirror, I focus on my chest and the way it looks in the push-up bra I reluctantly put on under my shirt. I'll admit I didn't really *need* a push-up bra, but it does display my perky, full B-cup breasts nicely within the deep neckline of the pale blue wrap shirt, and even though I'm embarrassed at having my boobs on exhibit, I can't help acknowledging they look pretty darn good.

Actually, my boobs look *great*.

Encouraged, I turn this way and that, checking out my boobs and ass in the mirror. The dark-wash skinny-jean capris are a pair I haven't worn in ages, so I was thrilled to discover they actually still fit my size five/six frame.

I didn't even have to lie down on the bed to zip them up—*there is a god!*

I strapped on some nude summer wedges, the leather straps wrapping around my ankles and buckling with gold hardware in the front. Very sexy. Very cute.

You know—sexy-cute. (Wink.)

Once I'm done wiping myself down, I neatly fold the washcloth in half and drape it over the towel bar next to the bathtub. Spinning back toward the sink, a pair of glasses catches my eye. I move to pick them up, biting down on my lip as I inspect them.

Thick black Ray-Ban frames with prescription lenses.

I close my eyes for a second, trying to visualize Caleb's

pensive, dark-chocolate gaze framed by these glasses, and I give a little squeak, followed by a wistful sigh. I catalog *sexy black glasses,* mentally filing them under *Abby's Kryptonite*, in the same category as *gaps in teeth.*

Setting the glasses back on the counter precisely where I found them, I take a calming breath and stare at the doorknob before inhaling and pulling the door open.

Squaring my shoulders, I walk back into Caleb's bedroom. He's lying across his bed, head resting on a ton of pillows—way more pillows than any guy should have and bordering on feminine—and feet hanging over the edge as he stares a hole through the bathroom door.

He straightens hastily when I walk out, runs his palms up and down his upper thighs a few times, and scoots himself on the edge of the large king-sized bed. "All good?"

"Yup. All good…" I answer absentmindedly, my eyes once again scanning his room.

First thought: it's much cleaner than I would have guessed. His bed has been made, a navy-blue duvet-covered comforter folded neatly at the foot of it. The many throw pillows of grays, blues, and greens are stacked in an orderly fashion at the headboard. On his nightstand is another pair of black-rimmed glasses, a water bottle, and a small stack of novels.

Silently, I read the titles from where I stand: *American Sniper, The 7 Habits of Highly Effective People, Shit My Dad Says*, and…is that *Harry Potter*?

Talk about a diverse collection.

Secretly pleased, I give a furtive smile.

Caleb stands, smoothing down his jeans and rumpled shirt, but I'm not ready to walk out into the party mayhem—not just yet. He watches me intently as I walk over to the desk, trailing a fingertip along the solid wood, glancing up at him briefly from the corner of my eye as I rest my hand on a hardcover copy of *Gone Girl*.

I pick it up, flipping through the pages, the familiar smell of freshly printed paper assaulting my senses. "I haven't read an actual book for pleasure in months," I say, twisting my wrist as I hold it toward him. "But I did read this one. What did you think of it?"

Caleb pauses, gathering his thoughts silently. "I think... the ending was fucked up."

I laugh and set the book back down. "I guess I thought so too, although I wouldn't have used *those* exact words."

"Sorry."

The dim light from his bedside lamp glows, casting a warm light in the cozy space.

"You're really quiet. What are you thinking right now?" I ask, because I'm still tipsy and because I really want to know what he's thinking.

"You're not supposed to ask guys that," comes his low reply.

"Why?"

"It's basic Guy 101. Even *I* know that." He's quiet for a few more seconds, eyebrows furrowed, concentrating hard. "Besides...you probably wouldn't like the answer."

"But maybe that's where you'd be wrong," I say, walking idly over to the bookshelf and studying the titles so purposefully arranged there. I glance over my shoulder before adding, "Maybe I would."

I hear him grunt, but he doesn't reply, so I momentarily

turn to face him.

"Well?"

His mouth opens, then closes, and I can sense his internal debate. Whatever is going on inside his beautiful head, he's afraid to say it out loud. And here I thought *I* was the awkward one…

With my back still turned to him, I continue studying the shelf—the books, the collection of hockey trophies and medals, the random knickknacks, and the dozen or so framed photographs of him in various states of hockey play, with his parents at his high school graduation, doing a flip while wakeboarding, and one with a gray-haired old lady that we'll assume is his grandma.

Everything is lined up and displayed tidily.

I pick up a Wayne Gretzke bobble-head, give it a gentle shake, and watch the head bounce back and forth on the small spring inside the neck, then quietly set it back on the shelf. "Hmmm," I mutter.

He hesitates. "Hmmm what?"

I chuckle as I continue my inspection. "Nothing. Just hmmm."

Caleb crosses his arms and scowls with a pout. "Tell me what you're thinking. Why did you say *hmmm*?"

I walk toward him—toward the door—and smile up into his frowning face. *So serious, this one.* "You probably wouldn't like the answer." I mimic his earlier response sarcastically, embarrassed to have even asked in the first place, and reach for the door handle.

I paste an uncertain smile on my face, and my long, lithe fingers slowly but deliberately turn the handle then give the door a gentle tug. "We should probably get back to the party," I state.

Suddenly, Caleb's large calloused hand is on my upper arm, stopping me from turning the knob farther, and I glance down, staring at the loose grip he has on my bicep but making no move to back away. Nevertheless, he yanks his hand back like I just singed him with a branding iron and apologizes. "Shit, sorry."

Just when I think maybe, just maybe, he is about to put the moves on me, he backs up to give me a wide berth, and I pull the door wide open. Music from the state-of-the-art sound system immediately pounds up the staircase, the bass vibrating the walls up and down the hall until it reaches his bedroom and assaults my eardrums—and probably his too.

"How can you stand living in a party house?" I ask as we step out into the hall, him shutting the door behind him and checking to make sure it's locked. "This is nuts."

If possible, there are even more bodies crowding the hallway than before.

Caleb is close, leaning in to whisper in my ear. His warm breath against my neck nearly causes me to shiver, but I'm able to resist the urge. Thank god. "It's not always this bad. The boys are getting it all out of their system before our season starts."

I feel his hand on the small of my back as we navigate our way down the long corridor, guiding me as we sidestep students along the way, getting shoved and jostled as people stand, dance, and yell to each other over the music, most of them blocking the direct path to the stairwell.

Eventually, we make it back to our friends, who are standing in the same spot in the living room, creating a small conversation circle near the fireplace.

I walk over to Jenna and Molly, inserting myself in between them. "What did I miss?" I ask, taking the cup of beer Jenna holds out to me and taking a sip to pacify her. It's warm and flat, but at this point, I don't care.

"Um, no. You don't get to ask us what you missed. First you tell us where you and Caleb Lockhart disappeared to," Jenna demands with a mischievous glimmer in her eye, her large silver hoop earrings shining in the dim overhead light.

"Nowhere. Just the bathroom." I avoid her eyes and chew on the rim of the red cup.

Stephan Randolph's girlfriend, Chelsea, has joined them, tapping Jenna on the arm and giving her a commiserating look. "*Just the bathroom*. That's what they *all* say."

"Seriously. He took me to the bathroom to, um, clean me off." I point to my shirt, which isn't as damp as it had been. "I mean, specifically, he let me use his bathroom. *He* didn't clean me off." They stare at me and I shake my head, flustered. "You know what I mean."

Molly giggles and puts her arm around my shoulders, giving me a reassuring squeeze. "We know what you mean."

"He took you up to his *bed*room?" Chelsea asks, her eyebrows shooting up into her forehead.

I shrug casually but my face is burning up. "It wasn't a big deal. The line down here was really long. He was being nice."

Chelsea smirks. "I'm sorry, Abby, but Showtime doesn't *do* nice. He does pissed off. He does angry. He does moody."

"Although!" Jenna stabs her forefinger in the air. "Sometimes pissed-off-angry-moody sex is the best kind of sex—not that you would know, sweetie." She pats me on the arm.

Okay, that was kind of mean.

Frustrated, I grit my teeth and ask, "Would someone please just change the subject?" *Before I have a coronary.* "Tell me what I missed while I was gone."

"All the good stuff. We were just planning a quickie in the Dells. Oops, did that sound naughty?" Jenna winks, taking her cup back and holding it to her lips. "The guys thought it would be fun to rent a cabin near the waterpark next weekend before school ends and they start pre-season training camp." She takes a drag from her beer. "*I* personally have always wanted to go to Yogi Bear National Park."

Molly rolls her eyes. "I told you, we are *not* going to Yogi Bear National Park. Stop trying to make Yogi happen."

"Why? I made *fetch* happen." Jenna smirks.

"You're kind of an idiot," I tease, lips pulled in a big grin. I tilt my head and catch Caleb staring at me from my peripheral view, but he quickly jerks his head away. My stomach plunges, and the butterflies that have recently taken residence in my belly flutter wildly as if they're trying to break free. "So, um…who's all going?"

I can barely get the words out of my throat.

"Everyone," Molly replies, giving me a knowing smile. "Blaze and his girlfriend, Shelby, are going to take care of the details. The plan is for everyone to stay in one cabin if they can find one with enough beds, probably at the Wild

Outdoors Resort or something. We'll split the cost and pitch in for groceries."

"Wait." I halt the conversation. "Blaze has a girl-friend?" He was such a flirt!

"Yeah. She's got him on a tight leash, too," Molly says at the same time Jenna mutters, "Unfortunately."

"Anyway," Molly continues, "if you want to go—and you *will* go—we have to let Shelby know by tomorrow afternoon so she can call the resort and book the place. It'll be fun. We'll hit the waterpark or whatever for a day and sit around playing board games at night."

"I call *Cards Against Humanity*," Jenna says, grinning wickedly and wiggling her eyebrows. "That game is wicked awesome." She shoots me a side-glance. "Hey, since we're both single, you can be my roomie. I promise to keep the hands to myself in bed." She makes spirit fingers for emphasis.

The simple mention of the word *bed* has me blushing all over again, and I cast a hasty glance at Caleb to make sure he's not looking our way. "Oh my god, shut up," I hiss.

Yes, my reaction is immature, but I can't stop myself.

I'm so awkward like that.

Jenna shrugs. "No, no. I get it—you're not a cuddler."

All right, I'll admit it—I begin laughing. I mean, she's completely and utterly ridiculous. And outlandish. And inappropriate. And let's not forget crude—but all in a fun-loving, hard-to-resist kind of way. Jenna would never embarrass me on purpose...well, she would (and has), but it's always (usually) entertaining, and she's never hurt my feelings.

I give in to her playful banter with a chuckle and take the beer out of her hand. "Fine. You can cuddle me."

"Well, I mean, unless Caleb over there makes a move, which…" She assesses him from across the room, tapping her chin. "Ugh, the odds don't look favorable. I bet his dick has moss growing on it."

See what I mean about her being inappropriate?

"Jenna!" Molly gasps. "Do you have to be so crude? Jeez."

Jenna shrugs again, shamelessly. "What? What did I say? Look, I did some digging, and it sounds like the guy is a hermit. Doesn't date, keeps to himself. Quiet." She digs in her pocket and pulls out a mint, popping it in her mouth and tilting her head thoughtfully. "It seems like he's into you. I see him watching you. But if you say he didn't try to make a move after getting you upstairs…"

They look at me questioningly, and I shake my head in confirmation.

"Right? Okay. What *guy* passes up the chance to get freaky-deaky when he's got a girl in his room? I mean, how much beer is it gonna take for him to loosen up?"

"He's got a perpetual case of the grumpies," Chelsea says.

We all turn our eyes toward Caleb, who stands ramrod straight amongst his friends, frowning at something a blond-haired guy wearing a knit beanie is saying.

Jenna nods, somewhat authoritatively, feeling that she's proved her point. "See what she means?"

Molly agrees. "Yeah, chances are he's not even going to come." Jenna snorts and Molly gasps, shaking her head and laughing. "To the Dells! Come to the Dells, not come in his, ugh, I didn't mean... You know what? Never mind. What I meant was, I don't think he likes crowds. Being cooped up in a cabin with however many people probably isn't his thing."

Jenna pokes at me with her forefinger. "But it's *our* thing, and you're *our* friend, so *you*, my dear, are coming with us."

Caleb

"Did you hear me, bro? You are coming next weekend," Miles Turner says, nudging me in the ribs with his behemoth arm. He's been standing next to me since I came back downstairs, too close for comfort, with his hulky frame and complete lack of social skills. "No excuses."

"And by coming, he literally hopes you're *coming*," Blaze says from across the circle. "Get it?"

Miles nods. "Agreed. We're not going to let you hole up another weekend fixing shit around the house. Besides, do you really want to give *dipshit* here a shot at Walk of Shame?" Miles throws his thumb in Cubby's direction. "She keeps looking over at you."

I resist the urge to look.

Blaze nods in agreement. "And she's doing a shitty job being covert about it. On second thought, maybe you should stay home. You know Aaron Beaumont thinks she's pretty damn cute, too—if you like the scared-as-shit virgin vibe she's got going on."

"Oh, come on now. We don't know for sure that she's a virgin," Weston charitably chimes in, coming to Abby's defense.

Not that she has anything to defend.

Being a virgin isn't the crime they're making it out to be.

Aaron disagrees. "Nope. Pretty sure she is a virgin. I mean, look at her. Crossed arms that scream *no entry*, that shirt my mom wore to church last Sunday…those jeans."

Everyone's heads crane toward Abby's denim-clad figure. I run a palm down the front of my face, trying not to lose my shit.

"What's wrong with those jeans?" Cubby asks, confused, beer halted halfway to his mouth.

Aaron shakes his head ruefully. "Isn't it obvious? They're button fly. That's worse than a chastity belt. Good luck getting into those babies."

Just when I think my friends can't get any dumber, Miles nods. "Yeah, good point."

"*Althoughhhhhh*…the wet shirt thing is pretty fucking hot. Ten points for originality," Blaze adds, reaching over to grab a potato chip from a random bowl perched precariously on the fireplace mantel. "Plus, I can't help but notice she's got great set of tits,like peaches on a windowsill. Fuzzy navel." He looks around guiltily and leans in. "Shit. Did I say that out loud? Don't tell Shelby I said that."

"Hey, Showtime, do you really wanna miss the opportunity to see those virgin tittays in a bikini top this weekend?" Aaron prods with a sneer.

God, they're pigs.

I grit my teeth but say nothing and force myself *not* to look over at Abby, who has been obliviously chatting away with Weston McGrath's girlfriend and some chick with purple and blonde hair while I stand here listening to my friends running their mouths about her fantastic, um, *assets*.

Jesus Christ, I can't even say the word in my head. What am I, five?

"I take it by the deafening radio silence, you're thinking about going," Blaze jokes, taking a swig from his bottle of Corona.

"Don't think, just *feel*," Weston advises, closing his eyes and putting a palm over his heart.

Aaron turns to him. "Wow. That made you sound like a goddamn pussy."

Weston grins. "Your sister wasn't complaining last night."

"Oh, funny guy's got jokes," Aaron grits through his busted-up teeth. "My sister is fourteen, pickle dick."

"All right, all right, enough. So, Lockhart, what's it going to be?"

In the end I agree, just to get them to shut the fuck up…

At least, that's what I keep telling myself.

Abby

Because the number of people who actually end up committing to the waterpark cabin weekend is so high, Shelby and Bryan end up booking our group two rustic log cabins, side by side, nestled in the woods a short walking distance from the actual waterpark, and a three-hour drive from campus.

There are thirteen of us in all, mostly hockey players and their girlfriends.

I don't really mind having been railroaded by my friends to shell out one hundred and twenty bucks of my hard-earned cash to share a bed with Jenna—but a double bed? Not a king, not a queen—a freaking double. Just so you know, that's only a tad bigger than a twin, and my idea of a good time is not sharing it with a self-proclaimed bed hog.

Seriously. Shoot me now. Please. I'm begging.

As I throw the last of my crap into a small carry-on suitcase and struggle to zip it shut, Meg pokes her head into my bedroom, her lively green eyes surveying the bag skeptically. "Er, that seems like a lot of stuff for such a short weekend."

Blowing a puff of air at the stray hair in my face in frustration, I sigh. "I know, I know, but since the weather isn't hot and it's not cold…" I shrug helplessly. "I wasn't really sure what to bring, know what I mean?"

I'm not about to mention that a certain someone might be going, and for once in my life, I want to have wardrobe options.

"Um, yeah, but it's still a lot of crap."

"Whatever, just get over here and hold this closed."

Meg walks over and places both palms on top of the red suitcase I got for high school graduation three years ago, gives it a few good shoves, and squishes it down into my mattress. At that moment, Jenna waltzes into the room with her car keys jingling from her index finger. She gives them a shake.

"Why aren't you ready?" she asks with a long sigh, like I'm a disobedient child. "We're carpooling with Molly and Weston and have to be at the Omega house in ten, so get your ass in gear." Her eyes go to Meg struggling with my suitcase. "Is that tiny carry-on all you're bringing?"

Meg loudly huffs in Jenna's direction as I finally get my zipper to successfully glide all the way around the suitcase. "No comment."

"Grab my pillow, will ya?" I point to it on the bed. "I just have to run to the bathroom quick, and we can be on our way."

Three hours later—after the most aggravating car ride of my life—we pull off the interstate, drive our way through the Waterpark Capital of the World, and pull into the gravel driveway of the resort Shelby booked for us. We find a spot at the main office and Weston runs in, emerging a few short minutes later without a set of keys.

"What's going on?" Molly asks him from the passenger seat, digging her hand into a bag of Jelly Bellys and picking through to find the cotton candy-flavored ones. They're her favorite.

Climbing back into the truck, Weston turns to check his blind spots as he starts the ignition and puts the truck in reverse. "Everyone else is already here and checked us in, so we're all set. The cottages are another few minutes down this road."

My anxiety level increases exponentially as we hit a gravel road moments later, and Weston slows the truck down so we're not kicking up dust. Quaint log cabins line the road, set back a few yards from the tree=lined avenue, and are far from humble.

Since I'm shelling out so much for the two-night stay this weekend, I'm secretly pleased that from the outside, the cabins appear to be worth every penny.

Rather than house numbers, each abode is indicated with a sign above the door.

Our home for the weekend is named "Bear Claw."

We pull into a short parking spot, and when Weston puts the truck in park, he takes his phone from the cup holder and thumbs through the texts. Still looking at the screen of his smartphone, he says, "Abby, I guess Shelby's got you rooming in the cabin next door with Jenna?" He says it likes it's a question. "Let's all go in and say hello before you head next door to put all your stuff away."

I nod and brace myself, ready for whatever the weekend holds.

Caleb

I can hear them before I see them—the newest arrivals—even above all the loud chatter and commotion in the cabin, and I tense at my place by the sink where I'm helping Shelby unpack the groceries we brought down.

Voices sound from the front entry hall, greetings and salutations exchanged as Weston, Molly, Jenna, and Abby descend into the main family room, where a fireplace is roaring—despite the fifty degrees outside.

Cubby just couldn't resist.

As I rip open a bag of chips and pour them into the large red serving bowl Shelby plunked down in front of me, she gives me a sidelong glance from the sink, where she's cutting up a tomato for some taco dip. "So...?" She lets her voice trail off suggestively.

I blink back.

She cocks her head at me and plants a hand on her hip. "Well?" Now she's got her eyebrows shooting up into her hairline, and she's gazing at me expectantly as holds the pronged knife that's now dripping tomato juice on the tile floor.

I'm confused as shit right now.

"Well...*what?*"

Shelby rolls her eyes and goes back to cutting the tomato. "You *know*."

"Pretty sure I don't."

"Oh, please. Hello...*Abby* is here. Are you nervous?"

I grab the shredded cheese that has been sitting on the counter in front of me, resisting the urge to rip the thin plastic bag in half like the Incredible Hulk and wondering how the fuck I got stuck helping her prepare the snacks to begin with. "Nervous about what?"

Shelby waves a hand airily to and fro then flips her long platinum-blonde hair before lowering her voice conspiratorially. "Blaze told me you haven't made a pass at her yet, and we all see the way you watch her. We don't know what you're waiting for."

Fucking. Blaze.

"Oh, *Blaze* told you that, huh?" I hiss, glaring at her. The thing is, she doesn't look the least bit put out by my mood swing…or maybe she's just that dumb. Maybe she just doesn't give a crap.

Another hair flip. "Um, yeah. He tells me everything, 'cause, *hello*." She strikes a pose, inviting me to ogle her by propping her knife-free hand on her hip, sticking out her impressive artificial chest and making a duck face with her cherry-red lips.

"I'm speechless," I mutter, mostly to myself.

"Why, thank you." She takes that as a compliment and preens a little. "Listen, can I give you some advice?'

"As if I could stop you," I respond dryly without the barest hint of a smile.

Shelby gives a twinkly laugh. "You're so hilarious." She begins spreading the diced tomatoes evenly onto the taco dip tray and continues. "Can you hand me that bag of cheese? Thanks. Anyway, as I was saying—just some friendly advice, since you're Blaze's best friend and all—"

"I am?" Since when?

She laughs again like I'm the funniest guy. "Just try smiling this weekend, 'kay? You look so angry all the time. We don't want you scaring the poor girl away."

Here we go again with the *we*.

"Is that your friendly advice?"

She rolls her eyes. "Well…yeah."

I suddenly feel really bad for Blaze, because Shelby can be such an airhead sometimes. Don't get me wrong, most of the time she's a real sweetheart, but sometimes I worry the elevator doesn't go all the way to the top floor. Even so, what she said made me think, and I glance back to where Abby stands, hovering on the fringes of the kitchen, looking as uncomfortable as I feel, even surrounded by her friends.

***

Abby: *Guess where I am…*

Cecelia: *Please tell me you're in the basement of a fraternity house doing body shots*

Abby: *GUH! Seriously. Why would you say that? You just ruined my fun.*

Cecelia: *Blah blah blah, stop keeping me in suspense.*

Abby: *We took a road trip to the Dells, and now we're all holed up in this rental cabin, getting changed into our pajamas, then watching movies.*

Cecelia: *And might I ask—who is WE?????*

Abby: *You know, the gang…Weston, Molly, a few guys from the team. Caleb…*

Cecelia: *I can see you blushing from here.*

Abby: *Ugh, I am! I can't help it. I feel like this is my very first crush…*

Cecelia: *…and what a wonderful feeling that is! Now go dazzle him with your brand of Abby awkward…*

Abby

"Jenna, where are the pajamas I put in here?" As I ask, I continue digging through my suitcase, which I've ransacked twice already.

No pajamas.

"Oh. You mean those hideous thermal bottoms and giant man shirt? They're gone." She emerges from the bathroom and leans against the doorframe, toothbrush poised at her bottom molars. "No freaking way am I letting you out there in that getup. Not with Caleb here, not when we're trying to get you laid."

She watches me and works the toothbrush back and forth.

Brush, brush, brush.

"Oh. My. God. Jenna, why would you *do* this to me? Why?" I try not to shriek, really I do, but unfortunately for me (and whoever is sleeping in the next room) my voice comes out breathlessly high pitched and scandalized. "This isn't a beauty pageant. We're camping."

"This isn't camping, you yuppie." The brat snorts at me, shaking her lavender ponytail. "I'm sure you think you're perfectly adorable in *man* jams, but it ain't happening. The clothes are gone. Poof! I smothered them in hot dog juice and fed them to the raccoons."

Brush, brush, brush.

I take a deep breath, count to five in my head, and mutter through clenched teeth, "Remind me again why I haven't tried to asphyxiate you in your sleep yet?"

The toothbrush stops moving, and Jenna lets it sit in her mouth while she talks around it. "Why are you fighting me on this? Molly and Cecelia were never half as argumentative when I was helping them." She disappears for a few seconds to spit in the sink, then returns. "Your problem is those hideous—and I do mean hideous—thermal pants, that for the life of me I can't fathom *why* you would bring along, along with the most asexual shirt you own—one that even your dad wouldn't wear."

I fold my arms across my chest and pout. "It *is* my dad's."

Jenna stops brushing and points the foaming toothbrush in my direction, dripping toothpaste bubbles on the carpet. "Exactly! That's my point. And how tall is your dad, exactly?"

Tall. My dad is *really* tall.

Which means his t-shirts are really big.

I purse my lips and stare down into the suitcase laid out on the bed, shrugging, and avoid her contemptuous stare.

"Yeah, that's what I thought. You *will* wear something I brought for you. Knowing you like I do—since I'm the resident stylist—I forbid you to go out there in *that*." She gives my jeans and well-worn sweatshirt a disdainful glance, disappointment written all over her sharp features, which have only been exaggerated by makeup. "While everyone else is chilling in their cute comfies, you want to wear your dad's hand-me-downs? No." As if she hadn't delivered that proclamation dramatically enough, she adds a shiver that racks her thin body, totally repulsed. "Not happening."

"Whatever," I scoff, refusing to hear any more lecturing, and stalk to the door, giving the handle a good, pissed-off yank.

Peering outside, I give pause when I catch sight of Molly entering the kitchen completely decked out in pale pink yoga bottoms, sparkly rhinestones running up each leg, and a cute coordinating tank top. Ugh, totally adorable. Moments later, Shelby rounds the corner from her bedroom and catches sight of me.

She too is sporting a coordinating set—heather gray leggings and a slouchy, off-the-shoulder gray cotton shirt that says *#NOFILTER* across the front in big, sparkly sequin letters.

Crap.

Shelby looks me up and down, dismissing me before flipping her long platinum-blonde ponytail over one shoulder. "Hurry and *change*. Jeez, slowpoke—we're picking the movie in, like, five minutes! The guys are in charge of the popcorn."

I don't have the guts to tell her this is what I *want* to wear, because I don't feel comfortable prancing around in actual girly loungewear in front of real-life, breathing boys.

I jerk my head in a nod, disappear back into my shared bedroom, and slam the door shut. I turn to face Jenna, whose cocky smirk threatens to make my blood boil, even as she points a bright yellow fingernail toward a small pile of neatly folded clothes at the foot of the double bed.

You can bet no spooning will be taking place tonight— no, sir.

Freaking. Jenna.

Caleb

"Sit down anywhere, bro. Pick a spot, we're starting the movie. Cubby, man, pass Showtime something to eat. Give him the popcorn."

I stand in the arched doorway of the great room under a bulky log barn beam, stuffing my hands into the warmth of my hoodie, uncomfortable with the dynamics as I debate my options. For the most part, everyone here is a couple. Molly is basically lying on top of McGrath, who is massaging her shoulders in a huge recliner. Shelby, Blaze, Stephan Randolph and his girlfriend, Chelsea, are sprawled out on the floor.

Cubby has claimed the other red leather recliner, arms behind his head and already half asleep, while four more people are lounging on the massive sectional sofa.

In addition, various snacks, soda, water, and beer are set out on the large coffee table that's been shoved to the side of the space.

So, I can sequester myself and sit on the floor at the outskirts of the room, *or* grow a pair of balls and sit next to Abby; the only other space available is beside her on the couch.

What a coincidence.

"Sit your ass down already, Showtime. We're watching *The Mighty Ducks*," Miles Turner informs me from his spot on the couch. His fuck buddy, Angelica, is on the floor in front of him, leaning back between his spread legs. She watches me intently from under her exotic Filipina eyelashes, her beautiful predatory gaze alive with interest.

Christ.

"Pop a squat or go sit by Abby. She promises not to bite too hard, and there's plenty of room on the couch," that girl Jenna calls out from across the room. My eyes—and everyone else's—go wide as I search Jenna out on the floor and find her wiggling her eyebrows my way.

She's got brass balls, that one.

I can't decide if I like that about her.

Abby, for her part, is snuggled up on the end of the sectional, elbow on the armrest, watching me with wary eyes and a tentative smile. I don't blame her; this whole situation with our friends trying to force us together is embarrassing.

I feel twelve, like I'm in goddamn middle school all over again—only back then I would have bolted out of the house and sworn never to attend another party again.

My feet stay rooted to the ground, uncertainty making me pause.

"Don't be shy. Go sit down."

I nod once, acknowledging Jenna's remark, and hesitantly begin weaving myself gracelessly through the room—stepping over lounging bodies and tripping on a blanket—toward Abby, with her eyes wide and lips parted in surprise.

Her long, shiny hair is in a loose, messy braid thing, cascading over her bare left shoulder, her smooth legs extending from a pair of bright white lace boxer shorts as she sits cross-legged on the couch. She's tugging at the hem of a gauzy white tank top as if it's too tight, even though it's, uh, *flowy*.

As she scoots closer to the arm of the couch to make room for me, I drop onto the beige corduroy furniture with an "Oomph," quickly taking note of Abby's visible cleavage, the delicate smell of her perfume, the sneak-peaks of skin in her crochet top, and, well…*her*.

My dick stiffens, and I quickly adjust myself and my gym shorts.

Shit. This is gonna suck.

I give her a nod in greeting, spread my legs to get comfortable, and sink lower into the broken-in cushions, clasping my hands in front of me on my lap to cover my boner, even though what I could really use right now is a pillow.

"Showtime, heads up," Cubby says, pitching me a beer from the cooler like he's lobbing a football through the air. I catch it easily, tap on the top before twisting the can cap off, and toss the cap behind the couch before taking a swig. I struggle with the urge to pound it all down in one breath when Shelby jumps up and clicks off all the lights.

Abby

I can hardly breathe when the lights go off. Caleb is sitting so close, and I'm wearing so…little.

His head is tipped back, and I hungrily observe the thick cords in his neck working as he swallows from his beer bottle. It's obvious he hasn't shaved in a few days, the stubble on his neck and chin casting a dark shadow over his already seemingly unhappy features.

He lowers the bottle and wipes his mouth, casting a quick glance over at me, his eyes flickering down over my chest, and I swear I hear him grunt grumpily.

As soon as the lights are turned off and the movie begins, my body is on high alert. Every tiny movement, from his shallow breathing and occasional discontented grumbling to the heat his imposing body is emitting, sends a tide pool of awareness through my nerve endings, and I'm unable to concentrate on the big screen television in front of us.

Self-conscious in what I consider skimpy shorts and a sheer top, I feel his dark eyes on me, lingering on my legs and arms from under the brim of that ever-present ball cap.

His enormous bear-sized palms rest on his steely, athletic thighs, and every so often he runs them up and down the length of his athletic pants, like they're sweaty and he's trying to dry them off.

Feeling him regard me now under that gray brim of his hat, I take a deep breath and angle my head to face him. Trust me, it takes every ounce of courage I possess to turn toward him, every bit of nerve. This small act that might be frivolous to some, but not to me. To me, it's an act of bravery.

What I want to do is get up and run—run out of the room, out of the cabin, and go home, because I'm scared. I'm scared shitless, pardon my French.

Having been caught staring, Caleb jerks his jet-black eyes back to the television, and he feigns interest while casually letting his hands—the ones so tensely resting on his knees—idly slide to the couch on either side of his legs, palms flat on the cushions.

Inches from my legs.

Inches from my bare skin.

His chest heaves in and out like his breathing is labored, and I automatically wonder if:

1. He's as nervous as I am.
2. He's as out of practice as I am—and by *out of practice*, I mean *inexperienced.*
3. He's trying to make a move but doesn't know how.

The thought softens my resolve and I coax myself into motion.

My arms, which have been crossed in self-preservation during the movie so no one can see my breasts, now slowly lower, uncrossing themselves of their own volition.

I gingerly finger the hem of Jenna's lace sleep shorts, and from my peripheral view, watch as Caleb's solid fingers begin gently massaging the corduroy couch cushion. Slow, slight circles with the tips of his fingers. The sight of those fingers tensely stroking the fabric is kind of driving me insane as I imagine them on my skin—can't *help* but imagine them on my skin—when all he's doing is stroking the *couch,* for crying out loud.

I hold my breath and exhale before letting my own hands slide down from my bare knees, limply thumping down onto the corduroy fabric next to Caleb's.

Our hands are so close—almost touching—and from the corner of my eye, I can see and feel Caleb's fingers inch closer to mine, *tap-tap-tapping* nervously on the fabric as if debating, before closing the space between our hands and sliding his hand, inch by inch, over mine.

I let out the breath I'd been holding with a sigh.

His hand is warm and coarse, and I can feel rough callouses on my knuckles as he skims them with the pads of his fingers. His feather-light touch isn't soft, but is almost enough to make me sigh again—and I would have, were our immature friends not present.

He holds perfectly still, gauging my reaction and breathing deeply, stoically staring at the TV in a trance.

With my heart fluttering in rapid palpitations within my chest, I flip my palm over, giving Caleb leave to trail his fingers over the sensitive pads of my palm.

He obliges.

He obliges, and I fight the urge to tip my head back and lean it against the back of the couch in a euphoric haze. I bite my lower lip and glance around the room at our friends; they are none the wiser.

Seriously though, it takes every ounce of willpower not to shout, *A boy is touching me. Caleb is touching me! Caleb. Is. Touching. Me.*

Idly, his index finger continues torturing me with its lazy little circles, until finally, I bridge our connection and lace my fingers through his, blushing when his body visibly relaxes next to me. His broad, tense shoulders sag as he gently squeezes my hand.

We sit like this for the next half hour or so, holding

hands, his thumb absentmindedly stroking mine, while *The Mighty Ducks* plays up on the big screen. Caleb's teammates criticize the film's depiction of hockey, and how it is inaccurately being portrayed.

"What!" Miles shouts at the screen. "I call bullshit. That is *not* how a foul is called."

"Duh, it's Hollywood, dipshit." Weston throws a Dorito at Miles from his spot in the recliner where he's snuggling with Molly. "Calm down." He gets a few snickers. "Rookie beyotch."

Beside me, Caleb quietly chuckles, giving my hand another squeeze. "Come on, McGrath. You can't throw down a cop movie reference during *The Mighty Ducks*. Not cool."

He chuckles at his own remark, and in the dark, someone coughs.

I turn my head in shock and gape at him. "Was that a… Were you *laughing*? Did you just make a…a *joke*?"

He shakes his head, his firm lips drawn in a straight line, but it's his eyes that give him away.

"Seriously, you thought *that* was funny?" I whisper, giving my head a shake in mock disappointment, and he gives my hand another squeeze. "Of all the things you could laugh at, you choose that."

"Hey, what are you two whispering about over there?" someone asks from out of the semi-darkened room, the only light being cast by the movie and the moonlight.

Suddenly the lights flip on, and Stephan—one of the hockey players I hardly know at all—stands by the outlet, staring over at the couch. It takes me a second to realize who he's gawking at, his eyes wide with disbelief.

Me.

Caleb.

Us.

Holding hands like two fifth graders under the jungle gym on the playground.

"Well, well, well, Showtime *does* know how to make a move. And here I was beginning to think you were homosexual. Check it out, guys." He points at us like he's just discovered a rare breed of animal, his laughing eyes wide with wonder. "Watch out, you two." He laughs at us. "Don't get carried away over there—that's where babies come from."

Caleb's grasp on my hand tightens.

Blaze rolls his eyes. "Shut the fuck up, would you, Randolph? And turn the damn lights off and sit your ass back down." I hear him mutter "idiot" before the room is dark again, and at the same time I hear Stephan's girlfriend, Chelsea, ask him what he was even turning the light on for to begin with.

"I wanted to catch someone doing something nasty." I hear him laugh.

"*Ugh*, you really *are* an idiot," Chelsea hisses at him angrily from their spot on the floor. "You're so embarrassing sometimes."

Stephan scoffs, loud enough for everyone to hear. "It doesn't *embarrass* you to be seen with me when I'm winning trophies, so why don't you stop nagging me."

I watch as Chelsea pushes herself up on her elbows and glares down at Stephan, who's lying flat on his back. "What the hell is that supposed to mean?" she all but screeches.

Oh boy.

He shrugs on the floor. "Take it however you want."

"I'm not such a *nag* when I'm blowing your tiny dick, am I, douche?" Chelsea spits out as she scuttles to a stand. She doesn't even scan the room before storming out. Her departure is punctuated by the front door being pulled open then slammed shut, the floral grapevine wreath swinging back and forth.

"Yikes," Cubby says from his spot on the recliner, and he bites down on an entire handful of chips, crunching noisily in the dark. "You know they have special pumps for small dicks, Randolph? It's called a cock pump. You should look into it."

"Shut *up*, Cubby," Stephan shoots back.

"Um…dude, aren't you going to follow her?" Weston asks tentatively.

"Fuck that shit. Chelsea's been a bitch all week," Stephan responds, but contradicts himself by rising to his feet.

"Okay, but was it really necessary to call her out in front of everyone? That was kind of harsh…"

Stephan stares at Weston with narrowed eyes. "What the *fuck*, McGrath?" He rudely flicks his gaze at Molly and dismisses her. "It's not on me that you're a domesticated little pussy."

Oh…*shit.*

Abruptly, Caleb drops my hand and pulls himself to a stand. He leans over and hauls me to my feet. "We're out of here," he announces to the room, tugging me gently behind him, across the living room and toward the patio door. "Come on, Abby.

Caleb

It wasn't my intention to drag Abby outside to the porch, but I wasn't about to sit there and have her watch my good friends get into a fight, either.

As we lean against the railing, I pull her in closer without giving it any thought, and we both turn to face the sliding glass window, toward the scene unfolding inside the house.

Stephan and Weston yell at each other in the middle of the living room floor, fingers pointed in each other faces, chests posturing. Molly's in on the action, arms flapping up and down, and she's yelling, too.

Cubby, clearly entertained, sits on the couch in the seats we just abandoned, stuffing his face with more chips. It looks like he's watching a movie.

"*What* just happened?" Abby asks softly, her back pressing into my front, the loose stands from her braid blowing in the slight breeze.

"Truthfully? This kind of thing always happens."

"Why would Stephan pick a fight with Weston if he's mad at his girlfriend? I don't get it."

I consider this. "Because he needs someone to blame for his problems? He's a hot head."

"*Oh*, is that why he has no teeth?" she jokes.

I almost give her an all-out grin, but stop myself. "Yeah, that's why he has no teeth." I pick a fallen branch off the wooden patio railing, peel the bark back, and then toss it into the darkness to the woods beyond the cabin. "He's tried instigating shit with me in the past, but so far, I've managed to avoid it."

"Not a fan of conflict, are you?" she asks curiously, turning her head to study at me.

"No. Not *this* kind of conflict. It gets too…ugly." I pause. "I don't mind a brawl on the ice, but that swagger bullshit going on inside? No thank you."

Another breeze kicks up, and Abby visibly shivers. Crap, how could I have forgotten that she's wearing next to nothing while I stand here in shorts and sweatshirt?

Instinctively, I close the space between us, pulling her into me and folding my long arms around her. Briefly stiffening, a few seconds pass before Abby lets her body relax in my arms. "Shit, sorry," I mutter the apology into her hair, relaxing my grip on her waist. "I just thought you'd be cold. Sorry for dragging you out here, but that whole argument was heading south."

She grabs my hands then, holding them steady about her trim waist. "No! I mean, I don't mind. My body is actually on fire. Wait, that's not what I meant. I meant that I'm not cold." She covers her face with her hands and groans through the fingers over her mouth. "Oh my god, I'm so bad at this." Even without seeing her face, I know she's blushing furiously. "I'm so out of practice."

"Thank god," I let out a laugh. "Seriously. I'm so bad at this I'm probably going to start chasing you around the woods and pulling your hair." Abby's light giggle makes my stomach flutter, giving me the courage to keep talking. "You're so pretty I hardly know how to act around you." I look off into the yard, making light of my ardent confession. "You scare me shitless."

She spins to face me, her large blue eyes gazing at me in wonder. The dim light from the porch casts a shadow on us both, and only her lips are visible in the dark. My hands, which now hover near her ass, just above the waistband of her lacy boxer shorts, itch to inch lower.

"*I* scare *you* shitless? Abby scares Caleb." Surprise etches itself across her face from this novel information, and I can see her clever brain processing the data, turning it around and around, the play of emotions evident on her pretty face. Unlike most girls, who would take my confession and use it to their advantage, the idea that I'm vulnerable seems to make Abby uncomfortable. "How is that even possible?"

"Believe me, Walk of Shame, it is," I tease.

Abby smacks my bicep and tries to give me a sullen pout, lip jutted out. "Why did you have to go and bring that horrible nickname up?"

"Because I have no concept of what's appropriate?"

An owl hoots somewhere in the woods, its creepy low melancholy bellow echoing through the crisp night air. It might be spring, but the last of the snow just melted, leaving behind chilly, autumn-like temperatures.

"We should probably go back inside. It looks like they're done bitching at each other." I nod toward the large sliding glass door to the living room, where our friends are dispersing, the fun having come to an abrupt halt.

"Do you, um…" She clears her throat nervously.

"Do you want to watch a different movie or something?" I ask at at the same time she says, "Are you up for another movie?"

Abby laughs nervously as we walk to the sliding patio door, and I watch as she begins twisting a finger on her right hand, presumably the spot in which she normally wears her ring. Reaching around her, I slide the door along its track just wide enough to squeeze through, and we both shiver again as we step over the threshold into the warm, cozy living room.

Abby runs her hands up and down her bare arms. "Brrr, I didn't realize how cold I was until we came back inside. I'm kind of glad they built a fire."

"Here, grab a blanket," I say, grabbing a fuzzy blanket from the couch and holding it open.

"Thanks," she says somewhat breathlessly. She beams up at me with her beautiful, smiling blue eyes before stepping into my open arms—into the blanket. My heart swells with pride, because I've finally done something right.

My arms fold around her, encasing her in the thick wool, and linger on her shoulders before she eases herself away and down onto the couch.

"Do you want anything from the, uh, kitchen?" Self-consciously, I stuff my hands inside my hoodie. Abby's eyes go to the pocket, then back up to my face.

She nods slowly with a shy smile. "Water, please?"

"Water? That it?" What I don't say is, *I'll gladly get you anything you want.* "Okay. So, uh, want to find us a movie while I'm grabbing drinks?"

I disappear into the kitchen and take a deep, steadying breath with my hands flat on the counter before going through the motions of filling up two glasses with ice water. It takes me less than ten minutes, but when I return to the living room, I note that, in that time, Abby has nervously smoothed out her braid, climbed out of the blanket, pulled the coffee table back to the center of the room, and repositioned herself on the couch.

I stand motionless under the barn beam arch, hesitating at the threshold of the room, and survey Abby lounging dead center on the sectional. Do I walk over and sit down next to her? How far from her do I sit? Or should I sit in the recliner on the other side of the room to give her space?

Shit.

As if she senses my indecision, she takes pity on me and pats the couch.

"Am I hogging all the room on the couch? Sorry, I'll scooch over." Abby makes a show of repositioning herself for me on the sofa, but in reality it looks like she's only moved over a few inches.

Which is just fine by me.

***

Cecelia: *So the two of you just watched a movie?*

Abby: *Yeah. We watched that chick flick, Pitch Perfect. He'd never seen it before.*

Cecelia: *NEVER SEEN IT?! Was he living under a*

rock?

Abby: *I don't know, but watching him try not to laugh was better than watching the actual movie.*

Cecelia: *Did he do anything besides hold your hand during the movie? Like, oh, I don't know…touch you inappropriately?*

Abby: *NO!!!!!!!!!!!!!!! He was a gentleman.*

Cecelia: *Well THAT'S boring!*

Abby: *Okay, now you're starting to sound like Jenna. Stop.*

Cecelia: *TAKE THAT BACK ^^^*

Abby: *You've been living with a boy too long ;)*

Cecelia: *Ugh. Sorry. Matthew is corrupting me with his hockey locker room talk. Let's blame that one on him.*

Abby

Have you ever had one of those dreams that was so vivid, it felt like reality? Have a dream that felt so good, you were content basking in it, slipping in and out of reality in a drunk-like state, oblivious to your actual circumstances, and just giving in to your senses?

Yeah. I'm having one of those dreams now.

"Mmm, that feels good," I moan in a low, groggy, sleep-filled voice that hardly sounds like my own, stretching lazily and rotating my hips against the hard erection pressed into my ass crack. I slowly become cognizant of a wide, warm palm resting lazily at my waist, and that same, solid palm grazing the flat expanse of my stomach beneath my tank, fingers traveling down to the waistband of my lacy white sleep shorts.

My breathing becomes labored, eyes rolling briefly back as I rotate my hips again, savoring the foreign sensation grinding against my butt crack. My arms come up, stretching to grasp the back of the head nuzzled in the crook of my neck. The lips against my throat emit a low, almost painful groan as the hand roams up my torso and the large palm runs over my breasts before giving one nipple a gentle squeeze while he grinds into me from behind.

It sets my already buzzing body a-freaking-blaze, the ache in my thighs throbbing unbearably as I gyrate my backside in slow circles, unknowingly looking for some relief.

"Don't stop…" An agonized curse trails off in a whisper. "Don't stop. Abby…"

Wait. What?

My eyes pop open, even though in my drowsy stupor I continue pulling the silky hair fisted in my palm, and I suddenly become aware of the following things:

1. 1. The hand and erection belong to Caleb, and we're both lying horizontally on the couch.
2. 2. Daylight pours through the large living room windows.
3. 3. Caleb and I are not alone.

"Bro, check it out," a voice declares. "They're dry humping in the middle of the living room."

"Shut the fuck up," another male voice demands. "You'll wake them before they get to the good part. Shit, this is better than soft-core porn."

The first voice laughs. "Do you think Showtime will jizz in his boxers?"

"Definitely. I don't think he's gotten laid in a while."

"Didn't he get a blow job from that butch lesbian on

the lacrosse team?"

"No, dude, that was me." They both laugh and I hear them high-five.

Oh. My. *Freaking*. God.

Once again, I force my eyes open, the fuzzy vision clearing after I blink a few times, concentrating my focus on the other side of the room.

Cubby and Stephan Randolph are sitting on the fireplace hearth, watching us, each with a mug of steaming hot coffee in their hands. I bury my face in the couch cushion as Caleb slowly removes his hand from underneath my shirt, pulling the hem down my hips.

"Shit," he moans. "I'm *so* sorry." The low pitch of his voice so close to my ear makes me shudder. "Well, sorry we got caught."

Unable to face his friends, I struggle with my movements, trying to flip over so my backside is presented to the guys *without* making eye contact and I can bury my flaming-hot face in Caleb's soft t-shirt. I maneuver this way and that, trying to balance myself and not fall off the edge of the sectional.

"Don't move. *Please*," Caleb grunts. "You're making it worse."

Right.

The overlooked erection is now pressed into the juncture of my thighs rather than my butt crack.

"If you don't finish him off, Abby, you're going to give him blue balls," Cubby says matter-of-factly, and I can hear him slurping obnoxiously from his coffee mug.

"Shut the fuck up, Cubby. Can you give us some privacy?" Caleb talks over my shoulder, his muscular arms wrapping protectively around me—and because I can't resist the temptation, I snuggle in deeper, giving his shirt a good whiff.

Mmmm, so, so good.

His hand timidly caresses my back.

"All I'm saying is, we weren't hating watching you dry hump," Cubby says, just as Stephan adds, "It gave me a giant boner just seeing you two." I hear the shuffling of clothes as he stands. "In fact, I think I'll go stick it inside Chelsea."

"Jesus Christ. Unbelievable," Caleb whispers. "Cubby, why are you still sitting there? Get the fuck out of here."

"All right, all right, I'll leave—but remember kids, abstinence makes the heart grow fondler."

"What a douchebag," Caleb mutters, aggravated. When Cubby clears the room, he gives my back a few more strokes. "Hey, are you okay down there?"

I pull back, tipping my chin to look at him.

I'm mortified, but I nod.

"Yes, I'm okay." I wonder just where the heck my courage is coming from to even respond. *My underpants, probably*, because the sight before me is like a wet dream. Caleb's often serious face is covered with the sexiest five o'clock shadow I've ever seen, and he's gazing down at me with his aroused, storm-colored eyes.

A deep gash that I've never noticed before mars the corner of his eyebrow, and a new, healing scar runs down the length of his rigid jawline.

And his hair—oh, his shaggy, beautiful black hair. It's

truly a crime against nature for this surly boy to have such thick, silky hair, and for him to hide it under a vast collection of baseball caps.

His full lips are pulled down over his teeth, and the outline of dark stubble surrounding that sexy mouth is a crazy, maddening, ovary-clenching turn-on—especially after all the rubbing, petting, and grinding we just sleep-walked through.

Our lips are but a whisper away, and morning breath be damned, I arch my back, stretching my lips toward his beautifully imperfect face and lay a single, soft kiss on his surprised mouth. He produces a low growl as a loud, annoyed shout rings out from the kitchen. *"Get a room!"*

Caleb

I'm in hell.

Struggling through a crowd of loud, obnoxious, un-supervised kids and teenagers, I barely manage to climb in line behind our friends for the water ride we all just stood in line to buy wristbands for.

Two little punks in front of me start a game of tag, and I seriously want to punch myself. Fuck, this is aggravating.

Whose goddamn idea was this?

I catch site of Abby at the top of the platform for a ride called *Tornado Waters*, one arm wrapped around a big yellow inner tube. She's laughing unabashedly at some-thing the purple-haired chick, Jenna, is saying, the action making her boobs jiggle in the simple navy-blue bikini top she's got on.

Boobs that I had a handful of this morning.

I run a hand down my face at the memory, and when I look up at her, she's watching me from her spot in line and listening intently to whatever Jenna is saying in her ear, eyes wide. They exchange glances, Jenna throwing an irritated elbow to Abby's ribs. I snarl and take a step forward protectively—because, *Hey, get your damn hands off her*—and before I realize what's happening, Abby is curling her hand in a shy *come hither* wave.

I stare.

I blink.

I'm shoved from behind by a big yellow inner tube.

"Get your big dopey ass up there," Weston says, rolling his eyes. "Does she need to send you an engraved invitation?"

"Oh," I reply.

He bumps me once more with the tube. "Yeah, oh," he mimics, rolling his eyes again. "Don't be such an embarrassment to the team."

The tube thumps me a third time in the back of the head, and it's enough momentum that I stumble on the steps.

I swat him away, scowling. "Enough already. Knock that shit off, all right? I'm going."

I don't mean to sound so begrudged, because I *do* want to get to Abby, but Jesus, man, enough badgering me about it. When did my friends get to be such pains in my ass?

Weaving my way up the stairs doesn't take me long—Abby is only about ten steps up—but navigating through the tubes was a pain in the ass, especially because my friends take douchebaggery to an epic level. Only a kid would find it fucking hilarious to pull someone's swim trunks down in a crowded indoor waterpark full of little kids.

I shoulder past Miles and Stephan, who are keeled over laughing at the sight of Cubby struggling to pull his board shorts back up over his narrow hips.

"I thought maybe you'd want to share?" Abby says when I reach her, Jenna looking on with a satisfied glint in her eye. Even at a waterpark, the chick is dressed outlandishly in a bright Aztec-print bikini, large gold hoop earrings, and a matching gold chain around her stomach—like she's not afraid that shit's going to get ripped off her body on one of the water rides.

Whatever. Not my problem.

Four people are ahead of us now.

"You kids go on ahead of me." Jenna balks when I join them. "I'll wait for that big hunky gorilla, Cubby, since he's flying solo too." She wiggles her eyebrows at Abby, who shakes her head in objection.

"No to Cubby. Just…*no*."

Jenna shrugs. "What do you expect me to do? Get *myself* off all weekend?" She laughs. "Oh, calm down, I'm kidding…sort of. You should see the look on your face."

"Put the lid back on your filter," Abby says with a blush. "And no one wants to hear about you getting yourself, uh…" She darts a look at me.

Holy shit. Do girls actually sex talk to each other like this?

We move up another rung on the steps and Jenna lets us pass, but not before swatting me on the ass. I scowl at her as Abby hands the tube over to the waiting attendant, a lanky teenager with a crap ton of zits, who looks bored. As. Shit.

"Have fun sticking it through the tunnel, lover boy."

Her innuendo isn't lost on me, and my mouth falls open. I mean, it's one thing for a guy to say shit like that, but a chick? Jesus.

"You sit down first." The attendant directs Abby and me, sizing me up before pointing down at the tube he's placed at the entrance of the dark waterslide hole.

It's a single tube for one rider.

"Don't we need a double tube?" I ask the kid, confused and wanting to follow the rules.

He sighs like I've just inconvenienced him and puts his hands on his hips, clearly irritated. "I don't *know,* bro. Do you *want* a double tube?"

Mother. Fucker.

I feel Abby staring me down, her face flushing from her chest up to her cheeks, willing me not to say anything to the little prick.

"Uh, no, I was just asking." I actually pout.

"Then sit *down,*" the little shit-ass says sarcastically, and I want to punch him in his arrogant fucking face.

I sit down, straddling the tube, not having a chance to adjust the mesh inside my swim trunks so it's not clinging to my junk before the kid takes Abby's hand and assists her onto the tube…*onto my lap.*

Horrible idea.

This is worse than "accidentally" grinding into her from behind on the couch this morning, because now she's sitting directly on top of me, her ass settling in right on top my cock.

I immediately get hard.

"You're gonna wanna hold *on* to her, bruh," the little

shit-ass says in another mocking tone, like he can tell I'm afraid to touch her.

I glare at him through narrowed eyes. "Thanks. I got it, *bruh*," I bark angrily through clenched teeth, my temperamental hockey player flare-up only made worse by the raging hard-on in my damp swim trunks.

Abby puts her hands on both my thighs and gives them both a squeeze, twice, imploring, *Could you not start anything, please?*

Fine. Messaged received.

Then, because I hesitate too long, she reaches down and takes my mammoth hands, directing them to her waist, as if she actually *wants* them there.

Her bare skin is soft, and before I can stop myself from acting on hormone-powered impulses, I lean forward and press a kiss to her shoulder blade, chuckling. "Sorry about my, uh…"

She shivers and looks back at me with a shy smile. "It's f-fine."

Jenna gives a loud-ass, dramatic, and wistful sigh from behind us, just as the little bastard kicks us forward into the tunnel with the heel of his resort-issue flip-flop and sends us plunging blindly through the dark.

We fly through the tube, my arms wrapped tightly around Abby's waist, hers securing us both to the tube. I grip her tight as we spiral down; she gasps squeals of delight with every plunge and turn we take in the dark tunnel.

Minutes—maybe only seconds—later, we shoot out into a shallow, waist-deep wading pool, water thrusting us out into the middle so the next tuber doesn't nail us.

I reach up, squeezing the brim of my wet, backward

ball cap into shape, then begin paddling us out a little farther.

We bob there for a few seconds before Abby cranes her head to look at me, embarrassed. "I guess I'll just... get off."

She hops down, the water pooling around her waist, and as she adjusts her bikini top, I readjust my hard-on.

Get off.

Sounds about right.

Abby

The day has been amazing. Exciting. Blissful.

I'm floating down the lazy river with all the girls while the guys are off doing...whatever they're off doing. I haven't seen Caleb since we went down that one ride together, since he hopped down off the tube, scooped me out of the water, and waded through it with me in his arms until the pool attendant made us leave the water slide dump zone.

I smile to myself and sigh, remembering Caleb's arms tightened around my middle and how they continued to linger there even after we were shot out of the tunnel and into the wading pool, holding me against him, brushing against my wet skin.

Double sigh.

"What part of relaxing were they thinking about when they decided to put a damn *waterfall* in the middle of the *lazy* river? Lazy my ass." Jenna's voice breaks sarcastically into my daydream before she hops down out of her tube, walking it over to the edge of the manmade canal wall to stay dry. "A man must have designed this stupid ride."

"This is freaking work," someone else complains, joining her against the wall.

We all laugh good-naturedly, half of us getting soaked by the waterfall Jenna took pains to avoid. After we pass it, she climbs back on her yellow tube, smoothing her hair back into its sleek ponytail.

Once more, we're drifting along contentedly, letting the current and a bunch of random kids float us around corners, through dripping caves, and over several rippling tide pools.

"So what are we doing tonight?" Chelsea asks lethargically, trailing her hand in the water as she bobs along, her question directed at Shelby.

Shelby lets out a yawn. "I was thinking game night? Or we could just hang out and relax, do a bonfire."

A bonfire sounds awesome.

Not everyone agrees.

"I thought we were going out downtown," Miles's friend Angelica says with a frown, a shadow of displeasure marring her pretty face.

"Nah. Blaze and I were talking, and we didn't think the downtown area here sounded like much of a nightlife. Too many little kids and tourists. Too many gift shops with souvenirs and not enough bars. So we thought we'd grill out and sit around the fire."

"Sweet," Molly says, paddling her feet and kicking up a small splash. Her thin gold ankle bracelet catches the sun shining through the overhead glass ceiling. "Wes and I love a good bonfire."

We round a bend of the lazy river, arriving at the beach entry marking the end of the ride. I don't immediately climb out of the tube like the rest of the girls. Instead, I let myself float idly by as the others stand and wade their way to the fake concrete shoreline.

My hands dip beside the tube, fingertips grazing the warm water, and I glance up to see Molly wading back toward me.

She paddles out in the shallow water, grabbing my yellow tube by the handle to steady me in place. "Hey," she says. "How's it going?"

I smile. "Good." *Real* good.

"So, I heard there was some funny business going down in the living room this morning."

"You're not very subtle," I tease.

"I wasn't trying to be." She splashes me with water and gives me a wide, toothy grin. "So? Give me a quick rundown."

"We watched a movie last night after everyone went to their rooms, fell asleep, and he woke up grinding me with his morning wood. It was amazing. Satisfied?"

Molly lets out a loud laugh and splashes me again. "Holy crap, I didn't think you'd actually tell me."

"I think it's easy with him because he's like me. You know, we're both…awkward. It's not intimidating."

Molly bounces up and down in the water next to me, still holding the tube. "Plus, he's easy on the eyes."

"Plus, he's easy on the eyes," I agree, throwing my head back and letting it rest on the tube. Staring at the ceiling for a few silent minutes, I let out another long, content sigh and dramatically cover my eyes with my forearm as I float peacefully in the concrete lagoon. "The gap in his teeth is divine. It's one of my favorite things about him. Swoon!"

"It *is*?" a deep voice asks beside me, the low rumble laced with amazement.

My eyes fly open and my body jolts, the motion so abrupt that, combined with the small waves from the lazy river, the gesture tips the tube and dumps me ass-over-tea-kettle into the water.

I go under and come up sputtering, tipping my head back into the water to get the hair out of my eyes before rising to a stand.

Why, why, *why* is this happening to me!

The water is waist deep, and we're in it alone.

My head whips around, frantically searching for Molly, whose bikini-clad figure is quickly retreating out of the wading area. With a jaunty little wave, the brat leaves me stranded to fend for myself.

"Caleb!" Water drips from my nose, and I wipe it away, mortified. "Where did you come from?"

He points to the opening of a water ride not thirty feet away in the opposite direction; it's shooting large quantities of rushing water and guests out of its tunnel into the same area we're standing in now.

He's gloriously shirtless, water dripping from his seriously powerful chest, wearing that backward ball cap and biting his bottom lip to stop himself from smiling with his teeth.

He couldn't *be* any hotter right now.

I lied before when I said he wasn't intimidating. It was a big fat lie, because seeing him standing there soaking wet...*guh!*

"I think that was the last ride. Everyone is going to start getting ready to head back," he says, stepping a little closer. "Unless you want to go down one more time?"

"I'm good." Good, but dying inside from my earlier proclamation about his teeth. *Dying.* "We can go."

He reaches out and grabs my tube, which had begun drifting away. I can't help it—I watch his powerful biceps flex as he retrieves it, my blue eyes assessing him appraisingly when his ripped muscles coil inside his powerful arms.

Don't even get me started on the rest of his body, especially not the dimpled indentations in his back, above the waistband of his swim trunks...

I swallow and wipe the water out of my eyes, giving him a weak smile when he starts back toward me, clutching his tube and now mine.

***

Cecelia: *Molly just LEFT you in the lazy river with him? That tricky little matchmaker!!! This is the SECOND time she's tried to fix her friends up. Although, I must say, her success rate is 100%*

Abby: *I did everything in my power not to hyperventilate or nervously giggle from the sight of Caleb in nothing but his swim trunks. Swim trunks and a baseball hat. OMG!*

Cecelia: *I'll have to take your word for it. Totally ador-*

able that you went down a water slide together. Lucky duck, going to the water park.

Abby: *Quack, quack*

Caleb

"I have an idea," Miles announces after the last of the dinner dishes are put away and everyone is gathered in the kitchen of Bear Claw. "Let's play a drinking game."

Some people groan, others cheer, because let's face it, none of us are above juvenile fun, even at twenty-one years old.

"Which drinking game?" Cubby wants to know. "I brought my beer pong paddles."

Blaze rolls his eyes. "This isn't a *frat* party, Cubs. Let's keep it classy but make it more interesting."

"Like strip poker?"

Shelby laughs. "Not *that* interesting…"

"And since when is strip poker classy?" Molly snorts.

"What about Spin-the-Shots?" Angelica says from a chair in the corner, her dark eyes scanning the room. Rising, she walks to the center island, hips sashaying, and grabs a nearby beer bottle, setting it in the center of the kitchen counter. "You take both liquor and non-alcoholic beverages and put them in shot glasses. Then, you arrange them in a circle, and in the middle of that circle you put your spin bottle."

"*Laaaame…*" Cubby groans, disappointed.

"I'm not done *explaining* it, Cubby. *God.*" Angelica skewers him with an icy glare and continues her explanation. "As I was saying, everyone gets a chance to spin. You drink the shot or choose someone around the table to make out with."

"Who wants to play?" Shelby asks. "Show of hands."

The majority of hands shoot up.

Weston grins and grabs Molly by the waist. "I'm in the mood for a sloppy make-out session."

"Why do some of the shots have to be non-alcoholic?" Miles asks.

"Yeah, what's up with that?"

Jenna rolls her eyes. "Oh my god, fine. We'll make them *all* liquor. Are you happy?"

Cubby grins at her, wiggling his eyebrows seductively. "I'll be happy when my tongue is down your throat."

"*Gross*," Molly whispers in mock horror at their display.

It takes a half hour, but we're finally setup in the living room, the couches and recliners pushed to the far recesses of the room, the big square coffee table in the middle. On the coffee table are two dozen shot glasses containing various boozes, and dead center, an empty beer bottle.

We all take seats, crowding as best we can around the coffee table, barely fitting but not giving a shit.

"I'll go first," Blaze announces. "Since I'm the host."

This earns him a few chuckles, and he steps forward, leaning across the table to spin the beer bottle. It only goes halfway around, landing on a clear liquid I assume is vodka.

"I'll drink the shot. Bottoms up, dick lickers!" he announces before tipping the shot glass to his lips and downing it in one swallow. The glass slams back down on the table with a loud clatter, glass against glass. "Boom!"

"Oh, jeez," Molly groans, amused. "You sure showed that shot who was boss, Blaze."

"Damn straight I did." He sizes her up. "Maybe next time I won't take a shot. I'll claim…a kiss!"

Molly crosses her arms and shakes her head with a laugh when he puckers his lips her way. "Forget it, buddy."

Blaze may be licking his lips at Molly suggestively, but he quickly turns and lunges at Shelby, knocking her to the ground and pouncing on top of her. "Get off me, you idiot." Shelby giggles as Blaze gives her neck a few playful nips with his teeth.

"*Okayyy*…" Angelica, the party pooper, huffs. "Guys, quit screwing around." She puts the bottle upright on the table. "Chelsea, since you're sitting next to Blaze, you can go next. We'll just go in order around the table."

Chelsea nods, moving to the table and giving the bottle a spin. "Ew, gross, that looks like the Goldschlager. I'm gonna have to steal a kiss, from…" Her voice trails off and her eyes dart around the room, passing over Stephan. "Weston! Come here, you freakin' panty melter."

"He is *so* a panty melter," Jenna agrees.

Weston blushes and shuffles to the other side of the

table, puckering his lips theatrically for Chelsea. The entire room erupts into fits of laughter as the two kiss briefly, awkwardly pressing their lips together before wiping their mouths afterward in mock disgust.

"Ew, get off. You repulse me." Chelsea pushes him away by the chest with a wink.

"Yuck." Weston makes sputtering sounds, returning to a bright red Molly.

After Chelsea, it's Stephan's turn. He grabs the shot, pounds it down, then spins around, grabbing Chelsea by the shoulders and sticking his tongue down her throat. Cubby does the same when he's up, drinking his shot and then pulling Jenna playfully to the ground with his hulky body.

Spin-the-Shots is a full-body contact sport—who knew?

"Kiss me, you sexy bitch," Cubby teases Jenna, yanking her to his broad chest. She tips her chin up and lets him devour her mouth right in front of the entire room.

Breathlessly, when they come up for air, Jenna puts a hand to her lips. "Wow. That was...*whew*!" She fans her face with her free hand.

That's all the encouragement Cubby needs, and his meaty arm snakes around her waist, pulling her into his side and planting a loud, wet kiss on her temple. "That's the Cubby Effect," he informs her loudly. "Pleasing the ladies since 1993."

Everyone groans.

Molly goes next, taking the shot, much to the disappointment of her adoring boyfriend. She is followed by Weston, who has us all keeled over laughing when he kisses a sputtering, indignant Cubby. After his turn, Miles grabs a revolted Shelby, planting a wet kiss on her disapproving, compressed lips. Jenna, who doesn't even bother to spin the bottle for her turn, locks lips once again with Cubby.

They continue making out, leaning over the coffee table until Angelica declares, "Hey, knock it off already, you two. It's my turn!"

A knot of unease forms in the pit of my stomach as her bottle spins and spins, landing on vodka. She glances up, a sly grin across her perfectly shaped mouth. "I'm claiming a kiss," she says, staring straight at me from across the table. "Caleb."

I shake my head and cross my arms. "I'm not kissing you," I firmly disagree, crossing my arms over my chest stubbornly. She eyes me like a female lioness, stalking her prey.

"Why not?"

"You *know* why not." Because I can barely tolerate being in social situations to begin with, let alone showing PDA to someone I'm even remotely interested in. No way in *hell* am I going to kiss someone else in front of Abby.

Not now, not ever.

Angelica's full bottom lip juts out in a pout. "That's not fair. Everyone else is playing by the rules."

"I don't give a shit what everyone else is doing."

"You don't have to be rude, you jerk. I'm not repulsive."

Yeah, you kind of are. "Whatever, Angelica. If you really liked Miles, you wouldn't be begging me to make out with you."

She scoffs. "Oh, please. We all know Miles is just using me for sex. Do you think I'm blind and stupid? He doesn't give a shit about me."

All right, I'd be lying if I said I didn't feel just a little bit sorry for her right now. Just a little.

Miles clears his throat and puts his arms around her shoulder. "Ha ha, good one, Angelica. If you're trying to make me jealous, it's working." His pseudo-girlfriend is glaring daggers at me. "Give me a kiss or take the shot." He leans over and whispers something in her ear that makes her eyes get wide, then a little teary.

"I'll…take the shot," Angelica finally agrees reluctantly, stiffening her spine and haltingly reaching for the glass. She tosses it back like a pro.

Shelby clears her throat. "Erm…I think this would *probably* be the perfect time to stop the game and switch gears, yeah?" Her question comes out somewhat apologetically. "Let's get the bonfire going."

Abby

The flames crackle loudly in the middle of the stone circle, and we're all gathered around the remarkable fire blazing in between our cabins, Bear Claw and Wolf Lair.

Let me just say that one more time: Bear Claw. Wolf Lair. How cool are those names?

Admittedly, it took a while to get the fire started. Stephan and Miles couldn't get it lit but refused to give up. Finally, a sighing, irritated Chelsea pushed them both aside, restacked the logs into a small teepee/pyramid shape, shoved a bunch of newspaper inside the pyramid, and started what looks like a crackling, holy blaze.

Afterward, standing back with her hands on her hips to survey her work, Chelsea declares with a satisfied nod, "There are two things my dad always said I'd need to utilize: how to start a fire, and the many uses for duct tape."

Her fire-starting technique *was* quite impressive, and while Chelsea dusts her soot-covered hands off on her jeans, I can't help but wonder what those many uses for duct tape actually are.

The night is quiet; our cabins sit at the very far edge of the vast resort property, the location surprisingly remote for a commercialized tourist destination.

Around the bonfire are red Adirondack chairs, logs styled as benches, and lots of warm, wool blankets provided by the resort. Just on the outskirts of the circle sits a large cooler filled with ice, beer, and a few bottles of cheap wine that are beginning to chill.

I admit I was much too shy to sit near Caleb, so I spent most of the evening surreptitiously sneaking peeks at him from across the fire, the high blaze occasionally obstructing my view, and, well…making my retinas burn.

I mean, I love a good bonfire, but I can't stand the smoke.

Just keeping it real.

We sit outside for a few hours in the dark. At some point, couples start returning to the cabins, one by one, as Chelsea's monster fire eventually whittles itself down to a smoky, crackling pile of embers.

Belatedly, I notice that Jenna has disappeared.

"I guess I'll go jump in the shower," I say to Cubby, Angelica, and Caleb, the only people remaining around the dwindling flames. I throw one last look over my shoulder as I walk up porch steps, catching Caleb's dark and penetrating gaze watching me retreat.

Once inside, I make slow work of the shower, unhurriedly standing under the warm spray of water, massaging the smoke out of my scalp with Jenna's delicious-smelling shampoo and conditioner. Because I don't think she'd mind, I also lather myself up with her organic seaweed scrub and shave my legs with her razor before deciding a steaming hot fifteen-minute shower is long enough. It's been heavenly, considering we have *one* water heater at our ransack rental, and our shower runtime before the water gets cold tops out at three minutes.

I step out, toweling off with a white, fluffy terrycloth towel, slather my body with lemon body cream, and blow-dry my long hair so my bedhead in the morning will be slightly *less* tragic, not outright horrific.

Still wrapped in the towel, I pad my bare feet to the bedroom but find it locked.

I rattle the doorknob and press my ear to the door, listening intently.

Nothing.

Knocking firmly, I hold my towel closed in one hand and clutch my dirty, smoke-filled jeans and sweatshirt in the other.

"Jenna," I hiss, knocking again. "Open. Up."

Still nothing.

"I don't think she's coming out," a deep voice intones behind me.

I whip around, and Caleb stands before me, freshly showered and holding a small stack of neatly folded (I squint to get a better look)…white pajamas.

My white pajamas.

What is he doing with my pajamas?

Oh my god, shut up, Abigail. Stop saying pajamas.

"She's in there with Cubby," he states matter-of-factly, tipping his head toward my closed cabin door. "Pretty sure they're not coming out any time soon. These were on the couch."

"I don't…get it."

But I do.

Jenna and Cubby *had* to have done this on purpose to force Caleb and me together. They're probably in that room laughing their asses off, quietly muffling their laughter with *my* freaking pillow.

I'm going to *murder* her in her sleep.

Freaking. Murder her.

"It's late. Why don't you, uh, take these into my room and get dressed," Caleb says. "Here. Give me those bonfire clothes. I'll throw them in the wash while you change."

I hand him my stinky pile of clothes, shivering when our hands brush while making the exchange, and steal away to his bedroom.

I see that Jenna has charitably left me the lacy white sleep shorts, sheer white tank top, and a white thong.

Great.

Since I usually wear granny panties—*no judging, this is a safe space*—and don't want anything riding up my butt, I skip the thong altogether and throw on just the shorts and tank top. I couldn't feel any more naked if I were actually, well…naked.

Glancing at the clock on the bedside table, I groan at the time: midnight. I'm tired but have no desire to sleep out on the couch—not after the way I woke up this morning, with Cubby and freaking Stephan Randolph watching me get felt up. Watching *us*.

When I finally get the courage to pull the bedroom door open, Caleb is leaning against the arm of the couch, arms crossed, waiting patiently. He takes me in from head to toe, eyebrows shooting up into his black hairline at the sight of me, his eyes abruptly finding the moose head above the fireplace the most interesting thing in the room.

"You can take the bedroom. I'll sleep on the couch," he mutters, still not looking directly at me.

I peer down at my chest and gasp.

My dusky nipples are visible through the sheer white fabric, leaving very little to the imagination without a bra on, and I let out a squeak of dismay.

Shit, shit, *shit*. If ever there were a curse-worthy moment, it would be this one.

Crossing my arms over my chest, I force out a nonchalant, "Nonsense." Ugh. *Nonsense? Nice one, Abby. Way to sound like Grandma Hazel, who said crap like that back in 1932.* "That wouldn't be fair. I'm the one who got booted out of my room. *I'll* take the couch," I prattle on nervously.

"As a gentleman"—I can see him inwardly groan at his own choice of words—"I *can't* let you sleep on the couch."

"But it's your bedroom."

"You shouldn't have to wake up tomorrow morning with Blaze, Miles, and Stephan fuc—I mean, undressing you with their eyes."

"Really, Caleb, it's fine. I insist." His eyes are still focused on that moose above the fireplace as I object yet again.

"No, really, it's not a big—"

"*For. Fuck's. Sake.*" An angry voice shouts from one of the two occupied bedrooms. "*Stop arguing outside our door and share the goddamn bedroom!*"

I'm not sure whom the voice actually belongs to, but talk about *rude*—and pardon my French, but there is no bleeping way I'll be getting any sleep tonight.

Not. A. Chance.

***

Abby: *Help. I'm in way over my head.*

Cecelia: *Want my advice? Just go with it.*

Abby: *You always say that!*

Cecelia: *That's because I had to learn the hard way to let myself take risks. So, try having fun and stop thinking so much*

Abby: *Easy for YOU to say...*

Cecelia: *Quit whining. AND PUT THE PHONE AWAY!*

Caleb

If I said I've never spent the night with a girl in my bed, never had a one-night stand, never gotten sucked or fucked at a party, I would be lying.

I might be anti-social, but as a young guy clearly in his prime, raging hormones have unquestionably lorded over my dick. I've callously used girls in the past to get myself off. Granted, I could count on two hands how many times it's happened, but when it did, it was all take and little give.

Contrary to popular opinion, I am no virgin.

That doesn't make this moment with Abby any less nerve-racking, probably because she does not have an agenda.

I hesitate when she enters the room, pausing to watch as she marches briskly to the far side of the bed, staring down at it, reluctance written across her creased brow. She falters for a few moments before pulling the forest green sheet back and slipping in quickly, probably because she knows I can see her tits through her top and wants to hide them under the blankets.

I slide the door shut behind us and automatically slide the deadbolt through the lock.

"Thanks again for letting me crash here," Abby says, and I turn to face her, drinking in the sight of her. Propped up on the mountain of elk-printed pillowcases, her crisp white tank and innocent girl-next-door vibe are as exhilarating as every opposing goal I've ever blocked on the ice—probably even more so.

Abby's silky hair falls in a loose cascade over her shoulders, her posture in bed causing the neckline of her shirt to dip low—really, really low—exposing the swell of her breasts.

She doesn't notice, but I sure as shit do.

I feel like such a creep for staring, but honestly, seeing her in that big bed is *seriously* fucking with my head. How the hell am I supposed to casually climb in beside her and act like this is no big deal when my dick is getting hard just from watching her climb in?

Timidly, she plays with the corner of the comforter and avoids my gaping stare. "You were right. I didn't really want to wake up with guys gawking at me in the living room. It was weird enough this morning."

Noted: gawking is disturbing.

I avert my eyes.

"Yeah, sorry about that. That was kind of my fault. But trust me, this"—I gesture around the room—"this isn't a hardship." I blurt it out before my brain can stop my mouth, and bite down on my lower lip. "I mean, no one will disturb you in here."

Abby chokes out an embarrassed cough and white-knuckles the blanket. "So, what's it like living with Cubby?" she asks, twisting the forest green sheet in her hands.

"It's a nightmare," I respond wryly as I reach down to pull the blue cotton t-shirt over my head. I hesitate, pausing with the shirt clenched in my fists and wonder if she minds if I remove it.

Aww, fuck it.

The shirt comes off, and I toss it haphazardly into the corner of the room with my other strewn clothes, noting that Abby's eyes go wide and she sinks deeper into the pillows, staring at the ceiling intently.

God, we're awkward.

"That kid is a pain in the ass," I continue, sitting on the edge of the bed and removing my athletic socks. I flex the muscles in my back, stretching as I lean over and flick my socks off. Straightening, I twist my torso to face her. "As you can see, he's a slob."

I motion with my arms toward the many jeans, boxer shorts, socks, and shirts strewn about the room, and not even in neat piles. There are enough clothes to last an entire week, let alone a thirty-six hour getaway.

In short, his shit is everywhere.

"At least you didn't have to sleep with him."

"That's true. Can you imagine? He'd probably try to spoon me, and the last thing I'd want is his coc—uh…him pressed into my back. Too bad he leaves his shit everywhere. Does it at home, too."

Abby giggles softly, her eyes sparkling in the dim lamplight. "You know, I've been wondering something. Why do you guys call him Cubby?"

I shrug. "It's short for Chester. Chester Billing the Fourth. He's a blueblood from Massachusetts. Been Cubby forever, I think."

She chokes back a laugh. "Yikes. They're both horrible, but I guess one beats the other…" Her voice trails off, and she swallows whatever she's about to say. I stand, readjust myself in my mesh gym shorts and trudge, barechested, to the opposite side of the bed.

With a little too much force, I yank back the bed covers too far, exposing Abby's smooth legs to the cold room and causing her to gasp. "Shit, sorry."

I yank the sheets up again toward the headboard. So far I just remade the bed. I sigh in frustration before giving it another shot.

"All that flapping around is making me cold," Abby teases with a laugh and rolls her eyes. "Just get in already."

I relax and let out an embarrassed chuckle. "I'm an idiot."

Abby

I watch as Caleb slides his big solid body in bed next to mine, and I marvel at the size of him. He's impressive with clothes on; without them, words can't describe how beautiful his athlete's body is.

The mattress dips when he settles in, arms going behind his head to busy himself by fluffing the pillows to the shape of his head. With his arms raised, my enthusiastic eyes have a chance to drink in the length of his naked upper body uninterrupted: the biceps, the ribcage, the perfectly sculpted pec muscles. Dear Lord, even his armpit hair is kind of turning me on right now.

Everything about his physical appearance exudes power.

Muscularity.

Strength.

Yet he's so very bashful and restrained with me.

Another turn-on.

"Are you done fluffing?" I ask, teasing as I give my own pillows a solid whack and roll over on my side to face him.

"Just about." He's on his back now, craning his neck to look at me, hesitating a heartbeat, then rolling over too, joining me on his side.

Hands tucked under his cheek, he observes me through those dark soulful eyes, roaming my face before quickly darting down to my breasts. I know without even having to glance down that he's getting an eyeful of boob—they're no doubt smashed together from the way I'm lying.

Caleb stares a few seconds too long and blows out a puff of pent-up frustration before rolling over and returning promptly to his back, muttering what sounds like, "*This was such a bad idea.*"

"Did you say something?"

He coughs. "Uh, no?"

Disappointed, I lie where I am, watching him. The dark mop of hair, the sideburns, the hard square of his set jaw. Once again, Cecelia's words from her last text suddenly stick out in my mind: *Just go with it… Just go with it…*

She hadn't finished the sentence, but it came through loud and clear: Just go with it *for once in your life.*

"Hey, Caleb?"

He stops staring at the ceiling to give me a tortured glance, brows creased together. "Hmm?"

"I think it would be a shame to be in this big bed and let it go to waste, don't you?" His eyes widen in shock, and who could blame him? Even to my own ears, that sounded so, *so* slutty. I hurry to correct myself. "I mean—I am *not* suggesting we have sex or anything..." Okay, that just made it worse. "W-what I mean to say is..."

He's staring at me like I've lost my damn mind, and yes, maybe I have.

But if he didn't smell so amazing...wasn't lying there half naked with that dark, angry scowl...that thick mop of shocking black hair...that oh-so-sexy gap between his front teeth that he hates...this wouldn't be happening.

Yup. All of this is his fault.

I watch as he pulls his top lip over his teeth and bites the inside of his cheeks to stop from grinning.

"Are you propositioning me?"

I gasp and sit up, pulling the covers up over my chest. "What! Pfft. No!"

Caleb closes his eyes and puts both arms behind his head, smiling. "Huh. That's too bad."

I flop back down, embarrassed, and reach over to flip off the lamp with a huff. Out of the newly dark rooms comes a low, sexy chuckle.

"Stop laughing," I scold, crossing my arms over my chest protectively.

Thank god he can't see how red my face is.

"Sorry. I can hear you pouting in the dark, and it's pretty damn cute." I can hear him smiling, probably a big ol' grin with his gap showing.

"Being awkward is part of my charm—or so I've been told."

The room is silent, then…

"I'm partial to it myself," he says quietly.

For a few minutes, we just lie there in the pitch-black bedroom, and I have nothing to do but relive the moment before, when it sounded like I was asking him to have sex, over and over in my mind, cringing in the dark. Until…

"Hey, Abby?" The mattress and blankets shift as Caleb rolls over on his side to face me.

"Yeah?"

"Where's your hand?"

It's really dark in here without the lights on, trust me. Pitch black.

My stomach does a little flip-flop, and my heart does too. Breathlessly, I extend my arm and slide my hand flat on the mattress, forward toward Caleb's voice, the sound of my palms skimming across the cool sheets permeating the air. "Here." I give my fingertips a wiggle, scratching them against the mattress.

Caleb's hand grazes mine under the covers and our fingers entwine.

"I want to kiss you, too." His voice is a hoarse whisper in the dark.

My breath hitches. "Then w-what are you waiting for?" Brave words, terrible delivery.

Gently tugging my hand toward him, he guides my fingers to his lips. I stifle a surprised gasp as he slowly kisses the pads of my palm, his warm breath on my skin only fueling my own need to touch him.

I resist the urge and am rewarded when the fingers holding my hand begin trialing their way up my arm, the calloused pads of his fingers wreaking utter devastation on my girly bits.

His large hand caresses my shoulder, my collarbone, and my neck, as if his fingertips could memorize every plane of my body. Caleb's hand cups the side of my face, and he tugs me closer still, his thumb seeking out and stroking my bottom lip.

I let out a sigh.

Holy shit, he's good at this.

Caleb

Holy shit, she feels good.

As my rough hands skim and caress the delicate skin of her arms, I let my senses savor every soft, sweet part of her: her narrow shoulders, her toned arms, her porcelain collarbone. I rub her glossy, satin hair between my forefinger and thumb before slowly trailing them along the column of her neck, my thumb caressing the underside of her tilted chin, then her bottom lip.

I found what I've been looking for.

Cupping her face in my large palm, I close the gap between us, lean in, and press my full lips against her trembling mouth.

The taste of her mouth is possibly the sweetest fucking thing I've tasted on Earth—this gorgeous girl with her pretty mouth muttering my name on a sigh in the dark.

The sweetest. Fucking. Flavor.

"Caleb," she murmurs quietly when I trail my index finger along the side of her neck, brushing her silky hair aside and whispering kisses down her jaw to that delicate spot just behind her ear.

Abby's fingertips tentatively trail along my stomach before flattening her palms against my skin—giving me goose bumps—sliding them over my fit torso, cupping the pec muscles I work so hard to maintain, as if weighing them and revering their strength. I cover her hand with my free one as her fingers roam, encouraging the exploration, and moan when her index finger traces a circle around my nipple.

"Abby."

I shiver, needing this girl, and tilt my mouth as she opens hers farther, our tongues cautiously, finally, introducing themselves.

I could kiss this girl for hours—and that's exactly what I do.

I found what I've been looking for, and I didn't even know it was missing.

We kiss—just kiss—until our lips are chapped and we couldn't possibly get our tongues any farther down each other's throats.

We kiss until we're tired and those kisses are nothing but whispers and sighs and breath across each other's lips.

We kiss until we're wrapped in each other arms, Abby's back to my front, her lips pressed against the thick bicep she's resting her head on.

I sigh, content, and run my hand down her hip before slipping into a dream.

18

Abby

It's like déjà vu, only this time, we're alone and the door is locked.

My eyes open slowly, adjusting to the sun that's flooding the bedroom with a brilliant morning light, and blink. Caleb peers down at me, chin propped on his palm, watching as I give him my first smile of the day. He dips his head and kisses my sleepy mouth, letting his lips linger there.

I raise my hand and run it along the whiskers of his face, my fingers stopping at his full bottom lip. Immobile as stone, he waits, anticipating my next move. I can see the anticipation building in his dark, stormy eyes, but rather than the typical brooding, I see nothing but desire.

"Morning," he whispers, his lips moving to my ear, flicking the outer lobe with his tongue.

With the tip of my finger, I trace his mouth, letting the tip remain at the crest above the bow, and whisper, "Let me see it."

He knows instantly what I mean: his gap.

Caleb's brows raise, and his shaggy hair gets a little shake.

"Please," I sulk. When he just looks back at me uncertainly, I add, "You can't hide it from me forever."

But I can try. I can *see* him thinking it so hard it's almost out loud.

"Fine, be that way." Rolling to my side, I face him, giving myself permission to cast my eyes downward to his mesh shorts and openly ogle his groin; the shorts do very little to conceal his erection.

Lazily, still too tired to be embarrassed by my bold actions, I trace his chest, flattening my palm on the hard planes of his abs and firm hips. There is barely an ounce of fat on this guy, which, to be honest, isn't necessarily a selling point.

In fact, I've always made it a point to stay away from guys who are in better shape than me. Call me crazy, but it makes me feel more self-conscious than I already am when a guy is ripped with a six-pack and spends all his time at the gym.

I know it's stereotyping, but those are the guys who will probably judge me later when they see me stuff my face with snacks and ice cream, and I couldn't handle that kind of pressure—the pressure of dating someone with the perfect physique when mine is anything but.

Not that I'm complaining!

Because Caleb's body…Caleb's body is a masterpiece that I couldn't possibly begrudge or envy. I'm *proud* of him for it.

"I'm…n-not wearing underwear," I announce. "It's too bad you won't show me your sexy gap."

"I'm not going to *barter* with you," he replies stubbornly, but his intrigued eyes give him away. His hawk-like gaze shoots down to my shorts, searching so intently for panty lines they're likely to catch fire. "This isn't an arbitration."

"What are you, a business major?" I reach over and play with a thick strand of his hair.

"No. Pre-law."

"Wow, how did I not know that?"

He shrugs. "I have to do *something* when I graduate."

"I just assumed, you know, the hockey thing…"

He gives me a nudge, and I'm quickly flipped onto my back again. "No. When I graduate, I'm done. I'm only playing to pay for school." He hesitates. "Would that bother you? That I don't want to play pro?"

Would that bother me…if *what*? If we dated? If he was my boyfriend? If we were in a relationship? I want to ask him for clarification, but I don't.

"No, I think it's incredible that you want to do something else. That you have to courage to do it," I whisper as he leans over, braced up on his arm, studying me. With him this close, I take the opportunity to study him back, beginning with his eyes: the darkest chocolate brown eyes that I've ever seen, with the tiniest flecks of hazel and thick, sooty lashes.

Mesmerizing.

The straight slashes of eyebrows above are the perfect indicators of what he's feeling, arching up and down curiously as he lets my intense gaze rake his face.

Other than the indent under a masculine nose that hasn't

been broken by any flying pucks, the only thing sexier than Caleb's pout is the shadow darkening his jawline.

I crane my head to note the time: eight o'clock. It's way too early for anyone to be up and in the kitchen yet—not with all the drinking they did last night.

Caleb shifts his hips, and when his erection rubs against my thigh, he cringes apologetically. "Sorry. I can't help it."

His voice is still so deep from just having awoken that I can feel the reverberation against the mattress, and I scoot closer, wanting to be near him.

Plus, the bedroom is cold.

Caleb doesn't hesitate to wrap his big, strong arms around me and pull me into the heat of his broad chest, and I close my eyes, breathing in the smell of him and relishing the lines of his hard body pressed so tightly against mine. I can feel all the planes of his athletic physique as he strokes my back, first over my tank top, then under it.

He moves over me then, one arm bent at the elbow next to my face, the other rough hand teasing the hem of my sleep shorts, before his fingers skim inside the waistband. "Holy shit, you really aren't wearing any underwear."

I gulp, suppressing a nervous giggle. "Nope."

Growling, his head dips down and our lips meet for soft, pliant, open-mouthed kisses that would have made me drowsy if I hadn't just gotten a full night's sleep. Caleb's teeth pull at my bottom lip, sucking, his tongue swirling erotically into my mouth.

I moan, my hips coming off the mattress when his hockey player hips rotate into the apex of my thighs in an excruciatingly lazy gyration. His palm reaches down into my shorts, sliding over my bare skin and cupping my derrière. He holds me firmly against his hard-on, fingers digging in dangerously close to my ass crack.

Caleb's hand leaves my bottom, firmly runs along my upper thigh, fingers tracing the lacy hem of my little white shorts before brushing the fabric aside and dragging his thick, mesh-covered shaft deliberately up and down the slit in my exposed crotch.

Holy…mother…o-of...*mmnnnuhhhhh.*

My head tips back, and his mouth presses kisses to the base of my throat, down my neck, on my collarbone.

Wet, open-mouthed kisses.

His thin mesh athletic shorts do nothing but deliver the weakest of barriers to our pleasure. The material provides the simplest chastity chaperone and is the only thing keeping me from tearing my shorts off and slipping him my V-card.

I spread my legs wider; he grinds deeper.

"Fuck, I'm gonna come," he growls in my ear. "Shit." His hips continue rocking into me, and I try to speak, but no words come out of my throat. The sensitive nerve endings in my body are exploding like fireworks, and I… *Oh! Mmmmuuh! Sh-shoot, oh, crap. Yeah, yes. Oh god, love his hips, they're s-so g-good at th-this…*

I draw out a moan as I come too. *Uhhh, so good…*

He braces himself over me, kisses my temple, then flops down on the mattress next to me and reaches for my hand.

We lie like this, side by side, for a few moments before a throaty laugh escapes my lips.

"Where'd you learn to dry hump like that?" I tease

breathlessly when we're lying there, my free hand resting on my chest above my heart

"Middle school." He laughs.

***

Cecelia: *So…congrats on your first orgasm! I feel like I should send you an edible bouquet…or a vibrator.*

Abby: *I'm going to ignore that last part.*

Abby: *(Sigh) I really really like him. Everything was so great until everyone started banging on our door, screaming out our names in fake ecstasy once they found the door was locked. Allllll downhill from there.*

Cecelia: *Lol. I bet Jenna was the leader of that pack. #obnoxious*

Abby: *Pretty much. His friends give him zero privacy. It's rude.*

Cecelia: *Yeah. That particular group is bad. Then throw OUR girlfriends into the mix. Chaos. So, what happens next?*

Abby: *Well, I asked him, "What next?" and he said, "Now I take you on an actual date."*

Cecelia: *(sigh) Abby, that is sooo romantic…*

Abby: *I know, right? My heart was beating so fast I thought he'd be able to hear it.*

Cecelia: *I am SO HAPPY FOR YOU (hugs)*

Cecelia: *Oh, before I forget, did you ever end up finding your ring?*

Abby: *No ☹ the search continues…*

Caleb

Tonight is the night of my first date with Abby, and I'm nervous.

Fucking. Nervous.

As all hell.

I make the mistake of having my door open as I'm getting ready, and both Stephan and Weston walk by, backtracking when they see me in front of the mirror, fumbling with an uncooperative button on the collar of my polo shirt.

I'm finally falling for a girl, and it's turning me into an awkward, edgy piece of shit.

"Dammit," I huff, giving up on the stupid button.

My roommates both stand in the doorway, staring at me like I've started a tilt on the hockey rink and they can't believe their eyes.

"What?" I ask irritably, finally slipping the white button through the small slit in my red shirt then straightening the collar.

"Nothing." Weston gives me a shit-eating grin. "It's just, we've never seen you look so pretty."

That's not true; we wear suits on the bus to every away game.

Stephan checks out my outfit and finds it lacking with a *tsk*. "Is that what you're wearing?"

I scowl at them both. "Fuck off." Nonetheless, I run a hand down the front of my shirt self-consciously. What the hell is wrong with a plain polo?

Instead of retreating, they take my hostility as an invitation to enter and shoulder their way into the bedroom, collapsing down on my king-sized bed.

"I hope for young Abby's sake you practice better manners on your date." Stephan flops on his side, watching me with—hey, is that a twinkle in his eye?

"Get out," I grumble, turning toward them and leaning against my dresser with my arms crossed.

They ignore me. Obviously.

"Where are you taking your lover this evening?" Weston asks with a smirk as he makes himself comfortable against my pillows. "Inquiring minds want to know."

"None of your damn business."

"Oh, come on now, don't be like that." Stephan snickers. "Give old Uncle Steve a little hint."

My lips clamp shut.

Weston rubs his chin thoughtfully. "Let's see, it's already past dinner time, so I'm guessing it's not dinner and a movie…"

"…and it's too dark for the chap to take her yachting…"

"Ahoy, matey!"

"…and the last time I checked, they only allow douche-bags at the bowling alley…"

"Hey, Molly and I like bowling!"

"Yeah, I know," Stephan snarks, snapping his meaty fingers together. "I've got it. You're going to the butt-packing district."

They both laugh, and I stifle a groan at their stupidity, regarding them stoically with only the barest hint of amusement on my face.

"Planetarium?" Stephan asks.

Weston shakes head. "Nah, too boring." He looks me up and down. "Roller skating?"

"Roller derby? Now that would be cool."

"Roller *blading*?"

I hold up my hands to halt their conversation. They're making me mental. "Stop." My demand comes out rigid and commanding.

They finally shut their faces.

For a second.

"So? Where are you taking her?"

Abby

I twist the bare ring finger on my right hand before sticking my soapy hands under the water faucet, giving myself a onceover as I rinse them off.

My dark brown hair is down, falling casually in glossy waves over my shoulders, my wide blue eyes decked out in black liner, a heavy application of onyx mascara, and a dusting of gray shadow—all compliments of Jenna.

I have a bronzy glow, and my full lips are a "very kissable" shade of deep berry.

Donning a pair of scored boyfriend jeans, I'm comfortable in a soft, low-cut but slouchy gray cotton tee, a few thin, delicate gold necklaces, and my feet are elevated in nude cork wedges.

According to Jenna, I am irresistibly cute.

I give my hair another fluff after drying my hands and walk back into the quaint little studio that Caleb's chosen for our date. Several couples and a few groups of friends sit around on stools, wine or beer glasses and canvases set on the tables in front of them. Soft music filters in from the ceiling, and there are paintings of every variety hanging on every square inch of wall, some of them amazing, some of them...not so much.

As I approach my date—can I say that again? My *date*!—the sight of him waiting there, waiting there for *me*, has me stopping briefly to admire him from behind, his broad back and sexy shoulders hunched over as he waits for my return. For once, he's not wearing a baseball cap, and as I brush past him to climb on my stool, I trail my fingers through the hair at the base of his thick neck.

His mouth crooks into a pleased smile that reaches his hypnotic eyes. Forget the wine; I'll just stare at Caleb all night.

As we're choosing which painting we want to work on—a sunset landscape—the door to the studio opens and two more couples walk in, and I startle as I recognize them.

Next to me, Caleb begins coughing on the beer he'd

been about to take a swig of, like it's gone down the wrong pipe, and I pat him on the back. Sputtering, his beer glass clangs on the table as the new arrivals approach us.

"Chelsea! Molly! What are you guys doing here?" I ask, rising from my chair and hugging them in greeting. Caleb turns to glare hostilely at Weston and Stephan.

"Yeah, guys, what are you doing here?" His voice comes out in a clipped, angry tone, and his now thundering eyes are narrowed into murderous slits.

He's so pissed.

The entire group moves past us, and I hear Caleb hissing under his breath, "You dickwads did this on purpose."

"Yup." I hear Stephan chuckle as he strolls by with his cocky gait.

The group moves to the service counter. They register, order drinks, and then move across the room to the sink area to get their painting supplies. I run my palm over Caleb's tense shoulders to soothe him, and his body retracts, relaxing instantly from my touch.

"Hey, it's fine. Let's just pretend they're not here." Resisting the urge to kiss him, I hop back on my stool and grab a paintbrush.

"They knew I was bringing you here," Caleb mutters with what looks like a pout. "I should have known this would happen. They're never going to let me get you alone. I have no privacy."

Poor guy looks miserable.

I look back to our group of friends in the back of the room and swallow my snicker. They're goofing off, and it's pretty hilarious. Stephan is holding a wine glass, his pinky finger sticking in the air, overdramatically oozing class while Chelsea smacks him in the arm repeatedly, already lecturing him to "grow up." My eyes also catch Weston smacking Molly in the butt, shouting, "Hee-yah!" before taking a dry paint brush and whisking it around her face, leering at her with a loud, "Just be glad it's not my pee pee."

She slaps him away with a loud laugh.

Oh boy.

Bravely, in a show of solidarity, I scoot my stool closer to Caleb's. He immediately spreads his thighs so our legs touch and flexes his fingers over my thigh, rubbing his palm up and down over my jeans. We automatically—as if compelled by gravitational force—lean into each other, our lips touching briefly.

All I can say is *wow*!

"Whoa, whoa, whoa! Moving a little fast for a first date, don't you think? Better slam on those brakes, and keep your grabby mitts where I can see them." Stephan stands behind us, holding a wine glass, a beer, and a can of paint, his remarks directed at me. My eyebrows shoot up into my hairline as he leans in to say, "Yeah, I'm talking to you, Ms. Grabby Hands."

I want to die.

Chelsea walks up, mortified. "Oh my gosh, I'm so, *so* sorry, Abby. Stephan, go back to our chairs and leave them be." She grabs him by the arm and drags him to a nearby table.

He casts a glance over his shoulder at me and winks.

When Molly and Weston walk by with their supplies, Weston leans over and pokes Caleb in the nose with the tip of his paintbrush. "Boop!"

I can't stop it; a burst of giggles bubbles up from deep inside and sneaks out.

"You think that's amusing, huh?" Caleb mutters, watching me squirt some blue paint onto the pallet we're sharing with a huge grin on my face. I add green, red, then white, before dabbing my brush into the water jar and blotting it on a rag.

"Oh, it was definitely amusing." I beam up at him. "The look on your face was like a surprised dog getting his nose batted by a kitty cat paw." I swipe at him and hiss. "Meow."

Then something remarkable happens. Wait for it. Wait...

Caleb's eyes crinkle, his head tips back, and a peel of laughter bursts out of him.

Laughing—he is *laughing*.

I can't even do the sound justice. It's an unhindered reaction; the baritone notes rumble out of his chest and are rich with emotion.

Caught off guard, I stare wide-eyed like a deer in headlights at the long column of his corded neck, his Adam's apple bobbing as he chokes out the deep roar, and his shoulders shaking. I catch glimpses of his gap and gleaming white teeth before he bites down on his bottom lip, and I want to tackle him off the stool, to the ground, and do naughty, naughty things to him.

Did you hear me? To. The. *Ground.*

Naughty, naughty things.

And this is *me* we're talking about here. *Ugh.*

I look away to hide my furious blush, clearing my

throat to disguise the fact that my thoughts have gone from only slightly lascivious to downright dirty. My nerves are creating absolute chaos in my lady parts. My body and mind are completely and utterly messed up—just from the sight of his unexpected laughter!

I *love* his laugh. It's rich and full and sincere.

I love his frown. It's real and thoughtful.

I love…

I…

I frantically dip my paintbrush back in the water and swirl it around for a few seconds, buying time as I select my paint color. Giving him a sidelong glance, I attempt to not undress him with my eyes.

Epic fail.

My blue eyes cannot help it; they are powerless against this side of him he only reveals sparingly, and if he were a smart person, now would be the opportune time for him to try to get in my pants.

I give him a feeble smile and gingerly take the wine glass in front of me by the stem, bring it to my lips, and take a teeny tiny sip.

Setting the glass back on the table, I consider what I'm about to say next, because it truly must be said. Inhale. *Exhale.* "That smile of yours…phew! It could get us both into big trouble."

He bites his lip again and his brows furrow. "What do you mean?"

I weakly smile at the ceiling, unable to look directly at him. "I mean, that was the sexiest thing I've ever seen."

There. I said it.

I said it, it's out there, and I can't take it back.

When he doesn't reply, I add, "Oh, please, don't act so surprised. You know how irresistible that gap is."

Nervously I slap more yellow on my canvas, aware that my painting has way too much yellow on it, dabbing it in circles like the instructor in front of the room is doing with small strokes…only hers looks nice. My canvas is beginning to look like it's been painted by a blind elephant at the zoo.

"It's my kryptonite."

Caleb's brush hovers over his white canvas. "Huh?"

I pause and turn to face him, swiveling on my stool. Our knees knock and I lean forward so he can hear what I'm about to say, loud and clear. "I am *mad* for that gap, so stop hiding it."

He props his palms on my knees and moves in. "I'm… uh…" He looks away, bites his lip with a frown, and takes a deep breath before continuing. "I'm.."

"Yes?" I breathe out the question in a whisper.

We're interrupted then by Molly—as in *Molly with the World's Worst Timing*—who stands over us, clearing her throat. "Whoa, you two are looking pretty chummy over here." She glances at our canvases and starts a litany of questions. "Shouldn't you be halfway done by now? What are you doing? Just sitting back here gawking at each other, or what?"

Yeah, pretty much.

"Yes," Caleb answers her seriously.

Molly looks at my painting, eyes wide. "*Umm*, what's with all the yellow? Never mind. Don't answer that." She shakes her pretty hair and titters. "I just got up to grab a bottle of water. You want anything while I'm up?"

We both give our heads a shake. "No, I'm good. We both have something to drink." I point to my wine and Caleb's beer.

Molly stalls a few more seconds. "Okay, just thought I'd ask. Hey, you guys wanna come out with us when we're done, or…" Her question trails off.

"Any idea where you're going?" Caleb wants to know.

"Best guess, Lone Rangers—you know, loud music, bad food, too many drunk undergrads with too little clothing."

Lone Rangers is a college bar down on State Street, and is the establishment most frequented by the Wisconsin Badger Hockey team. In other words, it's always packed. From regular students hoping to rub shoulders with the college athletic elite to the athletes themselves, Lone Rangers is *the* off-campus place to be.

It's also a complete dive.

The floors are so full of spilled beer that one cannot walk through the bar without putting effort into every step. It's much like trying to lift your feet to walk across a floor full of sticky, liquid honey. My best guess for the last time they scrubbed down or mopped the floors? Over three years ago.

The lighting in this place is dim and a tad—fine, I'll say it: rapey.

The place is *rapey*.

A young lady can't actually *see* whom she's talking to without squinting in the faint haze wafting through the air, and the hallway to the restrooms is dark and damp—

hence, a great place for pervy lurkers and rapists.

And let's not forget to mention that none of the stall doors in the women's bathroom actually lock, which isn't necessarily a bad thing. Think about it: not having the bathroom stalls lock actually forces girls to hover over the disgusting toilet if you want to take a pee, because you have to hold the door closed if you want privacy.

So if you're going to spin that into a positive, this means you can't actually *sit* on the toilet, because you're leaning on the door. The toilet seats are dirty, unsanitary, and riddled with who knows how many STDs. Gross.

Hovering over the toilet seat is #winning in my book.

Despite all this, the owner clearly feels no need to update—not with a packed house every night of the week. Sure, it's a total shithole, but why would the owner spend money doing repairs when its legal and underage patrons will come whether it's a rapey dump or pristine?

Caleb looks at me, countenance unreadable, and shrugs his broad shoulders. "It's your call."

With Molly's pleading stare and Caleb's passive expression—ugh! I'm torn about whether or not we should go. The bar scene really isn't my thing, never has been, never will be. Nonetheless, because I can't gauge Caleb's neutral expression, I nod my head slowly. "Sure, why not?"

After all, what's the worst thing that can happen?

Caleb

Lone Rangers is packed—and by packed, I mean wall-to-wall people. My personal preference is not to be caged into the corner of any fire hazard, but whatever.

In most cases, it would piss me off being here. Under normal circumstances I probably would have taken two steps inside the building, hit the vast wall of people, and walked back out the door.

But not tonight.

Tonight, my hand goes to the tantalizing curve of Abby's slim waist, and I firmly rest it there as we follow behind Molly, Weston, Chelsea, and Stephan toward the far end of the bar, to the place our teammates typically tend to congregate.

Tonight it looks like everyone has turned out, and I see many familiar faces in the crowd.

The music is too loud, the bass is shaking the walls, the floor is sticky from spilled alcohol, and the lights are too dim, but it feels damn good being here with someone.

Abby. A date.

The dating thing is a first for me.

I learned early on in the three years I've been at college that pretty girls would rather date an asshole than someone like me—moody, unsmiling, and aloof.

Greetings take place as we approach—high-fives, knuckle bumps, some back slapping. I'm relieved to see the group already has pitchers of the cheapest beer money can buy, which saves us from having to hoof it to the bar.

Maybe it won't be so bad being here.

A cold beer appears in my hand, and I lean down to whisper-talk in Abby's ear so she can hear me. "Is there something you want from the bar? Other than this shitty beer?"

"If you go to the bar, you'll be gone all night. I'll just stick with this." She holds up the cup in her hand and takes a sip, foam sticking to her upper lip. "Mmmm, yummy beer."

I'm not sure if she's being sarcastic or sincere. "Abby, if you don't want it, I can get you something else. I don't mind."

"Caleb, it's fine." She takes another sip, regarding me above the cup's ridge with a smiling, impish glint in her eyes. "See? Refreshing."

My eyes go to her foamy upper lip, which she immediately licks away with a flick of her pink tongue.

God, she is so unbelievably cute.

If this weren't a first date, I would lean down and plant a kiss on her pretty, foamy lips, run my rough palm through the wispy hair at the base of her neck…

True, we've already kissed a dozen times, already been in bed together—and to that point, my dick has already humped her pajamas until we both came in our pants like two horny, pubescent teenagers.

Which was totally awesome, by the way.

However, as fucked up as it sounds, being at this bar still seems far more intimate, probably due to my lack of experience with the actual act of dating. If I were any other dude—like any one of my friends—I would have had that shit with Abby locked down by now.

But I don't, mostly because I'm awkward, and reserved, and out of practice. I haven't had a steady girlfriend since eighth grade, when I dated Sarah Michelle Schroeder for seven whole days. I promptly dumped her one week later at the school Halloween dance for trying to kiss me during a slow song. I had to hide out from Sarah's vengeful friends in the bathroom until my dad came to get me. After that, well, I decided that having a girlfriend was *way* too stressful, and sticking to hockey and hooking up with the occasional nameless co-ed was the better path to follow.

It's served me pretty well. Until now.

Now, I wish I knew what the *fuck* I was doing. I feel like a douchebag. Twenty-one years old and still awkward as all hell. Besides holding my beer, I hardly know where to put my free hand. Should I touch Abby like Weston is touching Molly? Put my arm around her the way Blaze has his around Shelby?

Dammit.

I scowl, staring down intently into my cup of beer, like the answer to all my problems could be found floating in the foam.

A large, firm hand clamps down on my shoulder, jolting me out of my thoughts.

"Showtime, man, do my eyes deceive me, or did you bring a *date* tonight?" Liam Tielke, a teammate, asks at the same time he refills my cup with the pitcher of beer.

I avoid answering his question by giving him one of my famous non-committed shrugs.

"Come on, man, fess up. Legitimate date or blowjob artist?"

I give Liam a glare when Abby gasps, eyes growing wide and face getting red, but seize the opportunity to wrap my hand around her waist, keeping it occupied—you know, just in case I'm tempted to put it through Liam's already fucked-up face. He really can't afford to lose one more tooth.

Abby clears her throat and gamely replies, "Um, legitimate d-date."

Jenna, who is standing nearby, loudly adds, "She's too pretty to give blow jobs, don't you think? Everyone knows only ugly girl need to suck—"

"Jenna! Please!" Molly shrieks. "Good Lord, what am I going to do with you?"

Liam holds the pitcher of beer aloft like a prop, gesturing with it. "No, no, she's right. Ugly girls *do* need to suck cock more often." He looks down at Abby from his six-foot-two stature, his gaze lingering on her breasts. "You are a dime piece. I don't suppose you do anal?"

"Dude, too far." Cubby gives a low whistle from nearby. "Even *I* know better than to say shit like that."

"Know what we should do, Showtime? Change your nickname from Showtime to Preacher, on account of your vow of celibacy."

This kid has a death wish. I seriously want to punch him.

Lucky for Liam, he has the attention span of a toddler and abruptly turns his back to shout insults at Blaze and the team's forward, a great guy named Malcolm 'The Enforcer' Schwartz.

No matter. I'll make sure he gets what he has coming to him at practice next week—and it won't be pretty.

"What is *up* with that guy?" Jenna asks with a laugh, her long gold earrings dangling down to her shoulders. "What a pig."

Beside her, Molly snorts. "You little brat! You were encouraging him, so don't even start."

"Maybe." She takes a drink from her beer, shooting me a wink above the brim. "But you have to admit, I do have a point about them BJs." I feel heat rising up my neck and shift on my heels, uncomfortable with the direction this conversation has taken.

Cubby wraps his arm around Jenna's waist. "You're not really celibate, are you, Showtime?"

I give him a rigid stare.

"Enough. Leave him alone before he walks out of here," Weston interjects.

Cubby has the nerve to look affronted. "It was an innocent question! I really wanted to know!"

"Yeah right, d-bag. Go grab the pitcher from Foreskin over there and get Showtime's cup filled up."

Abby

All in all, the night went well—despite the continuous interference from our friends, who just cannot seem to stop themselves from embarrassing us. For example, at one point in the evening, Miles tweeted this:

@LoneRangersMadison Stop by and take a #selfie with #BadgerHockey goalie @CLockhart33 and his #lover @WalkofShame

So, yeah. We basically spent the entire rest of the evening fending off hockey fans and puck bunnies wanting to take selfies and pictures with Caleb, while his teammates laughed their butts off from the side—side-splitting, bent-over, gut-holding laughter while they watched Caleb ward off strangers.

Some friends he has.

Poor Caleb.

Despite how far out of my comfort zone I was earlier, I actually laughed harder tonight than I have in my entire life. Sure, there were some cringe-worthy moments, like when a touchy-feely blonde came over, wanting to pose with Caleb as she cupped his, uh, package. *That* pissed him off. He started yelling at Miles, shouting obscenities about the "fucking Twitterverse," and the blonde walked off crying—sans selfie.

But for the most part, tonight was awesome. I normally wouldn't admit it, but my friends help me not take life too seriously.

Just go with it.

Cecelia's advice has been resonating with me a lot lately. I'm normally so regimented. It's the only way I know how to behave, planning things down to the smallest detail and organizing my week, day in and day out. Studying constantly, tirelessly.

Here I am at the tender age of twenty-one, having all but forgotten what it means to be uninhibited and have fun. I've never had a boyfriend, never had sex, rarely go out.

Caleb and I gravitate toward each other because we have those things in common.

"So, tonight was…" Caleb starts beside me, his sentence trailing off in the dark cab of his pickup truck as we drive toward my house. He stops at a red light, waiting patiently for it to turn green.

It's late, and I give the clock on the dash one more glance: one thirty in the morning.

"Tonight was fun. You probably didn't think so, but I've never laughed so hard," I say with a crooked smile and a yawn, and he rests his elbow on the center console in between our seats. His fingers tap on it but he stares straight ahead, concentrating on the road.

I know what he's doing—I've seen this move before. He wants to make a move on me but is hesitant.

Emboldened by the two cheap beers I ingested at the bar, my hand slides over his and our fingers automatically interlace. Content, I lay my head back on the headrest, my face angled so I can watch him while he drives.

Study him.

He threw his baseball cap on in the parking lot of Lone Rangers, and his eyes appear obsidian cloaked under the gray bill.

I wish I had more time to watch him, concealed in the shadows of his truck, but it doesn't take us long to reach our destination, and before I know it, we're driving past Omega house, more rentals, and then pulling into the driveway of my house.

He releases my hand reluctantly to put the truck in park, and we both unbuckle when he cuts the engine.

I glance at the house. It's dark inside, and only the glowing light above the stove in the kitchen can be seen through the window. Caleb reaches into the back seat of the truck and pulls out the canvas he painted tonight. It's a sunset with reds, oranges, and a leafless, silhouetted black tree.

"Here. You take mine and I'll take yours?" He gives me a shy smile, unsure, the tiniest sliver of his gap visible between his lips.

Oh my god. *Swoon.*

Nodding dumbly, I fumble with the keys inside my purse and glance at him in the dimly lit cab. The planes of his face are nearly unreadable, his mouth and brows set in a thoughtful line as he watches me raptly.

"I'll walk you to the door." His deep voice rumbles close enough to my ear that I drop my keys then nervously trip my way to the covered back porch.

As I fumble to put the key in the lock, Caleb pushes on the doorjamb with the heel of his palm, testing and jiggling it under his weight. He looks up into the overhang then gives the porch steps a good, solid kick. They rattle from the impact and a wooden board pops up. "Structurally, your house is as bad as your cousin's. Do you have the same landlord?"

"Um…I'm not sure? My roommates and I are always joking about how easy it would be for someone to bust the door in," I joke, pushing the door open.

His scowl is back. "It's not funny, Abby. One well-placed kick, right above the deadbolt, would splinter this whole doorframe. Easy access."

I turn to look at him, ignoring his ominous warning and wanting to invite him in, but…not knowing how. He stands slouched, hands stuffed into his pockets, waiting.

I inhale a breath. "Do you…want—uh, to… Inside? I mean, do you want to, um…" I flick my wrist above my shoulder, indicating behind me to the dark pit that is the kitchen.

Caleb is grinning from ear to ear, gap tooth and all. I want to melt into a puddle of mush at his feet.

"Are you trying to invite me in?" He regards me, amused.

"No! I mean, yes. I mean. Only if you want."

He watches me for a few heartbeats, searching my face, his astute gaze lingering on my eyes. "I want."

"I don't think anyone has made it home yet," I blurt out, flipping on the light switch in the kitchen when he enters behind me and kicking my shoes onto the floor mat by the door.

Caleb does the same, pushing the door firmly closed behind him, sliding the deadbolt into the lock and setting his painting on the counter by the fridge.

"You can probably just leave that unlocked," I say, shrugging off my jacket.

This gets a reaction from him, and his eyes go wide.

"I'm sorry, but are you nuts? You can't just leave the door unlocked in the middle of the night. Wait, how often do you do leave it unlocked like that?" His hand is braced on a kitchen chair, leaning onto it for support and giving me a hard stare as he waits for my response.

Quietly, I gaze up into his dark brown eyes. "But... *you're* here."

That's all it takes. That's all it takes for his expression to soften and his resolve to disappear. Caleb steps toward me, lifting his hand to cup my cheek and bring his mouth down onto mine, tenderly. I raise up onto my tiptoes and press my lips full against his.

He walks me backward until my back is pressed against the stove, and his kisses whisper down my chin and neck.

Groaning, he buries his face in my neck. "You smell so good, like... like..." He searches for the words as he runs his hands slowly up and down my back.

"Baby powder," I fill in for him, sighing into his hair and threading my arms around his neck. My palms run lightly over his bent shoulders, memorizing every smooth contour of this boy's sinewy muscles—this shy boy who kisses me so sweetly that my heart could actually burst from the joy of it all. This shy and cautious boy who makes me feel beautiful.

Wanted.

Confident.

Like I steal his breath away.

The way he steals mine.

Caleb

But *you're* here.

But you're here.

Her words—those three simple little words—are a fucking arrow aimed straight at my gut. I reach for her, uninhibited now because of those three simple words, and walk her back, *back*, until she's pressed against the shoddy kitchen stove. Reaching to cup her face, I groan and bury my face in her neck, inhaling the sweet musk of her hair.

"You smell so good, like…like…" I search for the words and run my hands slowly up and down her back, imprinting myself on the delicate spine hidden under her thin gray t-shirt.

"Baby powder." She supplies the words, sighing into my hair when she threads those toned porcelain arms around my neck. Abby's palms skim lightly over my taut shoulders, and the pleasure from this timid gesture discharges sparks straight to my cock. This shy, beautiful girl who is tenderly kissing me in the middle of her shitty kitchen, in her crooked shamble of a rental, who overlooks the fact that I'm an awkward, edgy piece of shit.

She makes me feel…protective. Virile. Wanted.

Like I steal her breath away.

The way she steals mine.

Abby sighs into me, and my hands automatically go to her hips, pull her closer, and lift her off the ground. When I set her on the stovetop, she immediately scoots forward, pressing into me, wrapping her long legs around my hips. With a quick flick of her wrist, she knocks my ball cap to the floor and threads her fingers through my hair.

She kneads my thick strands, tugging.

"I'm never wearing that fucking hat again." A groan rumbles from my chest as my lips seek the soft, warm skin behind her ear.

She moans. "Shut up. I like it."

Whoa.

My nostrils flare and our mouths collide for wet, wide, open-mouthed kisses. Abby's tongue laps at my lips like they're covered with sugar. We kiss and kiss and kiss, and I rotate my hockey player hips, grinding my hard dick into the apex of her spread thighs. The motion rocks the stove, and it occasionally hits the wall behind it with a hollow, metallic bang.

Just as her hand begins tugging the polo shirt from the waistband of my jeans, the kitchen door flies open and Jenna stumbles in, holding up her keys and giggling. She halts in the threshold. Her hand flies up to cover her mouth, and her eyes widen with shock. Two seconds later, in walks...

Fucking. Cubby.

"Holy shit, Showtime. Do the two of you do anything but grind on each other with your clothes on?" Cubby asks without ceremony, breaking the stunned silence. Neither of our friends even have the common courtesy to look apologetic at having caught us, uh...doing what we do best.

His eyes dart down to my discarded hat on the floor, and he bends at the waist, scooping it up and dangling it toward me with his forefinger. He offers it over. "Here. You must have dropped this when you started fake fucking."

"Oh my god," Abby mumbles, mortified, burying her face in my neck.

I take the hat and place it on my head backward.

"What the hell are *you* doing here?" I ask through narrowed eyes, glancing from him to Jenna, who's watching Abby and me with open interest. She definitely looks buzzed, and so does Cubby.

"I'm here to *do* Jenna. What the hell are *you* doing here?" He cackles, grabbing Jenna by the waist. He tickles her and she slaps his roaming hands away with a, "Stop it, Chester, save it for the bedroom."

Chester?

Jesus. Christ.

"As much as I'd love to comment on this whole—Jenna waves her hand around—"*whatever* this is, we'll just leave you two kids alone. Come on, Cubby." Jenna takes his hand and tugs him through the kitchen. "My bedroom is this way."

Cubby gives me a salute then gives Jenna a light slap on the ass. They disappear down the hallway, giggling and bumping into the walls. A few moments later, a door opens and slams shut, leaving the kitchen quiet, save, of course, for the muffled laughter now coming from the other room.

"I can't even," Abby says, raising her head from my chest. Her pupils are still dilated and her cheeks are flushed, but she gives me a cheeky grin.

"That was painful," I chuckle, smoothing my palms down her forearms and leaning in to plant a kiss on the tip of her nose. "Granted, it wasn't as painful as you trying to invite me into the house."

She pokes a finger into my solid chest. "Hey now, watch it, mister. It's not like I have a ton of practice inviting guys over."

"But you're so good at it," I tease, and she bites down on her lower lip, dragging her teeth across it.

"Caleb?" Her voice is soft and full of hesitation.

I brush a loose hair from her brow and tuck it behind her ear. "Yeah?"

"I really like you." The way she says it—like an exhale, all breathy, like she's only just discovered it herself and had to blurt it out—it makes my adrenaline spike. It's the same rush I get whenever a hockey puck is flying toward my mitt: pure exhilaration.

"That's good, because I like you, too."

***

Abby: *…and then we headed to Lone Rangers*

Cecelia: *God I HATE that place. But that's where Matthew and I had our first fight, remember?*

Abby: *Uh, yeah. That wasn't a fight. That was foreplay.*

Cecelia: *Yeah. It was awesome… And tell me what you meant when you said Jenna is hooking up with Cubby? I hope you're wrong. Definitely going to have a talk with her about her unfortunate taste in men. I just threw up in my mouth a little.*

Abby: *Well you're not the one who had to listen to them having sex half the night. I had the honor of suffering through that.*

Cecelia: *Okay, but on a positive note—your date with Caleb tonight went well???*

Abby: *No, it went GREAT. He's amazing. Cece, I like him so much it scares me. I've never felt this way before and I have no idea what I'm doing. The good news is HE doesn't know what he's doing. Basically we're a hot mess.*

Cecelia: *Do you think he feels the same way about you?*

Abby: *Yes, I think so. Yes.*

Cecelia: *Then stop overthinking everything. What did I tell you before? JUST GO WITH IT. Take me for example: I moved across the country after "dating" Matthew only 2 months. WHO DOES THAT?*

Abby: *Crazy people* ☺

Cecelia: *Amend that to crazy people AND people crazy in love, and you are correct.*

Abby: *Love. There is that…*

Cecelia: *Wait, ARE YOU FALLING IN LOVE WITH HIM, ABBY???!!!!*

Abby: *Oh, come on. It's way too soon for that. But I am falling in LIKE with him. Definitely in like…*

Cecelia: *Before I forget, why on earth does everyone think he's celibate?*

Abby: *Best guess, because he's not a manwhore like his friends.*

Cecelia: *But he put the moves on YOU, right?*

Abby: *I mean, if you count him grinding into me while he slept as "putting the moves on me" then yes. He put the moves on me.*

Cecelia: *That definitely counts. And it's better than actual sex. Wanna know why?*

Abby: *Sure, why not.*

Cecelia: *It means he respects you.*

Abby: *How is that respecting me?*

Cecelia: *He's not pushing you to have sex with him, but he's still getting you, um…off?*

Abby: *Oh god!!! Could you NOT????*

Cecelia: *Sorry! Sorry. Matthew's open attitude about sex must be rubbing off on me…*

Abby

Campus is beautiful this time of year; the snow has completely melted, and with each passing day, the damp air and seasonal chill are replaced with new spring growth that begins brightening the places winter had forgotten.

Exiting the science building after my morning lab, I bend my head and pull out my phone, check my Instagram account, double-tap several pictures, check my email and Twitter, then respond to a few text messages.

Crossing the commons area, I follow the concrete path to the edge of campus, past a few administration buildings, and only look up when a voice calls out my name.

Tyler.

My cousin jogs toward me, looking like he's just rolled out of bed (which he probably did), and I roll my eyes as he approaches. Messy mop of hair, baggy jeans, even baggier sweatshirt, and backpack lazily slung over one shoulder.

"Abby, hold up," he says, breathing heavily when he catches up. For such a young guy, he really shouldn't be huffing and puffing from such a short jaunt; it was only a few yards.

"You really should lay off the pot. It's turning you into a complete Sally." I playfully lob the insult at him while hefting my backpack to the other shoulder.

"Got a minute?" Tyler asks, hunching over and resting his hands on his knees to catch his breath. Wow. He really needs to start taking better care of himself, or he's going to drop dead by the time we graduate.

I keep this to myself.

"Yeah, what's up?"

"Just wanted to make sure we're cool. You know, after that whole climbing-out-of-my-window thing." He rubs his nose with the heel of his hand and my face scrunches up. Gross.

"Of course we're cool. You didn't exactly shove me out the window, Ty. I did it myself." I pause before adding, "You didn't seem so worried when I was dangling out your window. Besides, that happened almost three weeks ago."

He scratches his head. "It did?"

Oh boy. Time to call Aunt Monica.

"Yup, sure did. But don't worry, as you can see, I survived." I give him a weak smile and readjust my heavy backpack. I'm sorry if it sounds harsh, but struggling through this conversation—or lack thereof—with Tyler is killing me softly. He's my cousin, but I've been a witness to his irresponsible and erratic behavior for twenty years. Therefore, I'm allowed to be irritated.

"Are you coming to the Kappa O 'Comeoniwannalayya' Luau this weekend?"

I laugh, shaking my head, and fan my fingers through my loose hair. "I think I've filled my yearly quota for your frat parties. Sorry."

"Seriously? You're gonna let one walk of shame keep you from coming back? That is weak. So weak."

Pfft. "I only came to the last one because you begged me to, and because you were celebrating your appointment to executive board." *And because my mom paid me fifty dollars.* "You know those things aren't my scene."

He looks about as disgusted as a stoner can get. "How is it possible that we're related?"

"Trust me, I wonder the same thing every single day."

I glance over his shoulder to the campus beyond, having lost all interest in the discussion, and give a start—Caleb is walking toward us, crossing the campus commons, his steely gaze fastened on me like I'm in his crosshairs.

I straighten and try not to completely ignore Tyler beside me, but it's hard.

Impossible.

This is the first time I've seen Caleb on campus, and it's disarming. Tall, broody, and determined, his stride is a relaxed gait, and the closer he gets, the more I can see a smile tipping his mouth into a curve.

And he's wearing his glasses.

Wow. Just...*wow*.

If I thought he was cute before, I was sadly mistaken. This Caleb...*sheesh*. He's a hybrid, athletic, and sexified version of Superman's Clark Kent. A studly, silent, glasses-wearing jock I've developed a big, fat, sloppy, teenage-style crush on all over again.

Ugh, he's so damn good-looking.

And he doesn't even realize it.

His eyes move from me to Tyler, and instantly his hooded stare gets moody from beneath the ball cap, hoodie, and black frames.

He approaches almost cautiously, removing his ear buds before arriving at my side and slightly bending at the waist to plant a quick kiss on the top of my head. "Hey."

If I died now, I would die happy.

"Uh…hey?" I blush from the tip of my toes to my hairline as his arm slips possessively around my waist. Guh! Physical contact in public! I swallow a nervous squeak.

"What the hell is going on?" Tyler interjects, his confused expression comical as he glances down between our bodies at the hand resting on my hip.

I clear my throat restlessly. "Tyler, this is Caleb. Caleb, this is…um, my cousin, Tyler."

Neither of them reaches out to greet each other with the customary handshake.

Tyler squints his weed-induced haze at Caleb. "Dude, do I know you?"

Caleb shrugs his broad shoulders, and I stifle a groan, knowing that this whole run-in is going to get back to my Aunt Monica—and hence, my parents.

I can hear the conversation now: *"Tyler tells us you're dating someone and that he is a* very *rude young man. Abby, your studies come first. First, you room with that inappropriate Jenna girl, and now you're dating a hoodlum? This is so unlike you."*

Tyler persists. "I know I've seen you before, I just can't

figure out where."

Internally, I groan and shoot Tyler an exasperated look that says *knock it off.* "Well, you *do* throw a lot of parties over at the Kappa house. Maybe you've seen him there." I give a tight-lipped smile.

"Maybe." He's unconvinced and looks down again at Caleb's arm around my waist, staring long and hard enough to make me fidget. I wonder what he sees as he peers at us and what he could possibly be thinking, because I've never dated anyone on campus, let alone a hulky six-foot-something athlete—and let's not forget the fact that I'm now partaking in PDA with the aforementioned hulky athlete.

"Abs, are you *dating* him?" Tyler asks me incredulously, jaw coming unhinged and gaping unattractively. "He looks like he could open a tin can with his teeth!"

Caleb's nostrils flare and his eyes darken at Tyler's insult. "I'm walking her home if she's heading in that direction," he interjects without ceremony or excuse, his voice low and gravelly. He shifts his mouth near my temple and continues for my ears only. "Want to join me?"

"Um. I…yes. Yeah. I'd like that."

He raises a dark eyebrow above the black frame of his glasses, amused. I can almost hear him thinking, *Wow. That was almost as awkward as you trying to invite me into your house this weekend.*

"Tyler, I guess I'll, uh…see you later?"

My cousin watches us for a few heartbeats then says with a jerked nod, "Yeah. All right."

But he's studying Caleb suspiciously, trying to place him. I can almost hear the rusty wheels turning inside that messy, bedhead-covered skull of his. A frightening thought.

Caleb steers me, his hand resting on the small of my back, to the curb, and we step down, crossing to the sidewalk on the opposite side of the street. When I risk a glance back over my shoulder, my cousin is still watching us, arms crossed, rooted to his spot on the sidewalk.

Caleb

Shit.

That was a close one.

Thank god that preppy little stoner couldn't place my face.

I thought for sure that little fucker was going to rat me out—call me out about the day I demanded Abby's information on his front porch. Threatened to bash his fraternity brother's face in. Okay, fine—and threatened to bash *his* face in. Refused to tell him my name. Lied when I said I didn't have her ring.

Her ring.

Shit, fuck, shit.

It's stashed in my bedroom, on my dresser, where it's been sitting, gathering dust since the day she showed up on the lawn next door, frantically searching the ground in between the houses—on her fucking hands and knees—because of its sentimental value, and coming up empty.

Because of me. Why didn't I just give the damn thing back when I had the chance? There's no way I can casually do it now.

I am so screwed.

God, why am such an asshole?

I reach between us and clasp Abby's hand, giving it a squeeze, desperate to ease my guilty conscience, worried that when she finds out I lied through omission that she's going to be pissed. Worry that she's never going to trust me.

Give up on me before giving me a chance.

Shit. What am I saying?

I look down at our entwined hands then back up at Abby's profile. Her lips are curved into a pleased smile. She looks so...*happy* that when her shining eyes meet mine, I stop walking, halting in my tracks.

She's jerked back and her backpack slides down her shoulder from the motion, falling to the ground with a thud.

"Caleb, what...?" She looks up, startled.

We're in the middle of the sidewalk, in the middle of our neighborhood, and only a few houses down from her shithole rental, but I don't care. I do the only think I really know how to do, the thing I do best—use my body to communicate. When I'm on the ice, playing hockey, I use my legs and hands to do my job, deflecting pucks and protecting the net. I can go an entire ninety-minute game without talking or uttering a single curse. The voices in my head are loud enough.

Now, I do the same.

Without using words, I loosen my own bag and lower it down off my shoulders, setting it on the ground and raising my hands to cup Abby's face between my palms. Her expressive eyes are huge. Clear. Blue. Questioning.

Shit, what I'm doing? I can't kiss her in the middle of the street.

Ugh! Fuck!

I release her and bend down, grab both our book bags, swing them easily onto my shoulders as if they weigh nothing, and keep walking. Abby doesn't say anything as she falls into step beside me, giving me a confused sidelong glance but grabbing my hand again.

I give it a squeeze and hold on tight.

***

Cecelia: *What do you mean he just stopped on the sidewalk and stared at you? That's kind of weird...*

Abby: *Well, it was kind of weird, but he looked like he wanted to say something. Like it was on the tip of his tongue but he couldn't get the words out.*

Cecelia: *Like he wanted to declare his undying love for you?*

Abby: *I wish! What was it like with you and Matthew?*

Cecelia: *Well. He said 'I love you' after only like, 2 months. But it's like I always say, "When you know, you know." You know? lol*

Abby: *Yeah, I do. I just... He's so hard to read. I wish he talked more.*

Cecelia: *You do?!?*

Abby: *(sigh) No. I don't wish he talked more. He's perfect the way he is. I just wish I knew what he was thinking.*

Cecelia: *Um, you probably don't. Knowing you, you'd be scandalized. He probably wants to rip your clothes off. Trust me, those hockey boys are walking, raging hormones.*

Abby: *Well, that's not likely to happen. A guy like that*

isn't going to wait around for me, and you know I don't sleep around.

Cecelia: *Oh, you're talking about "no sex before monogamy". Are you still watching that damn Millionaire Matchmaker?*

Abby: *Yeah, so?! Besides, I don't know if you've seen Caleb lately, but he's like...incredible. Girls are all over him. Why would he want to be with me when he could have any girl on campus?*

Cecelia: *Gee, I don't know—because he LIKES YOU??????? Maybe he even loves you? Because he's not a manwhore? Trust me. I asked around on your behalf. You're welcome.*

Abby: *I wish I were better at this. If I blush at him - or the thought of him - one more time, I'm likely to self-combust*

Cecelia: *Well whatever you're doing, just keep doing it. And Abby?*

Abby: *Yeah?*

Cecelia: *He's the lucky one here. Remember that.*

Caleb

I'm putting the last of the caulk on the trim by the kitchen sink when I hear the sound of the screen door off the pantry open, then bang shut shortly after. I turn to the soft sound of feet trudging up three stairs and a clearing of the throat.

Holy. Shit.

"Dad? Hey." I set the tube of caulk down and grab a dishrag, wiping my hands clean before moving into my dad's embrace. He pounds me on the back a few times and steps back to look at me.

"Hey. kiddo. Working on a project?"

"Um, yeah. The trim on the undermount was peeling." I glance out the window, tapping my middle finger on the woodgrain kitchen countertop. "Is Mom with you?"

"Yes. She's grabbing a few things from the car. Blaze is giving her a hand with some groceries."

"What are you guys, um…" *doing here*? I want to ask

but don't, because I don't want it to sound like I'm being rude or disrespectful. Don't get me wrong, I love my parents, and they've done a ton of shit for me and my hockey career, but they live two hours away.

They never just randomly show up without giving me a heads up first.

"Just a Sunday drive." My dad laughs, clamping his hand solidly down on my shoulder and giving it a squeeze. "Mom misses you, bud. We thought we'd drive down and take you for an early dinner. Is that okay, or do you already have plans?"

"Nope. No, that sounds great. No plans."

Just then, Blaze comes through the door, holding three paper grocery sacks and a blue IKEA bag, propping the door open for my mom with his foot, the only thing in her arms a six-pack of paper towels.

She pats him on the face as she passes. "Good boy."

Blaze grins. "This is why I love your mom, Showtime. That, and she's a MILF."

"No, you love her because she brings you food," my dad says with a laugh as my mom starts taking foodstuffs out of the grocery bags and setting them on the counter closest to the pantry. "I draw the line at letting your mom unpack everything. Wendy, let the boys do it."

My mom ignores him.

My dad rests his hips against the counter and folds his arms at the same time my mom hands him a box of garbage can liners without giving him a second glance. "Here. Go put these under the sink."

Dad unfolds himself and puts the garbage bags under the sink.

Well, I guess we know who wears the pants in *that* relationship.

Blaze snickers. "What are the Lockharts up to this afternoon, besides checking in on their baby boy?" he asks, taking the paper towels from my mom and unwrapping each roll as I get handed a ten-pack of spaghetti noodles from Costco.

"Maybe just an early dinner," Mom says, grabbing the Clorox Bleach spray and wiping down the kitchen counter. "If we don't get out of here soon, I'm going to end up scrubbing this entire place clean."

"None of the guys would mind finding you down here cleaning, Mrs. L. You're a total MILF."

"Hey, cool it with the MILF talk already," my dad warns him with an exaggerated scowl as he grabs an apple out of a nearby bowl, peeling the little sticker off and taking a bite.

My mom giggles into the washrag, her dark brown eyes gleaming with delight at being called a MILF like it's a goddamn compliment. You know what a MILF is, right? A "Mother I'd Like to Fuck." Yeah. And my mom *likes* it. How sick is that?

Dad swallows his bite of apple. "Blaze, you boys are welcome to join us. We thought we'd just hit The Brewery downtown. Grab a few beers and keep it casual."

Blaze looks at me. "Are you bringing Abby?"

My dad's eyes widen. "Who's Abby?"

Shit. Seriously?

"His new girlfriend," the traitor says casually over his shoulder, stacking some cans of Chunky Soup into the cabinet above the microwave. I want to grab him by the scruff of his black polo shirt and shake the living shit out of him.

Mom sets down the washrag and pivots on her heels to look at me. "Girlfriend? Caleb, how long... We'd love to meet her, of course." My mom's trying to play it cool, but I can see the excitement in her dark, expressive eyes. She's holding back a million and one questions and clamps her mouth shut to prevent anything more from spilling out so she doesn't spook me.

Fucking. Blaze.

I dig deep and shoot him the nastiest glower I can conjure up, my eyes practically sealed shut from squinting at him. Running my fingers through the hair under my ball cap, I exhale slowly.

"She's *not*. Abby isn't... Ugh, we're just. Shit," I mutter to myself "I mean, it's only been a few dates."

"And by a few, he means one. As in *uno*," Blaze adds helpfully, holding up his index finger to illustrate, and I want to tell him to shut his fucking face. "We did, however, catch them dry hum—"

I give him a quick jab him to the ribcage—with my fist. "Dude, I swear to god..."

"Damn, bro, someone is sensitive." He laughs as he rubs his side. My parents look on, both fascinated and confused. "But seriously, you should text Abby. Your parents would love to meet her." He looks at my mom and winks. "*Great* girl, Mrs. L. She's a peach."

I'm seriously going to kill this kid.

My dad levels me with a stare after Mom shoots him a hopeful glance full of expectation. I've see this look on my mom before; she expects my dad to step in and "handle me" to get what she wants. Since I know he'll do anything to make my mom happy, and what she wants is for me to call Abby, I'm not the least bit surprised when he demands, "Well, what are you waiting for? Go invite the girl to dinner."

Seething, I excuse myself, dragging my heavy legs upstairs to the privacy of my bedroom and all but slamming the door behind me. It might be a simple text, but this will be our first, and I need a minute to collect myself. She doesn't even know I have her number.

Fuck.

I hit *compose* on my phone and find Abby in my contacts list.

Taking a deep breath, I punch out a text, grateful that I can't stutter or sound like a fucking idiot via text. Right?

Me: *Abby, it's Caleb. How's it going?*

A few minutes go by that have me pacing the hardwood floors the length of my bedroom, and I wonder briefly if they can hear my nervous footsteps down in the kitchen.

Probably.

Abby: *Good! How about you?*

Exclamations are a good sign, yeah? I wipe my sweaty palms on the leg of my jeans before hitting *reply*.

Me: *Good.*

I pause, wanting to type *um*. Shit. This is harder than I thought it would be.

Me: *Good.*

Dammit. I just texted her 'Good' twice.

Me: *Listen. My pants are in town, and I was wondering... they were wondering if*

Accidentally hitting *send* before finishing the sentence, I groan after realizing it autocorrected parents to pants.

I lied. Shit, you actually *can* sound like a douchebag moron via text. I just proved it.

Me: *My PARENTS are in town, and we were wondering if you wanted to join us for an early dinner. If you're not busy.*

Me: *I totally get it if you have plans. Or think it's weird.*

Shit, I scold myself, *stop texting her*. Jesus, Caleb, get grip.

After a few minutes go by without any kind of response, I resume my pacing, stopping to tap my fingers on the ledge of my windowsill like a fidgety crack whore.

My phone pings and my heartbeat stills.

Abby: *What time?*

What time? Was that a yes? Holy crap. What. Time.

Me: *I can walk over and get you in a half hour? Is that enough time for you to get ready?*

Me: *My parents just kind of showed up and my dad is hungry. Sorry.*

Abby: *No, that's plenty of time. I went to church this morning, so all I need to do is change back out of these yoga pants. lol ;)*

Me: *Great. I'll see you in a half hour then.*

Abby: *It's a date.*

Abby

It's a date? It's a *date*?

Ugh, why did I put that! That definitely deserves a face palm.

Groaning, I cover my eyes when my phone pings a few seconds later and peek at the screen through my fingers.

Caleb: *It's a date.*

Yes!

Shrieking, I throw my phone down onto the bed like it's just caught on fire and dance around the room, arms above my head, hair sweeping wildly around my shoulders. I feel like the girl version of Kevin Bacon in the original *Footloose*—you know the part where he's dancing in the old grain mill? Yeah, that's me right now, but in a good way, not in the pissed-off, *this stupid town has outlawed music and dancing* way, but in a *holy crappers I'm meeting his parents* way.

I pop on Spotify and dance around to the beat of "Good Girls" by Five Seconds of Summer before stopping to look at myself in the mirror, taking inventory of my reflection, breathing heavily.

Flushed cheeks, animated blue eyes. My long dark hair is still wavy from having been curled early this morning, but I'm wearing black yoga pants, and those simply won't do.

I glance at my phone: seventeen more minutes to get ready before Caleb comes to pick me up.

Shoot.

Opening my closet, I peer inside, grabbing out a pair of worn boot-cut jeans and tossing them on my bed. I then thumb through my shirts, biting down on my bottom lip with indecision, but finally pull out a thin gray cable-knit sweater.

Gray heeled Frye boots complete the simple look, and just as I give my hair one last fluff and add some gloss to my lips, the rusty old doorbell croaks out a sickly *ding-dong*.

Grateful that both my roommates are out of the house, I smooth my hands down the front of my jeans, grab my phone off the bed and my purse from the hook behind my closet, and move through the living room to swing open the front door.

Caleb shuffles his feet on the front stoop, shoulders slouched, looking adorably embarrassed. "Hi." He shoves his hands into the pocket of his jeans, but today, he's missing the element of his hooded sweatshirt.

In its place is a flattering blue, white, and green button-down flannel, and I have to admit, it not only does his body good, but it's also doing my *hormones* good…but I can't go there right now when I'm about to meet his parents.

Stepping out onto the porch, I lock the door behind me and smile up at him.

He drags his teeth over his bottom lip. "You look… cute."

I feel the blush creeping up my neck at his halted compliment and cast my eyes downward, pulling back a few strands of hair and tucking them behind my ear timidly. "Thanks." *Oh jeez*. "Should we, um…"

"Yeah, we should go. My mom's kind of flipping out— in a good way," he quickly reassures me, his low snicker filling me with warm fuzzies.

He pulls his hands out of his pockets as we walk. His loose left hand brushes my hip, and then, after a few paces, grasps for my palm.

I love the fact that he wants to hold hands, and it somehow seems intimate.

I love it. *Love* it.

I love the feel of his large hand clutching mine, holding it tight, the rough, hard-earned callouses a stark contrast to my smooth, self-manicured palms.

Now that I'm being honest with myself, I'll be honest with you: I don't just love his hands.

I secretly think I love *him*.

All of him.

Every quiet, serious, brooding inch of him.

We stroll on without talking, our gait slow and leisurely. Caleb doesn't say anything, doesn't prep me or give me a pep talk. He just propels us forward to the stately Omega house, which sits in the center of the block down the street, its white trim and wraparound porch once belonging to a pillar of the Madison community.

Decades old, yet still just as impressive.

Obviously, I'm assailed with anxiety as we walk toward this uncharted territory. I've never met a boy's parents, let alone the parents of a boy I've only technically been on one date with—a date that we weren't even on alone.

He squeezes my hand when we get to the edge of the yard, and when we do, a figure in the front window catches my eye. The curtains hastily slide back into place, and beside me, Caleb gives his head a little shake and swallows a curse.

"Please just ignore whatever they tell you, and sorry in advance if they act weird."

A giggle escapes my lips as we ascend the front steps and cross the covered porch, and Caleb is pulling me by the hand through the front foyer. We're not five feet in the door when Caleb's parents walk out of the dining room, a huge, ear-to-ear grin spread across his mom's face.

Caleb drops my hand and stuffs his inside the pockets of his jeans.

I could have picked his mother out of a line-up; Mrs. Lockhart is tall with shoulder-length black hair neatly cascading over an aqua-blue running shirt, and she has the darkest hazel eyes I've ever seen, surrounded by lots of laugh lines.

With an expressive smile resting on her mouth, she is the spitting image of her son—or he's the spitting image of her.

Whatever, you know what I mean.

She's coming toward me, eyes darting down to where our hands had been joined on the way through the door, and, as if it were possible, her beaming smile widens. Then, as she's biting her lower lip, her cheeks dimple. "You must be Abby!" She enthusiastically embraces me in a hug.

Her cheeks will certainly be sore tonight from all the smiling.

Caleb groans.

"Hello, yes, I'm Abby." I laugh anxiously. "Thank you for the invitation, Mrs. Lockhart…ma'am."

Ma'am? Ugh—what am I, a southern belle?

"Oh goodness, call me Wendy. This is my husband, Rob."

Okay. I thought Caleb looked like his mom, but I was

wrong; he really is the spitting image of his dad. Rob Lockhart walks toward me and his presence in the room has my eyes widening into saucers. Just a hair taller than his son, he has shaggy black hair, dark brown eyes, and his mouth is set into a serious line.

Nervously, I extend my hand and he takes it. "Sir, it's good to meet you."

Mrs. Lockhart—*Wendy*—preens at Caleb. "Aren't you just the sweetest thing?"

"Mom," Caleb warns with a grimace.

"Sorry, sweetie." She's not sorry at all, because she looks at us both and sighs contently. "I'll grab my coat and we can go."

Caleb's dad walks to the bottom of the stairwell, grabs the newel post, and shouts upstairs, "Guys! We're leaving!"

Caleb groans again, and I look up at him. "What?"

"They invited everyone."

I gulp. "Everyone?"

He nods. "Affirmative. Everyone."

Oh boy.

Caleb

One by one, our friends and teammates walk through the heavy wooden doors of The Brewery, a local microbrewery and restaurant on the river, gathering in the hostess area. Collectively, it only ends up being eleven of us total, but given the size of half the people present, it might as well have been thirty.

Abby excuses herself to use the bathroom when we walk into the coat check area, and my parents use the opportunity to discreetly grill me as Blaze and Stephan excuse themselves to secure us a table. I shudder at the thought of having anyone else present when Mom pounces on me.

She is delirious with enthusiasm. "Caleb, she seems so sweet."

Has it escaped anyone else's notice that Mom has used the word 'sweet' at least three times in the last half hour? Yeah, I didn't think so.

Annoyed, I roll my eyes. "That's because she is."

"It didn't take her long to get ready from the time you texted her to the time you picked her up. Punctual. I like that," my dad says, taking a toothpick from the container on the hostess stand, unwrapping it, and sticking it between his bottom teeth.

He wiggles it around with his tongue, and it flops up and down as he watches me.

"That's because she was at church and her hair was already done," I point out.

My mom covers her heart with her right hand and whispers, "She goes to church?"

I cross my arms, and even though it's disrespectful, I glare at my mother. "I swear to god, Mom, if you start tearing up, we're leaving."

My dad clamps a hand on my shoulder and leans in close. "Give your mom a break, bud." He's called me bud since I was little-ish. "We've never seen you with anyone. We know you're not gay, but quite personally, I was really beginning to wonder—*not* that it would matter."

"I want grandbabies," my mom announces.

Oh yeah.

Every college guy's worst nightmare, and she went there.

"Mom!" I shush her, horrified. "Stop. Jesus, she could come back any minute and hear you."

"Fine, I'll behave." My mom has the decency to look shamefaced…sort of. Okay, not really. "I'm just so happy! My little boy finally likes a girl!"

Abby

After a lot of shuffling around, I end up sitting sandwiched between Jenna and Caleb, his mom and dad on one end of the table, Molly and Weston at the other, while Cubby, Stephan, Blaze, and Shelby sit across from us.

It's not long before the table is covered with appetizers—eight plates in all—and everyone is digging in, the waitress making her rounds and taking everyone's dinner order.

So far, so good.

That is, until…

Yup. Someone is definitely rubbing their foot clumsily up and down my leg, the rubber sole of a running shoe digging into my calf. As the foot grazes my shin, I look up, immediately fixating my gaze on Caleb, who has his head bent, eyes moving across the menu, elbows resting on the table in front of him.

Nope, not him.

My brow furrows, and I arch my back to get a quick look under the table. "Cubby, are you playing footsie with me?" I ask as quietly as I can across the table and bite my lip nervously. He doesn't hear me, so I ask again. "Psst. Cubby." I glance over at Caleb anxiously. "Are you playing footsie with me?" I half-mouth and half-pantomime this last part.

"No! I'm playing footsie with her," he replies at the top of his lungs, pointing at Jenna with his meaty middle finger.

My roommate laughs. "No, doofus, you have the wrong foot."

Cubby looks under the table. "Whoops. Sorry."

He certainly doesn't *look* sorry.

"I want to play footsie!" Blaze teases, putting his arm around Shelby and planting a kiss on her blonde temple.

Molly chimes in, "I remember once, when Cecelia came to dinner at my parent's house, Matthew tried playing footsie under the table with her but ended up rubbing my leg instead." She takes a sip of water. "He was so embarrassed. To this day he still won't admit it was him."

"If he wouldn't admit it was him, who does he say that it was?" Shelby wants to know.

Molly shrugs. "He just pretends it never happened. But I'm telling you, his foot was *up* my pant leg. I thought I was going to gag when I realized he had his shoe off. Cecelia was horrified. Of course, that was when they hated each other."

"Didn't take long for *that* train to derail," Weston says with a laugh as the waitress comes to take our food order. She lingers over Weston, pen poised above her notepad, smiling down at him with stars in her eyes as he continues. "Two months later they're shacking up. Who would have thought that douche canoe would be domesticated?"

I remember Cece texting that night, both horrified and delighted that Matthew was finally starting to put the moves on her. And, although my best friend wouldn't admit it—not to herself or anyone else—she had already fallen for Molly's brother at that point.

"So, Abby, tell us more about yourself," Mrs. Lockhart—Wendy—says after closing her menu, ordering, then handing the menu to the waitress. "How did you and Caleb meet?"

I clear my throat, readjust the napkin on my lap, and clear my throat again. The waitress catches my eye from across the table and her brows rise. Is she waiting for my answer to Mrs. Lockhart's question, or for my dinner order? I'm not quite sure.

"How did we meet?" I ask, glancing over at Caleb. He's blushing too, and he's staring holes into his napkin. *Great.* No help there. "We met, uh… How we met…*um.*"

Rob Lockhart tilts his head and studies me as I struggle to string together a perfectly normal sentence, like a normal human being, and my palms begin to sweat—profusely.

I mean, I can't very well tell him I met his son when I climbed out the window of the neighboring fraternity house. He'll probably think I'm easy. Or a puck bunny, or whatever it is they call those girls who chase hockey players for the popularity.

"They met when she climbed out the second-story window of the shithole next door."

At this pronouncement, all eyes go wide and everyone gapes at Blaze as he innocently pops a loaded tortilla chip from the appetizer platter into his mouth, chewing and gazing up at the ceiling.

Jenna swallows her water too hard and begins coughing. "Was." Cough. "Not." Cough. "Expecting." Cough. "That."

Wendy and Rob hesitate for a second, but then both start laughing. Maybe I'm being hypersensitive right now, because I'm not quite sure if it's *regular* or laughter of the uneasy variety, the kind of fake laugh you push out when you're hoping for the best but expecting the worst.

Laughing, laughing, laughter.

Oh god. I'm hysterical. Someone slap me.

"Good one, Blaze," Mr. Lockhart says with a chuckle, his eyes crinkling at the corner. It's not really a smile, but it's good-humored.

Caleb stiffens beside me as Blaze winks at us, popping another chip into his mouth, watching me with those hooded green eyes as he chews. It's unsettling and unguarded, but also hard with an underlying meaning, almost like he's challenging me to tell the truth.

Wendy's attention is back on me, her eyebrows now raised into her hairline as she waits patiently for an explanation. In fact, glancing around the table, I realize we now have the attention of our entire party. Our friends, who only moments earlier were ignoring us completely in favor of their own conversations, are now riveted to what I'm about to say.

Caleb beats me to it. "We met when Abby was walking by the house one Saturday morning. Then I bumped into her again that day at Walmart, and we started talking."

Thank you, God. Have I mentioned I've never liked him *more* than I do at this moment?

"Well, that wasn't so hard, was it?" Mrs. Lockhart

asks, relief that maybe I'm not a hussy spreading across her features.

"That's what she said," Cubby says with a cackle, slapping his palm against the tabletop.

"That's what she said," Shelby repeats, disgusted. "Why do you always say crap like that?" A sneer mars her pretty face.

Cubby snorts. "Der, because I like it." He throws a handful of salt packets at her. "Besides, Weston does it too."

Molly nods. "Yup, he does."

"*That's what she said* is my all-time favorite." Weston inhales a cheese curd, licking some ranch sauce off his thumb. "That, and pissing off her brother. Oh, and taco dip."

Cubby smugly turns to Shelby. "See?"

Both Wendy and Rob ignore the bickering. "With these yahoos hanging around, I don't blame Caleb for keeping you to himself, although a text telling us about your existence would have been nice."

Rob looks pointedly at his son but shoots me a grin.

"Not to mention a little reassurance to his folks that our boy here isn't batting for the other team," Blaze adds. "Swing batter, batter, swing!" Shelby elbows him in the gut. "Ouch, I'm kidding, like it matters. But trust me, he's hetero. It doesn't happen very often, but we've all seen Showtime getting his rocks off."

Shelby nudges him again, the pointy end of her elbow digging into his ribcage.

"Shit, stop," he says. "I'm kidding." He's shaking his

head and mouthing, "*I'm not kidding*," to the rest of the table.

He's kind of a dick, pardon my French, but kind of difficult to resist. Under the table, Caleb's hand finds my knee and gives it a squeeze.

"It's so nice to know Caleb has such a lovely new friend. He's always been so shy and focused on sports. We've always worried he keeps too much to himself." Wendy's smile hasn't left her face, and she directs her next comment to Caleb. "Honey, do you remember the last person you dated? Oh, what was her name…Sherri? Savannah?" She searches for a name.

"It was Sarah Schroeder," Mr. Lockhart supplies with a chuckle.

Caleb's face turns bright red. "How do you remember that? You know what. Never mind." He looks at him mom, pleading. "Just please stop. That was in eighth grade."

"Eighth grade, Showtime? *Yeesh.*" Blaze turns to me. "So do you see *now* why we wonder about his sexuality?"

Wendy doesn't stop. "But sweetie, you were traumatized. Remember? When Daddy came to get you from that dance, he had to come inside just to coax you out of the bathroom stall."

Caleb mumbles angrily under his breath, to the amusement of the entire table, about mean girls and harassment.

"What? Speak up, bud," his dad says.

"I *said* I was *not* traumatized. Sarah and her friends were just…overly aggressive."

Cubby shoots him a look of disdain, two plastic drinking straws dangling out of his mouth like a walrus. They flop around when he speaks. "An overly aggressive eighth grade girl? Is that even a thing?"

"They were pushy, okay?" Caleb practically shouts, crossing his ripped arms defensively over his muscular chest. He takes a few deeps breaths. "Whatever, I'm not going to argue."

Everyone at the table laughs, and Cubby lets out a loud, obnoxious snort, straws still sticking out of his mouth.

"Cubby, could you just shut the fuc—" Caleb glances at me and his mom, clamping his lips shut and scowling. "Let's just drop it."

His mom wipes a tear of mirth from the corner of her eye. "Oh, honey, you always were too serious for your own good."

Caleb

So all things considered, that went well.

It could have been worse. My mom *could* have told the story about the time I started pee-wee hockey at the tender age of seven and used to cry during practice to the point where it was distracting for the other kids, and Coach had to hold my hand while I skated.

Oh wait, that's right—*she did tell that story*.

Fucking. Hilarious.

She also told everyone about the time my childhood buddy Aaron thought it would be an awesome idea to bring ripped-out pages from his dad's pervy catalog of hot naked Russian teens to school and pass the pictures around on the bus. Of course, he didn't get caught with them by the bus driver—I did. School called my parents, they thought I was a closeted, masturbating little *freak*, and in turn—because I was sensitive at that age—I didn't talk to Aaron for three weeks after he let me take the blame.

Of course, Weston and Blaze spent the rest of dinner with my parents speaking and talking above everyone in these horrible fake Russian accents. Cubby, on the other hand, spent the remainder of dinner doing a made-up Swedish accent, sounding a lot like Chef from *The Muppets*—you know, since he's such a freaking moron.

Apparently it was the funniest goddamn thing anyone had ever heard, because they were falling all over themselves laughing.

Then they laughed at me because I *wasn't* laughing.

Assholes.

I remove the hat from my head and give my hair a shake, running my fingers through it and tussling it before pulling the cap on backward.

We're standing in the shared driveway between the Kappa O and Omega houses, waving good-bye to my parents as they back down the drive, when Blaze turns to me and claps a hand down on my shoulder, saying, "I need a drink. Wanna hit the bars?"

I huff. "What the hell do *you* need a drink for? I'm the one who had to deal with your bullshit without losing my shit.

Shelby laughs. "He's got you there, Blaze. You and Cubby were really obnoxious."

Cubby fans himself with his hand and bats his eyes. "Aw, I'm flattered."

Blaze scoffs. "Whatever. Are you guys coming or not? We'll go somewhere else, maybe O'Malley's. Lone Rangers is getting played out."

I turn to Abby, who stands next to me, biting her pinky finger and looking up at me with wide eyes. "Up to you," I say with a shrug. "I don't care either way."

Actually, I do care. I don't give two shits about going downtown and spending my Sunday night in a crowded bar. I'd much rather spend some time alone with Abby since we haven't had any. Every time we try to do something, we're either ambushed or rudely interrupted.

Being alone in my room so she could take a pee during a house party doesn't count, and dry humping in the bedroom of a rented cabin hardly counts, either.

Not really.

Shelby is bouncing up and down on the balls of her feet, grabbing Abby by the arm and whining, "Please! Please! You have to come with us!"

Once again, Abby caves. "Um, I mean. I don't *usually* go to the bars on Sunday night, but…I guess it's okay to make an exception?"

Shelby claps with glee, looking Abby up and down. "Yay! Why don't you run home and change real quick and we'll meet you out in a half hour, mkay?"

Abby looks down at the front of her feminine gray sweater. I can read her mind as she furrows her brow and glances back up at me with bright red cheeks and her lips part in a surprised O. *What's wrong with what I'm wearing?*

Nothing. Nothing is wrong with what you're wearing, I want to say. *Shelby is kind of being a bitch.*

"Maybe we should just stay home," I suggest with a hopeful voice.

"No! No. That's okay. I'll just go home, and, uh…

change. Then we'll go."

"Are you sure?" I ask her.

"Really, it's fine."

"She said it's fine, Showtime. Why are you being weird about it? Get your shit together and let's go." Weston smacks me hard on the ass and shouts, "*Hee-yah!*"

And just like that, we're back at Abby's house and I'm leaning against her kitchen counter, waiting for her to change—yes, change—even though I told her countless times on the walk over that she looks great and not to kowtow to Shelby.

It's the most words I've said to her all afternoon.

"First of all, what's kowtowing?" she'd asked, laughing at me. "Never mind, don't answer that. Whatever it is, I'm not doing it. I'm just…changing out of my sweater."

Abby emerges from her bedroom a few minutes later, looking cuter than she did when she went in. My breath hitches, because *man, is she adorable or what?*

Propping a hand on one denim-clad hip and chewing slowly on a salted caramel I found on the counter and popped into my mouth, I take her in from head to toe, not missing a single detail. Having changed out of her boot-cut jeans and into dark skinny jeans, Abby stands in the doorway of the kitchen, fingering the thin silver belt threaded through the belt loops and knotted on the end. It hangs jauntily off to the side, emphasizing her slim waist and long legs. The hem of her tight white V-neck tee is neatly tucked into the waistband, and naturally, my eyes land on her boobs.

I mean, shit. I did just mention it was a tight shirt, right? Hey, I might be a socially awkward bastard, but I'm still a guy, and I haven't gotten laid in…

Never mind. That's not anyone's damn business.

She is still wearing her hair down and has the silky strands pulled over one shoulder.

Abby is classy, understated, and sexy.

And smart.

And clever.

And sweet. Well, except in the instance where she was climbing out the second-story window of a seedy fraternity house then getting pissed at me for helping her not die—but that's hardly my point…

My parents loved her. I know this because my mom hasn't stopped text-bombing me to drill in the point.

Mom: *Abby is a doll.*

Mom: *Make sure you act like a gentleman. Hold her doors open. And tell her how nice she looks. She's so pretty.*

Mom: *Talk. Don't just mumble.*

Me: *Mom. Stop.*

Mom: *Don't just talk about hockey. Ask her about herself.*

Mom: *Take her out in public. I know how much you like your bedroom, sweetie, but please don't just stay home with the poor girl. She needs sunlight.*

Me: *Please stop.*

Mom: *What is she doing for spring break? When are you bringing her home? Dad wants to know.*

My dad wants to know? Yeah, right. No offense to my dad, but he could give a shit about any of my…girlfriends. Correction: girlfriend—as in, singular. As in, only having one.

Snorting, I shove my phone in the back pocket of my jeans and push off the counter as Abby approaches in heeled half-boots that have peep toes. I slide my large arm around her waist and pull her against my body.

Pressing a kiss to the top of her head, I give her hair a whiff, expecting it to smell like greasy burgers and food from the restaurant we were just at.

It doesn't.

It smells like…

"Why does your hair smell like cherries?" I ask, both confused and intrigued, because I sure as shit don't smell this good.

"Um…dry shampoo."

Dry shampoo? What the ever-loving eff is that?

Abby grabs her keys off the counter and puts them in her purse, a small rectangular bag on a gold chain with her initials stitched on it. "Ready?"

"As I'll ever be," I tease, kissing the top of her head again.

Abby

In the end, we don't end up going to O'Malley's.

Even though it hadn't been my idea to change my clothes in the first place, it takes me just shy of one half hour to change into something "better"—but it takes Shelby *longer*, causing Blaze to lose interest in going downtown altogether.

After that, everyone disperses, going their separate ways: Weston to Molly's apartment, Blaze and Shelby to argue in his room, Jenna back to our place, and Cubby... well.

Cubby is down in the living room, eating a burrito, watching *Mean Girls*, and I'm not entirely positive, but I *think* he may have just shouted, "*You can't sit with us!*" with what sounds like a mouthful of food.

I mean, if I had to take a wild guess...

As I follow Caleb up the dimly lit stairwell to his room, the dusky daylight outside has long faded into night and the house is quiet. Save for Shelby's bickering and Cubby shouting lines from the movie, everything is still.

How I ended up staying here and on this climb up to the second-floor master bedroom, I couldn't say. We didn't exactly discuss a plan of action when the living room was still crowded with our friends.

We just drifted toward the stairs when Blaze and Shelby started arguing and scaled them without a conversation, like it was the natural thing to do.

I don't regret it, *won't* regret it, and I refuse to have second thoughts.

Any second-guessing fades when Caleb punches in the keypad on his bedroom door and turns to face me with a hesitant, questioning smile, bending his lips.

We enter, and he pushes down the hood of the sweatshirt he threw on over his flannel, removes his hat, and tosses it onto his desk. Caleb fans his fingers through his hair and gives his head a shake. My eyes follow the action of his hands as they tug at the hemline of his sweatshirt, pulling it up and over his head, the action lifting the flannel shirt underneath and giving me a glimpse of washboard abs.

I try to look away, but I can't.

If Miley Cyrus came crashing through the wall on a wrecking ball, I still wouldn't be able to tear my eyes away from his solid athlete's stomach. I freeze, clutching my purse, face flushing as my brain processes the sight of him and devours that dark happy trail of hair disappearing into the waistband of his jeans.

I'm sure my eyes have gone wide, because Lord, he is so rugged. Rough around the edges. Unrefined in the best possible way.

Handsome.

You might think it's too soon, and I know this behavior isn't *me*. Contemplating jumping into bed with a guy after only knowing him three weeks, barely a single official date, and no history is not—nor has it ever been—my style. But...I *want* to stay.

I want to spend the night with Caleb more than I've wanted anything in a long time, maybe even *because* it goes against everything I've been taught—like no sex before monogamy—or maybe because it goes against everything I believe in—like no sex before monogamy.

Because, like Cecelia said, when you know...you know.

And I *know* I want this.

I want Caleb in my life and *in* my body.

Crap. Did that sound sleazy?

As inappropriate as that sounds, I have to admit, it's the truth.

Yes, I'm scared—scared witless—but I'm done being safe. I'm done being cautious. I'm done being scared, for once in my life. So what if I have absolutely no idea what I'm doing? I want to be here anyway, and I'm determined to fumble through it.

As long as it's with him.

This obviously isn't a fling. I can feel it when he looks at me. When he touches me. When he's watching me from across the room.

He wants me too.

Caleb

Abby is watching me from the doorway, a play of emotions etched on her pretty, flushed face. In the short time I've known and grown attached to her, I've come to recognize that look of determination mixed with a whole lot of uncertainty.

It's just one of the many reasons I admire her.

We're both socially awkward, yet here we are.

I stroll into my room and pull the hoodie off my head, removing my hat in the process, and run a hand through my thick black hair. Pausing, I drum my fingers against the solid wood surface of my desk, stare out the window for a few seconds, and chew on my lower lip.

I glance down at the digital clock next to my computer: eleven o'clock.

Not an unreasonable time to call it a day. Shit. How do my friends do this every weekend—bring an endless parade of women home and bang them without a second thought? Without knowing them?

All hours of the day and night.

Sometimes in the common bathroom. Sometimes repeatedly.

Loudly.

You get the picture.

I run a hand down my face in frustration and force myself to turn toward Abby just as Cubby's muffled shout booms up from the living room downstairs, causing Abby to softly giggle.

"Who's Glen Coco?" I ask, confused.

She giggles again. "It's from a movie."

"A chick flick?" I shrug cluelessly, sitting on the edge of my bed and then reclining all the way back.

"A cult classic," she corrects, bending to unbuckle and remove her shoes. Abby places them next to the door and sinks down into my mattress on the other side of the bed, next to my nightstand. She looks over at me with those baby blues that I swear get brighter as she watches me, and her pupils dilate.

I let my head fall back all the way to the mattress and rest my hands behind my head. I watch as she stands again, walks around the bed, and sits back down, falling back onto the comforter to lie next to me.

Our feet hang off the end of the bed, mine touching the floor, and for a while we're still, just staring at the ceiling in silence.

Mostly because I have no idea how to proceed.

Yeah, I've had sex before...not like my teammates, but enough that I shouldn't be lying here like an awkward erotophobic, which is someone with an irrational fear of sexual acts—and yeah, that's a real thing. Google that shit if you don't believe me.

Not knowing how to make a move on Abby is actually somewhat emasculating, and I wonder what she's thinking on her side of the bed.

Shit.

Say something, Caleb. *Anything.*

"Thanks for coming today and meeting my parents. They liked you."

Abby turns her head toward me and warmly grins, the gesture lighting up her entire face. "Yeah?"

Unable to resist the smile tugging at my mouth, I grin back, and her clear blue eyes immediately flicker down to my mouth. "Yeah."

She stares at my mouth, her gaze narrowing in on my gap for a few torturous heartbeats before she rolls onto her stomach—closer—and timidly reaches her hand over. I suck in a deep breath and hold it in as her fingertip lightly traces my lips and she whispers, "I've been wanting to do this *forever*."

My lips involuntarily part, and the tip of my tongue flicks the delicate finger now skimming the gap between my front teeth.

"Yeah?" My voice, barely audible, comes out low and husky.

"Yeah," she whispers again.

"Forever? That sounds serious."

My teeth nip her fingertip, and she pulls her hand back, surprised. Grinning, I tighten my abs and lift myself off the bed, tucking my large hands under her armpits and drawing her closer still, until she's leaning over me.

With her blue eyes shining, Abby leans down until our noses touch, and she brushes the tip of her nose feather light, back and forth, across mine. Her chin dips, and she pauses before placing a small kiss in the crease of my lips, first in one corner then the other.

"It seems I've acquired a taste for gaps in teeth, and other…things."

My eyebrows shoot up, interested. "Things? What other things?"

"You, mostly."

As a shiver runs up the length of my torso, starting with the twitch in my groin, my palms find their way to Abby's back, running themselves leisurely up and down her spine of their own volition.

My back muscles flex as I raise my head, pressing my lips against her neck. "I knew there was a reason I liked you." I speak into that smooth space behind her ear, giving it a nuzzle.

She emits a breathy sigh before pulling away and spreading out beside me, grasping for my hand. I capture it and thread my fingers through, giving it a tender squeeze.

Confession: if you would have told me two weeks ago that I'd be lying here, holding the hand of a girl I'd caught climbing out a second-story window, on the day I let her meet my *parents*…well, I would have laughed my ass off in your face then shoved you the hell out of my way.

"This is crazy," Abby says faintly, as if reading my mind.

"What is?" I ask, though I already know the answer.

"This. Us. It's nuts. What is happening to my life?" She gives a small laugh and I give her hand another squeeze. "I hardly recognize myself."

"I feel like I've entered a parallel universe," I tease, turning my head to face her. "I don't even like girls, and now I have one in my room."

"You seduced me with your awkwardness." She laughs.

Can't argue with that.

I nod. "Yeah, that sounds accurate."

Abby looks at me expectantly.

I oblige. "You seduced me by falling out of a window?"

She narrows her eyes.

"By spilling beer all over your shirt at that party and pretending to need my bathroom?"

"Stop it!"

Yeah, no. This is too much fun. "You seduced me by crawling around my yard on your hands and knees?"

She sputters indignantly before shrugging my hand off, sitting up, and giving me a playful shove. "You..." She takes a deep breath, her cheeks tinged in the most adorable bright pink.

"You...what? Say it."

"Smartass." Abby's face turns bright red when I laugh—a loud, booming laugh that has me rolling over on the bed and her attempting to give my solid body another shove. Too bad I'm built like a fortress of steel.

I resist the urge to flex.

"I'm sorry. Swearing like that must have killed you." Over the past weeks, I've noticed she has a deep affinity for avoiding any kind of profanity—not including the pissed-off ranting after she dropped out of the Kappa Omega Chi fraternity house window and reeled at me for being a cocksucker...which was totally understandable, given the circumstances.

I'd be lying if I said I didn't find her pure mind refreshing—and disarming, which is most likely due to the fact that I'm surrounded by lewd assholes on a daily basis.

Abby looks down at me, and I reach up to rub a strand of her rich mahogany hair in between my thumb and forefinger. It's silky and smooth, just as I imagine her skin is under her white cotton shirt.

"It's, uh, getting late. Do you want me to walk you home, or…" I won't push her to stay—I would *never*—and yet…

"I mean, unless…" I hesitate.

Abby sucks in a breath and bites down on her lower lip. "Unless what?" she blurts out loudly.

I open my mouth, but no words come out. Big shocker, I know.

Fucking. Awkward.

Instead, I shrug uncomfortably, raising my torso to a sitting position and resting my sweaty palms on my spread knees, rubbing them up and down nervously.

We remain side by side, both of us too chickenshit to actually make a move one way or another. Abby hasn't made the move to leave, yet she hasn't exactly gotten comfortable as she sits ramrod straight at the edge of my bed, one of her hands fisting my comforter.

Suddenly I'm envious of my teammates and their balls-to-the-wall attitude with women. Cubby would have his dirty paws all over Abby by now and his tongue down her throat. He wouldn't be pussyfooting around like I am.

Frustrated, I run a hand through my hair and let out a loud groan.

Abby

This is pitiful.

I've never wanted to be one of those girls, but I wish I were one right now, because then maybe I'd know what to do, and how to act, and what to say, and…a hundred other things.

What would Cecelia say?

Then I think: What would Jenna do?

Oh my god, I'm delirious. I must be, because why the heck else would I be thinking about what *Jenna* would do? Could someone come slap me, please? I swallow a nervous giggle, because I know *exactly* what Jenna would do: she'd be all over Caleb by now.

Obviously.

She'd most definitely have her tongue down his beautiful, thick column of a throat, hand fondling his tight, corded thigh and maybe even his…his…

Ugh.

He lets out a deep groan next to me and runs one of his large hands through his hair, glancing at me sideways before staring straight ahead out his bedroom window.

That nervous laugh finally escapes my lips. "We're ridiculous. How are we allowed out of the house?"

A chuckle rumbles from his broad chest. "Now you know why I keep to myself." He continues rubbing his palms over the top of his pants, but he give me a sideways glace with his dark smolder. "I don't know how I live like a monk when I'm surrounded by manwhores."

My eyes go wide.

"Shit, sorry. I didn't mean it like that. They're not all manwhores. Mostly just the single guys." Again, he rakes a hand through his hair, tugging at the ends.

"If you don't stop pulling at your hair, you're going to give yourself male pattern baldness by the time you're twenty-two."

Wait, back up—did he just say he lived like a monk?

Cautiously, I ask. "What do you mean by 'live like a monk'?"

"I would think that was obvious," he mumbles. "I'm not exactly Chanandler Tatum."

I stare at him, confused. "Uh. You mean *Channing* Tatum?"

"Was that a bad example?"

I wrinkle my nose in distaste. "Horrible example. Pretty much the worst."

"What's wrong with Chanandler Tatum?" This earns me a bashful grin, and Caleb's ruddy five o'clock shadow gets a little pinkish.

"First off, *Channing* Tatum is a stripper—or he *was*. You can't compare yourself to him—he's way too pretty. Plus, he isn't getting any younger."

No offense, Channing.

"You don't think I'm pretty? That hurts my feelings, kind of." Caleb wipes away a fake tear then huffs a sigh. "Fine. James Franco's brother, Dave."

"Where are you coming up with this?" I throw my hands up, charmed by his playful banter. "We are *not* having this conversation…"

"Oh, but we *are*."

"Stop it." I chop my hands in a time-out motion and shake my head from side to side in laughter. "First I can't get you to talk, now I can't get you to stop."

"I know, right?" He buries his face in his hands then

lifts his head. "What's my problem?" Running his tongue back and forth over his front teeth, Caleb bites down on his lower lip out of habit as his pointed gaze sparkles at me.

"Caleb?"

"Hmm?"

"I'm a virgin," I say it matter-of-factly, like I've just told him it's raining outside or that there's a new movie playing this weekend. I don't know why I announced it this way or what I'm expecting him to say.

He says nothing; the silence in the room is deafening.

"I'm only telling you b-because..."

He waits patiently for me to finish my sentence, but it's caught in my throat. I can't say the words; I don't even know what the words *are*.

So intead I brave through it. "Does my being a virgin make you feel more comfortable?"

He clears his throat. "Don't you mean *uncomfortable*?"

"No. I thought that, you know, *two* virgins being awkward together would make it easier."

He looks up at the ceiling and clasps his hands behind his head, moving it slowly back and forth. "Abby, I'm not a virgin."

Oh.

Oh!

Oh. My. *God.*

"I...I... Can we *please, please* pretend that didn't just happen?" I beg with a nervous giggle.

"Pretend what didn't just happen?"

"The whole virgin announce—" I clamp my mouth

shut when the lightbulb goes off. "Okay, I see what you did there."

He chuckles softly beside me.

Nervously, I clasp my hands together on my lap and stare at my feet, which are barely touching the floor. "Sooo, I guess I should…"

Get going? Get staying?

Get a clue.

"Stay—I mean, if you want to, uh…" Caleb clears his throat again. "If you want to stay, that's cool. No pressure. I'm just throwing it out there. Since it's late."

Sure, it's late—but it's not *that* late. Eleven o'clock on college student time is when parties are usually just getting started. Besides, I only live a few blocks over, so his walking me home isn't a big deal. It's three minutes away.

I might not have a lot of previous experience when it comes to guys and their intentions, but I know this: Caleb's nonchalant attitude isn't fooling me. He wants me to stay, and *that* makes me nervous.

Abruptly, I stand and wipe my clammy palms on the front of my jeans. "I'm just gonna use the bathroom if you don't mind?"

Shutting myself in his bathroom, I pull out my phone and frantically tap out a quick text to Cecelia.

Me: *HELP! SOS! I think Caleb wants me to stay the night at his place. AM I READY FOR THIS? Is this moving too fast?????????????????*

She responds within seconds.

Cecelia: *Okay, first of all, cool it with the ALL CAPS and hundred question marks. You're not texting me while you're with him are you??*

Me: *No. I'm holed up in his bathroom like a big scaredy cat. We were sitting on the end of his bed, and I said it was getting late, and he said I could spend the night if I wanted to.*

Me: *So I got up and shut myself in the bathroom. I'm so awk, Cece!!!! I don't know if I can go back out there and act suave.*

Cecelia: *I'm going to pretend you didn't just use suave in a sentence.*

Me: *WOULD YOU BE SERIOUS?????????????*

Cecelia: *SORRY! Okay. Chill. Deep breath.*

Cecelia: *Go out there and rock his world. Dude deserves to get laid. Might I recommend starting with the classic blow job.*

I stare at my cell phone screen, face turning red and mouth hanging open.

Cecelia: *OMG I'm so sorry! Matthew stole my phone.*

Me: *I can't stay in here all night. What should I do?*

Cecelia: *What do you WANT to do?*

Me: *I want... I guess I want to spend the night.*

Cecelia: *Then what are you waiting for?? Abs, remember, just because you stay doesn't mean you have to have sex with him.*

Me: *I know. I'm just nervous. My palms are sweating. My face is red. My neck has a rash. I'm A HOT MESS.*

Cecelia: Awkward is part of your charm.

Me: *So NOT what I wanted to hear.*

Cecelia: *Well, it's true. You're never going to be one of*

those girls who just goes for the guy. That's not you, let's face it. But what you do have is charm. And you're sweet. For the most part.

My phone dings again as she continues.

Cecelia: *I know it's hard for you because you're shy around guys, but I don't think you have to worry with Caleb. He might not be a virgin, but he knows less than you do.*

Me: G*ee, why doesn't that make me feel better?*

Cecelia: *It should. If you're worried he's going to judge you, don't. DO NOT. He's putting himself out there. Why don't you do the same?*

Me: *God, I hate when you're right...*

Caleb

What is taking her so damn long?

I stand and walk over to my dresser, dig into the pocket of my jeans, empty the contents onto its surface, then kick my shoes off and push them under my desk with the side of my foot.

Glancing again at my bathroom door, I pull out my desk chair and sit, rolling it back and forth on the hard-wood floors while rapping my knuckles nervously against the solid wood of my desktop.

What is she doing in there?

There's no window, so I'm assuming she didn't go in there to climb out.

The thought sobers me.

Wait. *Shit.* What if she spends the night and tries climbing out my window in the morning? That would be a crushing blow to my ego. I can handle her not wanting to be with me tonight, but I couldn't handle it if she tried to sneak out.

I'm not overly worried, but let's be honest, she does have a history.

The sound of the doorknob turning garners my attention and has me shooting straight up and off of my desk chair, the rapid motion propelling it backward on its castors across the hardwood floor and smashing it into the end of my bed.

Fucking bull in a china shop.

I grab it and push it back in place as Abby flips the bathroom light off behind her and walks demurely back into my room, head cast down and hands clasped in front of her solemnly.

She looks up at me then, a small smile on her lips. "Okay."

Um…could you be more specific?

Apparently my confusion is evident, because she gives a shy, tinkly little laugh. "Sorry. Yes. I'd love to stay. O-overnight. Um. With you."

I do my best to remain indifferent, despite my racing heart. "Great. I'm really freaking tired—not that I wouldn't walk you home. It's just that I'm dead on my feet."

Her bright blue eyes assess me, head tilted to the side. "Mmmhmm. Yeah, me too." To illustrate her point, she gives a loud, dramatic yawn, lifting her hands above her head and stretching her arms. "So tired."

My eyes go to her white t-shirt pulled taut against her high, round breasts, and I pivot on my heel, roughly yanking open the top drawer of my dresser. It shakes on its rickety legs from the jerking motion. Digging through haphazardly, I pull out the smallest shirt in my arsenal and chuck it at her. "Here."

It hits her in the face.

She fumbles, just barely catching it, and holds it up to her chest, burying her face in it and faintly giving another quiet laugh. "Thanks." Her shiny blue eyes, now sparkling with mischief, peer up at me as she bites down thoughtfully on her lower lip before retreating back into the bathroom. "I'll just be a second."

As soon as the door closes, I go to work undressing, starting with my jeans, yanking them down and draping them over the large chair in the corner. I look down at my navy boxer briefs—at my straining erection—and pull those down quickly in favor of a pair of red Wisconsin Badgers sleep pants.

I strip off both my shirts, first the plaid flannel then the t-shirt underneath, and begin pacing as I wait for the door to swing back open, wondering if I should stay bare chested or toss something else on. I mean, Jesus H. Christ, my nipples are so hard they could cut glass. You'd think it was twenty friggin degrees in here.

Should I be putting that shit on display?

I glance at the bed and groan, wondering how the fuck I'm supposed to act when Abby comes back out that door wearing my t-shirt, and if I don't stop running my fingers through my hair, I *am* going to give myself male pattern baldness. One glance in the mirror shows me my hair is standing on end.

Giving the dark locks a tug, I smooth them down with the palm of my hand and let out a frustrated breath.

The bathroom door creaks open.

My breath catches.

It's just an old ratty t-shirt, but...*damn*.

The smallest shirt I own skims her thighs and does an outstanding job being snug in *all* the right places, her white underwear playing peek-a-boo from under the hem.

"Do you want boxers or something?"

Please say yes.

"No. I think I'm good." Her freshly washed face glows, makeup free, and her long, dark hair falls in a straight curtain, framing her face and cascading around her shoulders like a waterfall. She glances at the bed, uncertain, fiddling with the hemline of my gray cotton tee.

Stop fucking with the bottom of your shirt, I want to shout, because the fidgeting is giving me a clear view of not only her smooth, bare stomach, but also a shot of her cotton-covered crotch.

Whoever said basic Hanes hipster panties can't get a guy's dick hard was a goddamn liar.

Let me assure you, they fucking can.

"Um. Which side...?"

"I sleep on..." Lamely, I point to the side next to the door, and then I stick my hands in the pockets of my sleep pants.

Abby nods, takes a deep breath, and gingerly walks robotically to the opposite side of the bed. She pulls back the covers and stares down. "When's the last time you changed your sheets?" she jokes as she climbs in.

"My mom washed them today, smartass."

"You never know. My cousin Tyler hasn't changed his since fall semester when he moved in, and the worst part is, my aunt's been to visit him twice."

"That's kind of disgusting."

She gives a visible shudder, scrunching up her nose. "Not *kind* of—it totally is."

I still haven't gotten in the bed yet.

"Crap. I forgot to brush my teeth. Be right back."

Abby

Why, oh why am I going to lose sleep tonight? Let me count the ways:

1. Bare feet.
2. Bare chest.
3. Happy trail.
4. Abs.
5. Ripped biceps.
6. Aftershave.

Repeat.

Oh my god, even his freaking belly button is sexy, and I mentioned the happy trail, right? Yup, there it is, number three.

I can't even handle it right now.

Shrinking down deeper inside his goose-down comforter, I pull it up to my chin and resist the urge to squeal out loud and kick my feet with both excitement *and* horrification. Horrification—who knew that was even a word?

My silky legs glide beneath the bedding, the crisp sheets cool against my smooth skin, creating an awareness of how bare I actually am beneath the blankets—nothing but undies and a shirt that's not even mine.

Nostalgic and self-aware, I tip my chin down and give the soft gray threadbare shirt a whiff, inhaling the clean smell of fresh laundry, slub cotton, and Caleb.

Content, I decide that no matter what happens after tonight, I'm going to steal the shirt and *live in it*.

Is that weird?

So intent am I in indulging my senses in Caleb's big cushy bed, I don't notice him standing bare-chested, framed in the threshold of his bathroom door, until he clears his throat. He's watching me wide-eyed as I have my nose buried deep in the collar of his shirt.

"This…isn't what it looks like," I murmur, cheeks on fire.

"It isn't?"

"No. So please don't look at me like that."

"I didn't say anything." He grins, gap on full display. "However…" He pauses to torture me. "If I had to speculate, I'd say you were smelling my shirt—but that's just a guess, because I'm not wearing my glasses or my contacts." He chuckles at his own joke.

At the mention of his glasses, I shiver, remembering how flipping gorgeous he looks in them, all Clark Kent-y and whatnot.

Embarrassed—no—*mortified*, I dive under the covers then, bury my face in a fluffy pillow, and yes, take a whiff of that too, nervous laughter finally bubbling over.

"Fine. Yes! I was smelling your shirt," I shout from under the covers before coming up for air. Folding the covers over and smoothing out the wrinkles in the duvet, I sit up and pat the air out of the goose down in an attempt to avoid eye contact.

"Would you please, please just get in bed so my breathing can go back to normal?"

I'm fairly certain my heart is beating at a rate of one thousand beats per minute.

Far more casually then he slipped into bed when we were sharing a room at the rental cabin, he folds back the coverlet and slides in, then begins his routine of pounding and shaping pillows. I watch, mesmerized, as his sinewy muscles flex and bulge and swell with every languid movement, the tendons in his back and neck so defined... my mouth might *actually* be salivating.

I manage to tear my eyes away just long enough to readjust my position on the bed so I'm lying on my side, and I give him a guilty smile when he finally turns to face me.

Like I wasn't just undressing his undressed body with my greedy, lecherous eyes.

My wanton, covetous, *virgin* eyes.

As Caleb settles in beside me with his arms bent behind his head, I can't tell if he's feigning indifference or if he isn't feeling what I'm feeling—complete inner turmoil.

"Can you really not see without glasses?" I ask, breaking the silence.

He tips his chin to glance over at me and chuckles. "Yeah, I'm pretty blind."

I wave my hand through the air in front of his face. "Can you see that?"

Another chuckle. "I'm not *that* blind. Saw it *and* felt

it."

"What about this?" I stick out my tongue at him and he emits a "Pfft."

"Why don't we do an experiment? You get closer and I'll let you know when I can finally see you clearly," Caleb suggests with a mischievous grin, his dark eyes raking over my hair, face, and his t-shirt…I think. I mean, the guy did *just* say he was blind without his contacts…

"Okay, I'll play along." I lean in until I'm a foot from his face. "Can you see me now?"

He squints, and his hands feel around as if grasping through the thin air. "Abby, dear, is that you?" His voice croaks and scratches as he attempts to make it sound like that of an old lady.

I move closer still, and his dark brown eyes crinkle at the corner in amusement as he watches me move in on him. I'm at a near crouch, hovering a mere six inches or so from his face, hands braced on my knees.

"Is this better?" I whisper.

"Well, I can't say for certain, but…I see lots of little dots. And is that—did you—Lisa, do you have a *beard*?"

God, he's so freaking cute.

Closer still…

"Better?"

If I'm not mistaken, I watch his pupils dilate and his nostrils flare as he stares at me with those big, beautiful chocolate-brown eyes. His dark eyebrows lower in concentration as he studies my mouth.

"You know what I think?" I whisper.

"What?" His torso leans up toward me a fraction, and

his arms come down from behind his head.

"I think you're a big faker." Our lips are a fraction apart. I gulp back a sigh. "A big…fat…phony."

"How. Dare. You." Caleb lets out a small gasp of indignation as he envelopes me in those strong arms, hauling me against him. Then, before I know it, I'm flat on my back, staring up at him. "Now what do you have to say?"

His low voice vibrates in my ear as he drags his mouth from my ear, trailing it along my jawline. My eyes flutter closed and I turn my head, presenting him with the slim column of my neck in a silent invitation to graze. He accepts eagerly, the tip of his nose running the length of my neck before giving the tender skin there a gentle nip, then a suck.

"Oh, *Lisa*, you smell so good," he teases, nuzzling the neglected spot behind my ear before peppering it with kisses. Caleb's large fingers run through my long hair, which is fanned out around the pillow.

"Mmmm, oh, *Clark*, that feels so good."

His muffled laughter fills my ear. "Clark? Who the hell is Clark?"

"Who the hell is Lisa?"

We lie there laughing until our laughter fades into smiles, and those smiles turn into kisses—steamy, wet, open-mouthed kisses.

Slow. Unhurried.

Kisses that steal my breath away.

Kisses that consume us both.

Kisses that continue when Caleb's hand slides up my bare thigh, his fingers flirting with the trim on my white cotton panties before palming the warm heat between my legs and sliding up my stomach.

A soft puff of air leaves my lips, and he captures it with his mouth, sucking on my tongue as he holds my naked breasts under his gray t-shirt, cupping them in his hands. I can feel the hard calluses marring his skin, the rough pads a contrast to my unblemished skin, and I marvel at our differences. I suppress a moan from beneath his large body.

My hands find their way to his back, and I run them up his spine. Our pelvises meet, the solid weight of Caleb's stiff erection digging into the valley between my thighs.

He tugs at the hem of my shirt, drawing it up over my stomach, and I give him permission to remove it by lifting my back off the bed so he can pull it over my head.

This is the first time in my life I've even bared myself to a man, and I blush from head to toe as Caleb looks down at me, exposed from the waist up.

Desire and passion and longing fill his eyes as he watches me, slowly rotating his hips, his hooded gaze a slow burn as it drops to my breasts.

My breathing is labored as his hand reaches for me again, one forefinger tracing the underside of one full breast, then the other, round and round, back and forth, deliberately, *painfully* slowly.

The feeling is…

Indescribable.

Empowering.

Bliss.

My head tips back as his mouth finds purchase on my body, kissing and suckling, and I close my eyes, prepared to lose myself in Caleb.

Caleb

Abby isn't a sure thing, and I'm not sure I'd ever want her to be.

Resting both hands on either side of her head, I prop myself up and stare down, running my abrasive palm over the silky flesh of her flawless breasts, loving the weight of them in my hand and marveling at how perfect they are as I stare at my reflection in her sapphire-blue eyes.

They get glazy and hooded when I run my thumb over a hard, dusky nipple, her pink lips parting and head tipping back when I lower my mouth to taste her.

My arms quake when I bend down to run my tongue over the perky tip of her right breast, and Abby moans when I suck it into my mouth, greedy for her, hungry for her.

Her hands go to my hair, those delicate fingers tenderly threading themselves through my shaggy locks, down over my shoulders, and pulling me closer.

Our mouths collide when I pull my mouth off her nipple with a pop, and she licks the moisture from the corner of my lips before our tongues tangle in a rushed frenzy.

I begin kissing my way down her neck. Jawline. Behind her ear.

Lower I go, kissing her breasts, down to the flat planes of her stomach. I give her belly button a lick and suck the skin of her hips before my wet tongue trails down her navel. She shivers, her hands back in my hair. I can physically feel her ab muscles tighten as I go lower.

A short, stunned squeal flies from her lips. "Caleb," she breathes. "I-I don't…I…"

"Is this okay?" My large hands splay on her stomach, and I draw a circle around her belly button as she gazes down at me, eyes glassing over.

"You don't h-have to…you know…" Her head thumps back down on the pillow, and she covers her face with her hands. "Oh god."

"Go down on you?" I growl into her belly, fingers toying with the thin waistband of her virginal white cotton panties. "Baby, I want to. *So* bad." I take a deep breath. "Tell me what you want me to do and I'll do it."

I give her stomach another lick, eyes trained on her, waiting.

"I've never… Please don't make me say it."

"Yes or no, Abby." Another lick. Another growl.

She bites her lip, and I bite her panties. Moaning, her head flails to the side as she squeezes her eyes shut. They flutter open, and she lifts her head, parts her lips, and breathes, "Y-yes."

"Thank *god*," I snarl, caressing the elastic band of her underwear and burying my nose in the apex of her thighs before running my nose up and down the seam of her crotch.

Above me, Abby lets out a surprised yelp, her hips lifting slightly off the bed. The sight of her thrashing on the bed is mind-altering, and I suck on her underwear, wetting them with my tongue, just to get another reaction from her.

"Oh! Oh Jesus, Caleb." I suck her through her panties harder when she gasps my name. "Are you t-trying to k-kill me?" Her words come out in a low, long, and tortured pant, and she grapples for a handful of sheets, knuckles turning pale pink as she grips them like her life depends on it. "I don't know if I can h-handle this."

Have I mentioned how much I fucking love her stammering? She only does it when she's turned on or nervous, and I've noticed that's only with me.

It's fucking intoxicating. *Addicting.*

"Shhhh. Relax," I cajole, voice raspy and on the verge of cracking. "You're so fucking wet, baby."

As I pull back the waistband of her pristine underwear, I look up at her naked and withering in the center of my big bed, and I almost cream my sleep pants from the sight of her pale pink tits jiggling when she squirms her hips impatiently.

Grinding my dick into the mattress for some temporary relief, I pull down the only thing stopping me from making her come down her hips, tossing the discarded panties to the side.

I can't stop the grin spreading across my lips when I'm finally able to hook my arms around her legs, spread her wider, and lower my face between her trembling thighs, giving us both what we've wanted since setting eyes on each other.

Abby

ear Heavenly Father, please forgive me for—ugh. Oh god. Wait. Not you. Him. Yes, right there. Don't stop. Shit, oh shit, oh god. Father, p-p-pleasssse...forgive me for my sins. This sinning. Th-th-this, oh...the sinning. Yes. Ooohh...that tongue. I'm so sorry, God. I'm s-sor... Deeper! Yes! I mean, no!

"Deeper! Yes! I mean, no!" I slap a hand over my mouth, horrified by the loud moaning and incoherent babbling that slips out. "Caleb, oh god." I gasp at the top of my voice. "Mmmnnugh. Right there."

I'm embarrassed.

But—oh god—does it feel good.

His face is buried deep between my legs, his long, eager tongue doing things to my body that I couldn't have imagined in my wildest fantasies. As my eyes roll back in my head, it occurs to me briefly how my friends can have casual sex—sleep with someone just for an orgasm. I get it now.

Because this. Feels. *Incredible.*

Addictive.

Intoxicating.

Intoxicating.

Crap. I'm repeating myself.

I try praying again, to beg forgiveness for having pre-marital sex, but I can't concentrate with Caleb's teeth and tongue thrashing down by my core. I clear my throat and give his hair a tug. "Ca... Caleb. Please. Stop."

He lifts his head, mouth glistening, disoriented eyes on fire...on fire *for me*. He crawls his way up my body, sliding his rock-hard groin against my legs, resting it between them.

My head tips back and he kisses my neck. I can taste myself on him when he presses a kiss on my lips, murmuring, "Tell me what you want, baby. I don't want to push you."

"You." I can feel my eyes shining as I try to focus on his face, but I haven't come and I can't...won't. "Inside me. I want you inside me. Please."

His nostrils flare, and his mouth slams down on mine, sucking my tongue into his mouth and running his hands over my ribcage, up to my breasts, squeezing and molding them with his palms.

"I want you so fucking bad, Abby. So fucking bad."

I do my best to nod. I might have lolled my head to the side—who the hell knows.

In record time, Caleb slides his pants off and kisses me again. Without breaking contact, his long, powerful arm reaches over, pulls open his nightstand, grapples around, and pulls out what I assume is a condom.

Oh jeez. I've never actually seen a guy put one on before, and I'm fascinated as he rips open the package, tosses the foil aside, and rolls the condom over the hard length of himself.

My cheeks are red hot, but I can't *not* look. I'm mesmerized.

"This is going to hurt." He pauses, referencing my virginity. "Are you sure you want to do this? With me?"

"Yes." I stroke his face. "I trust you. I…"

Adore you. Admire you. Am baffled by you.

His lips find mine, and through an open-mouthed kiss, he says, "Just hold on to me, okay, baby? This is probably going to hurt," he repeats with more kisses. "You're so beautiful," he whispers.

The sheets rustle as he reaches down and inserts his fingers into me before lining himself up. Pushing forward, he pulls his fingers out and lays his face in the nape of my neck. "I'm just going to get the worst part over with, okay? On three?"

I give a shaky nod. "Yes. Just do it. I'll be fine." *I hope.* "Promise."

Caleb lets out a long, frustrated breath. "I'm scared shitless," he admits with a nervous laugh.

"Me too."

His dick twitches at my entrance and I wiggle my hips. He blows out a puff of air. "All right. This is it, baby. Hold on."

I hold on. With one hard thrust, he pushes all the way in, and I inhale a loud gulp of air.

Holy. Mother. Of. God—and *not* in a good way. Honestly, that freaking hurts. And burns. I whimper and Caleb stills, his lips crooning reassurance into my ear.

It's *not* helping.

"I'm sorry, Abby. I'm sorry," he mumbles into my hair. "That's it. The hard part is over. I won't…I won't move." His strained, erotic groan fills my ear. "I swear. Just…tell me when you're ready."

Pouting, I give my head a stubborn little shake.

I don't want him to move. Like, ever.

Crap, whose stupid idea was this? Anyone who says their first time doing it was magical or good is a flipping liar.

After what feels like an eternity but is probably merely a few seconds, I push at his shoulders to give myself some space, and I take a deep breath.

"Okay." Grimacing, I mutter, "Okay. Just…take it slow."

Or I will *murder* you.

He does. He takes it slow, and eventually…*eventually* the stinging subsides.

Yeah, I said stinging.

Caleb works his hands under my ass, pulling me into him and pushing into me deeper, my hips digging into the mattress as he gently moves in and out, and I'm hating sex a tiny bit less. Notice I only said a *tiny* bit.

I'm not going to lie and say it's earth shattering, but at least it doesn't feel terrible, and it's done.

I, Abigail Darlington, am no longer a virgin.

Caleb gives one last thrust into me, and his groans fill the room as he comes. Alone.

Well, at least *one* of us had fun.

He hovers above me, planting kisses on my temple and forehead, bracing himself on his elbows and running his fingers through my hair. I feel cherished, special, and not the least bit regretful.

"You okay?" I nod and he rolls off me, giving me another quick peck—this time on the lips—and easing out of bed. "Don't go anywhere—be right back."

Caleb

I slide back into bed after washing off and disposing of the condom in my bathroom. I reach over to pull Abby closer, laying a hand on her naked hip before jerking the blankets up and over us.

She shivers and trails her fingers lightly over my chest, seemingly mesmerized by my well-defined muscles. I let her explore, watching her intently, taking in the rich cascade of brown hair, the bright blue eyes now weary with fatigue, the pink lips set in a content line.

So pretty. So sexy.

So…*mine*.

She raises her eyes, giving me a lazy smile, still tracing my chest with a lazy finger. "What was that?"

Ah shit. "I, uh…said, mine? You…if you want."

Her eyes get wide, and she leans in, dragging her mouth down over my bottom lip. "I want."

"You are ah-fucking-mazing," I whisper into her lips.

"You're not so bad yourself," she whispers back. "You know, since we're on the subject, I was kind of wondering something."

"Hmmm?" I roll onto my back, pulling her with me, the crush of her naked breasts on my ribcage and her bare pussy rubbing against my thigh making my dick twitch.

She lays her head in the crook of my neck and my hand idly rubs her bare back. "Have you ever had a girlfriend?"

I chuckle, chest rumbling. "Are you serious?"

"What do you mean?"

"I mean, look at me: fucked-up teeth, freakishly tall, pissed off all the time."

"But that's...*ridiculous*. Why would you say those things about yourself? Those are the things I like about you."

My chest releases a low grumble in protest.

"Wow. That middle-school Sarah girl really did a number on you." She laughs at her own joke.

I snort. "Whatever. *I* broke up with *her*..."

"Oh, that's right—at the eighth grade Halloween dance."

"Hell yeah. Who's the badass now?"

"Um, I'm going with Sarah Schroeder for barricading you in the middle-school bathroom like a boss."

"The little she-devil."

Abby taps her chin in thought. "I wonder what she's doing now..."

"Probably emasculating her poor bastard of a boyfriend."

Abby laughs softly, her hand disappearing under the covers and roaming over my tight abs. Pulling her hand back out, she gingerly lifts the bedcovers and peers underneath.

"What are you looking at?"

She gives her head a little shake and bites down on her lower lip. "I just haven't really ever seen one up close before." She laughs, staring down at my hardening dick like it's a museum exhibit. Not to brag, but it is pretty damn impressive.

"It's a little late to be curious, don't you think?" Ignoring me, she continues ogling my groin. "Better knock it off or you're going to get yourself in trouble," I warn.

Abby manages to peel her eyes away and wiggles her perfectly manicured eyebrows at me. "Or maybe trouble is exactly what I'm looking for."

"Aren't you sore?" My hand trails down her stomach and I gently caress her inner thigh.

She looks sheepish. "Well…yeah, a little."

Damn.

"Well, then I hate to be the one saying this, but…maybe we should just go to sleep." I look over at the clock on my bedside table. "It's one."

"Do you mind if I just sleep like this? I don't feel like getting out of bed to hunt down my clothes."

I stare down at her like she's lost her damn mind. "Do I mind if you sleep naked? What the hell kind of a question is that?"

I slap her on the ass then reach over to flip the lamp off.

We settle in like we've been doing this for years.

Abby

I don't know what woke me first: the early morning sun shining through the blinds in Caleb's bedroom *or* the hard erection pushing into my bare butt crack.

I stretch through a yawn as a large arm moves from where it had been resting on my naked waist, snakes slowly around my stomach, and cups one breast while his thumb strokes the other. Yes, his hand is that big.

With his hard groin grinding into my backside, I can hardly resist giving my hips a little gyration, causing the hand on my breast to give it a squeeze and hot breath to caress my neck.

"Is this going to be a thing?" I ask breathlessly.

He groans and continues massaging my breasts. "Mmm, what?"

"Us groping each other constantly like teenagers."

"Fuck yeah." His baritone voice is deep and gravely. "I hope so."

"Oh!" I gasp as he pinches a nipple.

"Hockey players are horny bastards. Insatiable. Didn't you know that?"

Horny. Bastards. Insatiable. My cheeks flush.

His hand trails down my flat stomach, circles my belly button, and cups my vagina. "Um...uhhh...n-no..."

"Are you still sore?"

"I..."

"I love naked Abby in the morning." His chest rumbles as he buries his face in my hair, his fingers sliding up and down the slit of my crotch. "I love naked Abby, period," he repeats, humming in my ear. "So fucking sexy."

"Language," I chastise, my head tipping back. I can't stop the flow of words spilling out of my mouth even though they're not exactly romantic post-coital bedroom talk. "Watch your mouth." He pushes a finger inside me while grinding into me from behind. "*Oh! Oh g-geez...*"

"Want to give the sex thing another try?" he whispers low into my ear. "Practice makes perfect. Besides," he continues, planting a wet kiss on my neck, "it usually (kiss) lasts (kiss) longer (kiss) than (kiss) it did (kiss) last night."

I bite down on my lower lip, trying to nod. "K."

"K?"

"Yes."

A relieved breath whooshes out of him and onto my bare shoulder. "Yes."

Seriously.

I've gone from total virgin status to certifiable hussy in less than two weeks' time. I don't even think Cecelia got this much action when she started seeing Matthew, and they were in a committed relationship. Caleb and I are just…

Actually.

I don't know what we are, or what our status is, but as I'm contemplating my questionable life choices while basking in a sexified stupor, I'm unceremoniously flipped onto my back. Caleb stares down at me, ten—no, *twenty* kinds of sexy.

Tousled, shaggy hair. Piercing, smoky eyes. The hint of a beard surrounding his full lips and jaw. Sculpted upper body with a light dusting of chest hair.

My hair is fanned out on the pillow, my half-hooded eyes gaze up at him drowsily, and I'm not sure what picture I'm presenting, but judging by the way he's devouring me with his eyes, he likes it.

He bends down and kisses me slowly before he reaches into his bedside table. A condom is rolled on, and now he's slowly sliding into me for the second time in a matter of hours.

I'm still sore, but the barrier of my virginity is no longer there. When his hips begin a slow roll, I can do nothing but marvel at the incredible new sensation. He isn't hitting any of my erogenous zones, but it actually feels…*good*.

Wait.

No. It's starting to feel…better than good. Delicious? Amazing. Spectacular.

"Do you want to be on top?" His throaty request sends a shiver up my spine.

"Huh?" My head lolls on the pillow.

"Get on top." He grips my ass like a vice and rolls us, groaning when I'm finally straddling him. "I read…somewhere…yeah…like that, baby…I read that girls…" He gulps then pauses, working my hips with his hands, pulling me over him back and forth, doing most of the work. "Shit…Abby…"

"Shhh," I hiss at him. "Shut up."

I'm trying to focus.

He squeezes his eyes closed and sighs, licking his lips in concentration as I move over him. "I read that girls have a better…chance…of having an orgasm…on…top." He drags out the sentence between pants. "You feel… Don't stop. Are you close?"

He read *what* somewhere? Why the hell is he still talking? I'm trying to have my first sex orgasm, for Christ's sake.

I must have spat the words out loud, because he sputters out a startled laugh, his head rolling to the side before a guttural moan escapes his lips. I undulate my hips, finally finding a rhythm that works for both of us.

I lean forward and am rewarded with a hungry, openmouthed kiss as Caleb's talented fingers fan out precariously close to my back door—there's no delicate way to say it—and I'm sorry, but that feels…it feels…s-so gooooood.

Keep doing that th-thing. Yes, Caleb, right there, th-that spot a little harder. Yes, like that…deep, s-so deep. Are my toes actually curling? Why does this—oh shit, oh shit— feel so good? Oh! O-ohh… Uhhhhhh… Oh my god, I'm going to have an orgasm, are the last intelligible thoughts I have before, well, having an orgasm.

"H-holy shit." A puff of air leaves my throat at the ripple of pleasure shooting through my body. "Now you have me swearing." I admonish myself as Caleb drives his hips upward, immobilizes my hips with his giant hands, and impales himself deeper.

"Keep moving, baby. I'm gonna come," Caleb demands with a rasping groan before his entire body tenses up with a hoarse, primal grunt. He pulses inside me a few times as his fingers slide to my shoulders, pulling me in for another kiss.

I sit up with him still inside me, gingerly stroking my fingers lovingly across his strong jaw and gazing down at him in satisfied wonderment.

And that's…

Well.

That's when I hear the four soft beeps of a keypad.

That's when the door flies open.

Caleb

"Dude. What the…fuck? Holy shit. Dude." Cubby stands in the doorway as my bedroom door ricochets against the wall, staring down at the bed. "I didn't know you had company, bro."

"Get the fuck out, jackoff!" I roar as Abby chokes out a horrified squeak. She scrambles frantically for the blankets but is still impaled on my now flaccid dick, so it's basically the most fucking awkward position I've ever had the misfortune to be in.

Her hands quickly cup her naked breasts, her face and neck turning red and covered with a bright rash.

"Wow, Showtime, she's got a great rack." Cubby's eyes roam Abby's creamy skin approvingly, and I all but throw her off me so I can climb out of bed and beat the ever-loving piss out of my roommate.

I look around for my pants, pointing furiously toward the door. "Get your fucking eyes off my girlfriend's tits and get the fuck out, now."

"Dude, I was giving her a compliment." He continues to stand in the doorway, immobile, captivated by the free porno show. "I stopped by to see if you're going to the rink tonight."

Why is he still standing there?

I am seething through clenched teeth. "I'm going to beat the shit out of you."

Cubby's eyebrows shoot up into his hairline. "Bro, why are you yelling? You're the one who gave me the code to your door. How am I supposed to know you're in here having sexual relations?"

Abby disappears beneath the covers, burrowing herself deep as another voice joins the party, chanting, "Oh my god, oh my god, oh my god," over and over.

"Whoa, whoa, whoa!" Miles halts next to Cubby, clearly on his way to the gym, keen eyes focused on the lump in my blankets. "You got someone in there with you, buddy? Don't tell me. Let me guess…" He taps a finger on his chin. "Brielle from the campus IT help desk?"

Arrogant prick.

"You idiot, it's Abby. I caught them *boning*," Cubby tells him matter-of-factly, like Miles is the idiot here.

"No shit it's Abby." Miles rolls his eyes. "I could hear him moaning her fucking name last night." He gives me an appraising look and adjusts the duffle bag draped across his shoulder. "Good for you, man."

I pinch the bridge of my nose between my thumb and index fingers and calmly exhale. "Close the door and get out."

Miles ushers Cubby out into the hall, closing the door behind him. "You might want to check the lock next time, bro!" he yells from the other side of the door, giving the solid wood a few raps with his knuckle.

I sit on the edge of the bed, sheet wrapped around my waist, and fall back onto the bed, reaching behind me to tap the maniacally giggly lump in the center of my bed.

"You think that was *funny*?"

"No!" Her head pops out from under my white sheets, dark hair falling around her bare shoulders in sheets. "Th-this is hysterical l-laughter. I can't h-help it. This only happens when I'm stressed out or terribly n-nervous."

"Are you going to be okay? Do you…need anything?"

"No, I'll be fine. It could have been worse, I guess." Abby hiccups. "At least I didn't start crying."

"Uh, yeah. I'm going to pummel their faces in. But don't worry, I'll make it look like an accident."

She blinks at me and leans forward, placing a kiss upside down on my Adam's apple. "You should really go and…throw that *thing* out."

"Oh shit!" I jump up and race naked to the bathroom.

I toss the condom in the garbage and rinse my hands, bracing both hands on the counter as I stare at my reflection in the mirror and take an inventory of myself that I haven't done in a long time. Dark eyes that aren't scowling, eyebrows relaxed, mouth in an upturned line for the first time in *fucking forever*.

For once, I feel carefree and young.

I run the sink again and splash cold water on my face, toweling off my neck and chest before wrapping a terry-cloth bath towel around my narrow hips.

For the hell of it, I splash some cologne on my neck before walking back into my bedroom, and call me crazy, but I was fully expecting and hoping to see Abby still sprawled out in the center of my big bed.

Instead, she's standing in my gray cotton t-shirt, next to my dresser, hand extended in front of her, two delicate fingers grasping her gold ring.

Oh shit. Oh fucking shit.

Her ring.

"What are you doing with this?" She holds it out high, eyebrows curved in a patronizing arch, bare foot tapping on my cold, hardwood floor. "Care to explain?" Her lips are pursed tight, and her other hand is on her hip.

"I…"

She stares at me impassively, waiting.

My palms go out in front of me, beseeching. "Abby, let me explain."

Still nothing.

"I meant to give it back."

"When, Caleb?" Tears form in the corner of her eyes, and she swipes them away angrily. "When you saw me pawing the ground on my hands and knees? Or when I told you about it that day you walked me home. *Answer* me."

Shit. Sweet Abby is kind of scary.

And if she weren't gearing up to chew my ass out, I'd applaud her for sticking up for herself.

"I don't know what to say."

"Clearly not." She stalks over to the chair where she stacked her clothes and begins angrily pulling on her jeans and muttering under her breath. She flops down, pulling on her shoes and zipping them both up the side. "Stupid little virgin. Way to fall for the big, angry, *lying* jockstrap."

My hands shake as I hold them out, imploring. I am way out of my league with this one. "Have I ever been anything but honest with you?"

She stands up and shoves the ring right in my face. "Gee, I guess not!"

"Be fair. Everything I've ever said has been honest."

She rolls her eyes. "Oh brother, like *that's* real hard—you scarcely ever *talk*, Caleb!"

"Come on, stop. Please, I tried. Don't be pissed at me." I shake my head and run both hands through my hair, frustrated. I don't miss Abby's eyes flicker to the waistband of my loosening towel with a guilty spark, and she gulps before jerking away.

"How do I know I can trust you with my *heart* if I can't trust you with my possessions? Or my privacy? Is this all just a big joke to you?"

A joke? Okay, now I'm getting pissed. "What the fuck is that supposed to mean? It's a goddamn ring, for Christ's sake. It's not like I fucking cheated on you. Chill the fuck *out*."

Okay, so *that* particular choice of words might have

been a mistake, because her face gets so red that her bright blue eyes look aquamarine. They're sexy and erotic and unnerving and all kinds of fucked up—especially when narrowed into slits and fixated on me.

She levels me with a stare, hurriedly gathering up her folded shirt from last night. "Okay. Fine. I'll *chill the fuck out* if you can tell me why you didn't tell me about the ring."

She irritably screws the ring onto the middle finger of her right hand.

I proceed cautiously, knowing from watching my dad argue with my mom that there's little reasoning with a woman who's hell bent on being pissed. I keep my voice steady. "I just...forgot, and that's the truth. I swear."

"You forgot," she says flatly. "Even after I brought it up, *multiple* times?"

Oh boy.

She sounds like a prosecutor cross-examining a witness, and I know that I'm losing her but am ill-equipped to stop it.

"Wait, who's the pre-law major here?" I try joking with her to lighten the mood; judging by the disgusted look marring her pretty face, it's an epic fail.

"That's all you have to say?"

"I don't know what to tell you. I'm sorry." I shrug helplessly. "Is this about the guys walking in on us? Seriously, what are you really upset about?"

"No. Yes! This whole thing is freaking me out, Caleb! Cubby saw my...my...boobs!" She opens and closes her mouth a few times, but nothing comes out. Then, "That was mortifying for me. Absolutely mortifying. Words cannot describe. And do you want to know something else? I don't think your roommates have any respect for you. If they did, they wouldn't have barged in here."

Huh? "I know you're upset—"

"My *boobs*, Caleb. He saw. My. Boobs. No one but you has ever seen them before!"

Feeling cornered, I shout, "I said I was sorry! What the fuck more do you want?"

"I want him to *un*-see my body! That's what I want! And I want you to have been honest and given me my ring! That's what I want!"

How did this escalate so quickly? "Wait," I ask slowly. "Are you mad that my friends saw your boobs, or that I had your ring?"

I know it's lame, but I really need her to be clear on this. Instead of responding, she stares at me like I've lost my damn mind. Like I'm an idiot. Like I don't *get* it.

"Caleb, maybe we're not cut out for a relationship." Her hands flutter, gesturing around the room. "Maybe this whole thing is a mistake."

I don't even know what to say to that, so I say nothing.

Abby inhales a deep breath. "I'm sorry. I'm just so… Maybe we wouldn't even be having this conversation if those jerks hadn't charged into the room and humiliated me. But they did, and…" She pauses. "I'll probably regret saying this, but I c-can't do this right now, not when I'm still embarrassed."

I run a hand through my hair, tugging it in frustration.

Mind made up, Abby stalks to the door, turning to face me as she yanks at the doorknob. She pauses as tears well up in her bright, expressive eyes. She wipes them away with a quick flick of her finger and lifts her chin a notch.

"And I-I'm *keeping* this shirt, asshole."

With a flounce, my favorite shirt *and* my would-be future girlfriend slam out the door.

Abby

" **H**ey, Abby, wait up."

At the sound of my name, I turn to see Tyler jogging briskly toward me, across the lawn of the Kappa house, in a wrinkled cut-off t-shirt and basketball shorts. His brown hair hangs in his eyes, and he's barefoot.

He's holding a blunt in one hand and a pair of brown leather flip-flops in the other.

"Hey," I mumble, sniffling.

"Where's the fire?" he guffaws at me, catching up and falling into stride next to me. "Please don't tell me you just climbed out the window of the Omega house."

I frown down at the weed pinched between his thumb and forefinger. "It's barely eight thirty and you're already smoking a joint? Can't you get arrested for walking around with that thing?"

He disregards my comment with a shrug. "It's a clove cigarette. Relax. Here, take a drag." He holds it out and I slap both his hand and the *clove cigarette* out of my face.

He only laughs. "You gonna answer my question or what?"

"You didn't ask one." I continue walking, wanting desperately to distance myself from Caleb. I need to be alone. I need to think.

"Why you coming from the Omega house?" my cousin asks, throwing down his flip-flops and stepping onto them before we hit the sidewalk and start toward my house.

"None of your business."

"Whoa! Why are you in such a rush and why do you look so…pissed off?"

Hmmm. He's pretty astute for someone so *high* this early in the morning. I march on, determined to ignore him, and catch him glancing back toward the Omega house from the corner of my eye.

I follow his gaze, and I can feel the yearning etched across my face.

"I *knew* it!" Tyler all but shouts into the cool morning air. "I fuckin' knew that guy was a douche." He takes another hit off his joint and blows the smoke up toward the sky. "I knew it the first time I met that loser trespassing on our property."

I halt, pivoting on my heel to face him, my arm shooting out to clothesline him. "Trespassing on your property," I ask so very slowly. "Tyler, what are you even talking about?"

"I finally figured out where I know the guy from. Couldn't figure it out the other day."

I clutch the white t-shirt I wore on our date in my arms

nervously, wringing it in my hands as I cross my arms, rolling my eyes at Tyler to keep the pleading tone out of my voice. I'm in no mood for his stoner BS. "Please, enlighten me."

My cousin scratches his sparse goatee. "He came over that night. Or afternoon." I sigh, exasperated. "You know, that day you climbed out my window. He came over and wanted your number."

Stunned, I breathe out quietly, my whole body going still. "What?"

Tyler takes another drag off his joint and blows out a gray, billowy puff of smoke.

I cough dramatically as his small cloud of carcinogens floats in my face, waving the toxins out of my clean air space. He takes one more pull and throws the joint on the ground, grinding it down into the concrete to extinguish it with the heel of his leather sandal. "Yeah. He came over and threatened to kick my ass if I didn't give it to him."

My mouth falls open in shock. "What did you do?"

Tyler looks only slightly abashed. "I gave it to him?"

"What! Tyler!" I punch him in the arm and start stalking toward my house at a brisk pace. Tyler hustles to keep up, and when he does, I whack him again. "Why would you do that?"

"Dude, stop hitting me." He rubs his arm. "That guy is huge, man. I didn't want him kicking my ass. "

"So it didn't occur to you that he could be a stalker? Or a psycho? Or, gee, I don't know, a *rapist*?"

Tyler's dazed eyes get wide as saucers. "Is he?"

I stop walking to smack him again. "No, you idiot, he's

not."

"Anyway, dude ain't right in the head. He reminds me of, I don't know, a lumberjack, or a hitman...or whatever."

"Don't be mean. You don't even *know* him."

"When a dude threatens to kick my ass on my own front porch, I can say whatever I want. Shit, maybe he *is* a psycho."

"He's not a psycho. He's just an introvert."

"Why are you defending him?" Tyler puts his arm out and stops me halfway up the block, looking me over from head to toe. "And why are you walking funny? Like you have a rod shoved up your ass."

Walking funny? Oh crap, am I?

I wouldn't be surprised. The soreness between my legs from the recent eight-hour sex marathon—which is more action than I've seen in my entire twenty-one years on Earth—probably *does* have me walking bowlegged. Mortified, I pick up the pace, hoping it will straighten out my stride, trying not to wince when my crotch starts to burn.

Peeing is going to suck.

"I'm not defending him, Ty." I let out a breath. "Okay, so maybe I am, but so what? I really thought I liked him."

"Then why did you bust out of his house like you had the hounds of hell nipping at your heels?"

"None of your business."

He doesn't take the hint and follows me up my driveway and into the yard. "Does it have anything to do with why he threatened to kick the shit out of me?"

"I wouldn't know anything about that."

"He said he had something of yours. Guess that's why he wanted your number."

I look down at my ring, which sits glistening on my hand in the warm spring sun.

"Dude, if you're gonna get all girly and weird, I'm gonna split." He throws me a sullen frown. "Peace out."

Lost in my own thoughts, I barely hear his retreat, his shoes crunching on the loose concrete driveway.

An uncomfortable knot forms in the pit of my stomach as some of Caleb's pleading words came back to haunt me: *"Please, I tried. Don't be pissed at me,"* he'd implored, standing in his bedroom, looking as lost as I'd felt. Then I remember him dragging me outside when Stephan and Weston started to fight at the rental cabin when we'd been at the waterpark. *"Not a fan of conflict, are you?"* I'd asked him in private. *"No. Not at all, and not this kind of conflict. It gets too…ugly."* He'd paused. *"I don't mind a brawl on the ice, but that swagger bullshit going on inside? No thanks."*

He hates confrontation, and that's exactly what I've given him, because I was embarrassed and horrified. Not ten seconds after we had sex, his friends busted into the room. They have no respect for his hard work around the house or his privacy, and certainly none for me.

And don't even get me started on how they constantly mock him for being an introvert…and he lets them, like being quiet and observant is a bad thing.

Stupid jerks.

I huff loudly, banging through the kitchen door to my house. Why the heck should *I* be the one feeling guilty? I mean, come on, *he* is the one who took my ring—and virginity—and didn't give it back.

What was he doing with it, anyway? Carrying it around in his pocket? Shaking my head as I shove my bedroom door open, I toss myself across the bed, kick off my shoes, and let my feet dangle off the end.

He must have been, because one minute the dresser top had been empty, and the next...he'd emptied his pockets.

But...*why*? Why was he holding on to it? Why didn't he just give it back when he had the chance?

It just doesn't make sense.

***

Cecelia: *I don't know if you recall, but Matthew picked a fight with me about blowies before we started officially dating. Remember?*

Abby: *Kind of, but not really.*

Cecelia: *He told me blow jobs were non-negotiable, and I said I didn't do those, so he broke it off with me. My point is: Guys are CLUELESS. 99.99% of them. And if you don't cut them some slack for being dipshits...then you're in for a lot of grief.*

Abby: *I guess...*

Cecelia: *I just don't think what he did is that big a deal. He's socially awkward, you said so yourself. I personally think you're punishing both of you for one little screw up.*

Abby: *So what do I do????*

Cecelia: *Well, first you give it some time. Give YOU some time. You've never had a boyfriend, so it's normal to feel confused. So, time, and then...everything will fall into place.*

    Abby: *I hope you're right.*

    Cecelia: *Trust me.*

Caleb

"So, let me get this straight. You find a ring she lost in our yard and don't give it back?"

I snap my head up at Weston's words and narrow my eyes as he coolly pops a cashew into his mouth. "Who told you?"

"Who do you think? Abby cried to Jenna, Jenna told Molly, and Molly told me." Unapologetically, he tips his head back and takes a swig of beer, not realizing my insides are in turmoil after his pronouncement.

"And who did *you* tell?" It's more words than I've strung together in hours, wallowing in self-loathing as I've been.

"Just me," Cubby chimes in from the barstool from my other side. At his declaration, I shoot him a murderous look and he holds his hands up in mock surrender. "What! I overheard parts of his conversation with Molly. Swear it was an accident. Okay, so I might have been—"

"So anyway," Weston interrupts, giving Cubby a *shut*

the hell up look. "Is that what happened? You kept her ring?"

"Pretty much." I'm hunched over a pilsner glass of beer after they dragged me to Lone Rangers with the intention of cheering me up. "Did she tell Jenna…*everything*?"

Weston has the decency to look chagrined. "About the sex and stuff? Unfortunately, yeah. She gave Jenna an earful." He rests a large hand on my shoulder and bears down. "Sorry, man. I know how much you like her."

Not as sorry as I am.

Feeling left out, Cubby opens his mouth again. "*Women*," he grumbles, sounding repulsed. "I'll bang 'em, but I'll never understand them. Speaking of banging, I kind of assumed Walk of Shame was a goody-goody. Girls like her make you wait—at the very least—a five-date minimum before letting you slice that pie. Props for popping that cherry, bro."

"Hey, watch it," Weston quietly warns.

Cubby soldiers on, unfazed. "And then she flipped her shit?"

"Pretty much." Dejected, I peel at the label on my beer bottle.

"She found the ring *after* you fucked her?" More from Cubby.

"Dude, enough already," Weston hisses. "What the hell is wrong with your filter, man?" He's quiet for a few seconds, thinking, finally letting out a low whistle. "Molly would have my ass if I did something stupid like that, and let's be honest, I'm always doing stupid shit like that!"

Weston plasters a fake smile on his face and elbows me in the ribcage cheerfully while I shoot him a glower, no longer in the mood for their company…not that I was to begin with.

Weston shrugs off my insolence in the jovial manner I've grown accustomed to since he joined the hockey team as a frosh, and I watch as he takes a drag from his beer, smacking his lips after swallowing with a loud *Ahhhhhhh!*

Cubby swivels on his bar stool, thinking. "You know," he starts wisely. "You probably should have chased after her. Her oxytocin levels would have still been elevated and bonded so her attraction level after sex with you would have been through the roof." He glances skyward, as if the universe above our heads holds all the answers, curtly nods, and continues, speaking to the ceiling. "Yeah. That would have been smart. You would have had a better chance getting through to her while she was still riding high on the oxytocin and dopamine from her orgasm."

Weston and I both stare at him with open-mouthed astonishment.

"Where the fuck did that come from?" Weston laughs.

"What? That's pretty common knowledge," Cubby says, looking affronted by our incredulity before stuffing his mouth with a handful of cashews from the bowl on the bar. "Christ, I know *some* shit. I'm a bio major. Climb down off my nut sack."

"Do you want some advice?" Weston finally asks.

Cubby palms my head like a basketball and pushes it up and down so it looks like I'm nodding. "Say yes, bro. Your brand of relationship suckfuckery is at a climactic high."

I shrug when he releases my head, not sure that I *do* want their advice. I'd rather stumble awkwardly through self-loathing and pity. "I don't know, guys, maybe I should just call my mom."

"Did you seriously just say that?" Cubby slaps me upside the head and my hat flips off, landing on the bar. "Are you turning into a pussy? I mean, Jesus, are you even listening to yourself? You do *not* call your mom."

Weston agrees. "Yeah, that's pretty messed up."

I look back and forth between them. "Well, what do you expect me to do? Abby thinks I lied to get in her pants." I glance over at Weston before resting my chin in my hands, dejected. "I'm never going to get her to come back to the house after Cubby and Miles busted in on us. She's…really upset."

Weston frowns, leaning forward to glance at Cubby, who is stealing and eating olives from behind the bar. He holds one up, rips it in half, and licks out the pimento before he notices we're watching him. "What?"

"Did you hear what he just said?" Weston asks him, now taking on the role of mediator. "You embarrassed the shit out of Abby when you busted in. Why didn't you knock, you shit bag."

Cubby's furrows his brow, confused. "Because? Oh, come on, don't give me that look. He never has people over!"

"So? I would beat the crap out of you if you walked in on Molly and me having sex, and that's only after she beat the crap out of me for letting you."

"All right, fine, sorry. I should have knocked. Jeez." He doesn't look sorry, but this is probably the first and last time the word has ever cross his lips.

"Know what?" I start, then I hesitate, clearing my

throat before starting again slowly. "It's not fucking okay. You guys are always doing this shit to me. I don't say anything, because why would I? You assholes never listen. But this time...Jesus."

I rake my hands through my hair, frustrated and about to lose my shit. Now that the words are spewing out of me I can't stop the floodgate. "She literally falls into my life, and now I can't get her out of my head. She makes me— Christ, I don't know...*happy*. She's all I can think about and now she's fucking *pissed*, and you jackasses made it ten fucking times worse. I don't know how to fix it. Now you're giving me a piss-poor apology that's supposed to make me feel better? Well, it fucking *doesn't*."

I'm breathing hard, head bent, crestfallen.

Weston's solid arm finds its way across my back, and he drapes it over my shoulders. "Caleb..." From the corner of my eye, I can see him shooting dirty looks at Cubby. "I get it. *We* get it."

"Do you? Abby deserves respect. She's not some..." My voice trails off. "She's not a goddamn puck bunny or a party girl just in it for a good time or a quick fuck. She's shy and quiet and didn't ask to be humiliated."

"Humiliated?" Cubby rolls his eyes. "Dude, get real. Chicks are so dramatic." He pops another olive into his mouth and chews.

Heat rises in my face, and I push back on the barstool, rising to my full height. "Fine. If that's how you feel then pack your shit and get the fuck out of my house."

They both stare at me, slack-jawed, but I'm not done yet.

"Know what else? All you jerk-offs better start pitching in around the house. Can either of you blowhards tell me why the hell *I'm* the one patching up holes *you* put in the walls? Start pulling your weight or I'm going to add a dickhead fee to your rent."

Weston speaks first, but not in a full sentence. "Whoa..." His eyes are bugging out.

Cubby sputters, the intensity of my glower causing a blush to creep up his neck and color his high cheekbones. "Seriously? Shit. You *are* serious." He scratches the five o'clock scruff along his jaw. "Showtime, dude, I honestly didn't realize you gave a shit about the kid."

I ignore that he just called her *kid*.

Fuck it. No I don't.

"When are you going to get it, man? She's not a kid. She's not a random hookup. When are you going to stop acting like a douchebag and start acting like my friend? You don't treat Molly this way, and you better stop treating Abby this way. Start showing some respect, or you've got to go."

Cubby rests his elbows on the bartop and leans forward. We all sit silently for a few minutes, the gravity of the situation setting in.

Finally.

"So what are we going to do about it? Let's ask Yoda here," Cubby ventures out loud, and it doesn't escape me that he used the term *we*. Casually, he goes back to eating olives, turning to Weston. "Bro, what did you do when you and Molly got into *your* first big fight?"

"What did I do?" Weston takes a drag from his beer, wipes his mouth, and laughs. "Shit, man. I had my little sister write her a letter and then I read it out loud in public, in a restaurant." His lips curve up at the memory. "But I was desperate."

"Did it work?" I don't mention my own desperation as I sit back down on my stool.

He scoffs. "Duh."

Cubby makes a choking sound and bangs his hands on the counter. "No. No, no, no. We are *not* fucking writing this chick a letter. That's faggy." He peeks around me at Weston. "No offense, man."

"Are you even listening, you idiot? I didn't tell him to write Abby a damn letter. I was only telling him what I did. Focus."

"I was just saying..."

"Well, don't."

I clear my throat, agitated by their bickering. "Guys, this isn't helping."

Cubby slaps his hand on my back, giving it a few obligatory thumps for good measure and a show of solidarity. "No worries, Showtime. We'll get her back. She won't be able to resist our charm and *tit*illating conversation for long. Get it? Tit?"

Why does he keep saying *our* and *we*?

"Will you grow up? Seriously."

"God*damn*, McGrath, you're such a buzzkill. Seriously. I think Molly turned you into a pussy-whipped Sally."

"That's a lot of words for you, Cubby, and not a single big one."

"Thank you. It's a gift."

Abby

It's been four days since I last saw Caleb.

Four.

I'm still sore, emotional, and miserable.

Twisting the golden ring newly restored to my right hand, it cradles the finger that's felt barren for the past few weeks. I slide it back and forth on my finger, the metallic weight of it a heavy reminder of all I've gained and lost in fourteen days—a reminder so heavy it's actually become a burden.

What was once a symbol of my parents' love and support has become a symbol of my embarrassment. My humiliation. Caleb's childish, petty lie.

Three and a half weeks ago, I climbed out of that window. Twenty-four days. Five hundred and seventy-six hours. Thirty-four thousand, five hundred and sixty minutes.

But who's counting?

Twenty-four days is all it takes, apparently, for your emotions to be broken/shattered/torn/obliterated into a million fragile fragments. Twenty-four days ago a heart—*my* heart—that was so filled with expectation and passion and anticipation, is empty, wrecked, and desolate.

And lonely—lonely for Caleb.

So very aching and lonely for him that it physically *hurts*.

How did this happen? When did I fall so hard that it pains me to get back up?

All right, I need to stop being so dramatic. How utterly ridiculous I'm being. He freaking lied. He took my virginity, something I can never take back and will never forget, knowing that he had my ring. Then he sat there as his friends ogled my breasts. What a...what an ass-face. Sorry, but there's no polite way to put it.

Shake it off, Abby.

You hardly know the guy. So what if he□s just as naïve as you—he knew he had your ring. He lied by omission, and a liar isn't worthy of you, even a clueless one. A lie is still a lie, no matter how small. Yes, but wasn't he trying to give it back? Yes, but he didn't, did he?

I scoff, staring into the mirror and inhaling a deep, cleansing breath. I remove a foundation brush from my makeup caddy and begin to apply concealer around my eyes to hide the shadows looming there along with blush so I don't look so pale.

I have to hurry.

My classes aren't going to pass themselves.

***

Cecelia: *Hey, sweets. Just checking up on you. How you doing?*

Abby: *Considering that Cubby Billings saw my naked ta-tas?*

Cecelia: *But he liked what he saw, right? Tee hee*

Abby: *(crickets)*

Cecelia: *Sorry. Was that too soon?*

Abby: *Yeah. A little too soon. The wound is still fresh. Caleb hasn't tried to call or text or get ahold of me. So that bums me out.*

Cecelia: *He will. Have some faith.*

Abby: *I'm trying, but…it's not easy when Jenna is all over me, trying to cheer me up. She downloaded Tinder on my phone and was swiping right while I was in the shower last night…*

Caleb

Cracking open another thick textbook, I finger through the table of contents, quickly find what I'm looking for, and flip to page 489. I run my finger down the small text, searching for the definition of *ombudsman.*

Lost in thought, I jot down the description and categorization of the word in a separate notebook, giving a start when a loud knock bangs at my door. It sounds like two fists are battering in tandem and the door casing creaks from the excessive force. The walls also vibrate and my lamp shakes on my bedside table.

"What the hell," I damn near shout, hitting *save* on the seven-page ethics paper I've been working on for the past four hours. I minimize the Word document and rise, stalking to the door with a huff.

I yank the door open to a chagrined Miles standing in the hallway, leaning against the wall opposite my room. "What the hell, Turner? Are you *trying* to bust my door down?"

He gives an eye roll. "What's with the look, man? I'm just following orders—Cubby said we had to start knocking, said you wanted *privacy* or some shit." He lowers his voice to a whisper, glances up and down the hall, and uses air quotes around the word privacy like it's a conspiracy only we're in on.

I stand, regarding him silently, arms crossed, shaking my head in disbelief. These guys are un-freaking-believable.

"Do you have any tape? I'm out."

I keep expecting Miles to push his way into my room, but he doesn't.

Huh. Weird.

My frown narrows in on him suspiciously, and I give a stiff nod of acquiescence before disappearing to fetch the black hockey tape we use to wrap our sticks from my closet. He waits patiently in the hallway and thanks me when I slap it down in his outstretched palm curtly.

"Anything else?"

"No." He studies me curiously, and I nod again, grasping the doorframe in my hand, ready to close it in his face. His large hand darts out to stop it. "Wait." Miles chews on his bottom lip. "Is it true you're going to charge us a dick fee?"

"A *what*?"

"Cubby said you're charging us, uh, a dick fee."

Fucking. Cubby.

Miles looks so disturbed by the idea that I almost burst out laughing.

Almost.

I arrange my face into an impassive mask. "Dick fee? Yeah, I'm giving it some serious thought," I deadpan. It occurs to me that I should be asking, *And you believed that, douchebag?* But I don't. "Why, are you worried?"

"Pfft, no," he guffaws, but his face is solemn. "I mean, only if you're charging by the inch."

Wait—the *hell* is he talking about? "What exactly did Cubby tell you?"

Miles leans back against the wall and scratches at the roll of hockey tape with his fingernail absentmindedly. He shrugs. "Nothing. Just that if we wanted to live here we had to start knocking on your door and leaving you alone and shit. And if we don't you're going to kick us all out or charge us, and he's the one who'll be measuring our cocks and keeping track of all that shit." He rambles on. "I mean—that's not really cool, man. Dick size isn't something you can control."

Unable to keep a straight face any longer, the laughter erupts out of me in a deafening sputter. I bend over and clutch the doorframe with my right hand to keep myself from falling over, tears spilling out my eyes. "Oh my god, dude. I c-can't... You fucking idiot... Oh, Jesus Christ, did you just admit you have a small dick?"

I'm wheezing and coughing now, and when I squint up at Miles's angry scowl through teary eyes, I laugh even harder. "Small dick... Turner, how am I going to take you seriously? Oh jeez, this is a good one."

"Shut the fuck up already! Stop saying small dick!" Miles implores, glancing down the hallway again. "God, you guys are assholes."

I hold my hands up in surrender, biting my entire lower lip between my teeth as I struggle to regain my composure. "*Why* the hell would you believe anything Billings has to say? He's a complete moron."

Miles crosses his arms, pissed. "You know I wasn't being serious about my dick. I knew the whole time it was a crock of shit."

"Yeah, yeah, yeah, whatever you say, man." I chuckle. "Except the privacy crap. You guys need to stop treating this place like it's a frat-house free-for-all, because it's not. You scared off my, uh...Abby. That shit is no longer acceptable."

"Okay, *Dad*," Miles mocks sarcastically. Then he gets a good look at my face. "Okay, okay. Yes, fine. No more barging in."

I point a finger in his face. "And start picking up your own shit around the house."

"Baby steps, Showtime. Baby steps."

***

Cecelia: *You've been texting me a lot lately. I don't mind, but you're making me worried.*

Abby: *There's nothing to worry about. I'm just trying to figure all this out without having to spill my guts to Jenna.*

Cecelia: *Do you want me to drive up this weekend? It sounds like you need a hug and a dose of BFF...*

Abby: *You would do that?*

Cecelia: *Are you crazy!? Of COURSE I WOULD. I heart you. Besides, it's only a little over an hour drive. I can be there in two days, by the time you get done with classes on Friday!*

Cecelia: *Heads up, Matthew was reading that over my shoulder and he says he's coming with...*

Abby

I can't stop watching out the front window of our crappy student rental, waiting anxiously for that familiar white Tahoe to pull into the gravel driveway.

"Watching out the window on the couch like a damn cat isn't going to get her here any faster," Jenna points out sympathetically from the kitchen while wielding a cast-iron pan. She's been frying up pot stickers for the past twenty minutes and is totally stinking up the joint.

My nose scrunches up as I sniff the air. "Can you light a candle or something? It's starting to reek in here."

Rolling her eyes, Jenna goes back to her task, unscrewing a bottle and shaking a generous helping of soy sauce into the pan. It sizzles and sears, and I can see the steam rising from my spot by the window.

A popping sound whizzes.

"Oops," I overhear her mutter. "I don't think that was supposed to happen."

I crane my neck to catch a glimpse of her at the stove, waving a hand in front of her face. "What are you *doing* in there? You're going to burn the house down."

"Then I would be doing our landlord a huge favor. And don't come in here!" Jenna sticks her head in the living room from around the corner. "Um, incidentally, where do we keep the fire extinguisher? A friend of a friend wants to know."

I roll my eyes and look back out the window. "Cabinet under the sink."

"We're going out tonight, right?"

"Yes!" I shout, pulling back the curtain again and flying off the couch when the familiar white SUV appears around the corner.

"Was that a *yes we're going out tonight* or a *yes hooray my friends are finally here*?" Jenna questions over the loud hissing of the pot stickers. I hear coughing and watch as she flaps a kitchen towel through the air and the smoke alarm begins blaring. "Crap!"

"Both!" I laugh. "Yes to *both*."

***

There are no words to accurately articulate how jazzed/elated/pumped/excited I am to have my best friend in town. Granted, she's dragged her overbearing, vulgar, live-in boyfriend along, but beggars can't be choosers, and occasionally, Matthew Wakefield isn't all that bad.

Except for one small fact: like his UW-Madison alma mater progeny, the hulky professional hockey player *loves* Lone Rangers.

So that's where we end up.

And instead of it being a girls' night out or a reunion between two best friends, the night has inexplicably transformed into a hockey player reunion between Matthew and his buddies.

Messages sent out. Texts exchanged. Statuses checked-in. Tweets twittered. Combine all that and what do you get? A crap ton of people piled into a tiny, dilapidated dive bar, probably violating thirty different health codes and restrictions.

The elation I felt at having Cece and Matthew in town has turned into reticence because I know with certainty, just like I know Caleb's hair is black and the sky is blue, that I'm going to see him tonight.

Full disclosure: I don't just know I'm going to see Caleb tonight, I *hope* I'm going to see him. Call me a glutton for punishment, but I would never in a million years have slept with him if I didn't care about him.

And you don't just stop caring about someone overnight or because they mistreat you. Emotions aren't a switch you turn on and off.

I stare at my reflection in the women's bathroom mirror at Lone Rangers from my place in the tiny room as I wait for Cece to pee, holding the stall door closed for her because it doesn't latch.

"Stop fidgeting. I can see you through the crack. Quit playing with your hair," Cecelia teases from inside the stall, and I hear the toilet paper dispenser rolling.

It's incredible to have her back in town, even if she is scolding me.

"Sorry, I can't help it," I say, turning to peek at her

through the gap. She sticks her tongue out at me as she zips up her jeans and buckles her belt. I twist my body, leaning my back against the stall door. "Did I tell you that Cubby Billings sent me a message?"

"What?" Cecelia's surprised gasp wafts over the top of the stall. "No way!"

"Yes way. It was actually kinda funny, sort of. He texted saying he was sorry for invading my privacy and his mama raised him with better manners, but in his defense, the door to Caleb's bedroom was unlocked."

Cecelia snickers, chagrined. "Okayyyy."

"He went on to say next time he needed Caleb, he would knock first. Then, of course, he ruined the apology by telling me I shouldn't be embarrassed because I have a really nice rack."

"Yup, that sounds like pure Cubby."

"It was nice to get a message from him though. Totally unexpected."

"At least he's trying?" Cece raps on the door with her knuckle and I release it, stepping back so she can exit the stall and head to the sink. She glances at me over her shoulder as she scrubs her hands and pulls down a piece of brown paper towel. "You know, many a relationship was solidified in this seedy establishment, and the night is young."

"Is that…some kind of code talk?"

Cecelia laughs, her merry green eyes sparkling with mischief—or from the beer she drank before. "No. I just meant this is the place where Matthew and I finally, you know, had our first real kiss. It feels lucky."

"Erm, yeah. I remember. I also remember the crowd

and the jeers because you and Matthew took so long to do the deed."

Just to clarify, when I say *do the deed,* I'm not even talking about sex. Cecelia and her boyfriend didn't even *kiss* each other for the first few months they knew each other, and when they finally did, it was because Cecelia lost a bet.

It drove everyone around them crazy. The sexual tension was off-the-charts, through-the-roof ridiculous.

My best friend tips her head back, laughing, long brown hair spilling down her back in a silky cascade. "Well, I couldn't seem *too* eager. Have you met the guy? He was so full of himself I had to keep him in check. Still do."

She reaches for the door, hand grasping the cool metal handle.

I stop her from walking out. "Do…do you think that maybe Caleb and I…that we moved too fast? Should I have waited? To sleep with him, I mean."

What I need right now is some reassurance, and Cecelia is ready to give it. She takes her hand off the door, resting it on my shirtsleeve. "Abby, *don't* have regrets. This thing with you and Caleb—it isn't over. In fact, if you want my opinion—and I think you do—it's only the beginning for the two of you. I get that you're freaking out, but these things have a way of working out." She gives a short laugh. "God, listen to me, talking like I know what I'm doing. Remember how I questioned myself and my relationship with Matthew every day? I questioned my choices forever, texted you constantly. Giving up everything to move in with Matt—hardest decision ever, but I did it, and eventually I stopped worrying about it. So don't do that to yourself. Please."

My arms open wide, and when she steps into them, I rest my chin on her shoulder, our arms enveloping each other as she whispers in my hair. "It's not just going to be okay, Abs. It's going to be *awesome*."

A throat clears in the bathroom, and both our heads shoot up. A redhead wearing a tight silver midriff top and an even tighter smile is just exiting the other stall and grimaces at us.

She is so not amused. "Uhhhh, am I interrupting something?"

Cecelia laughs and releases me. "Nope. Not anymore." She gives the girl a wink, and a blush creeps up my neck before she clasps my hand and pulls me out the bathroom door.

Music assaults us when we enter the bar, and the crowd immediately swallows us up as we walk with the flow toward Matthew, Jenna, Molly, and Weston. Lone Rangers is nothing but deafening music blaring from its speakers and wall-to-wall people—drunk students and students *looking* to get drunk. Guys trying to get laid, surrounded by an unlimited supply of girls who're going to let them. Tight groups of cliques. Singles ready to mingle.

Cecelia is still firmly grasping my hand as she pulls me through the throng, her mere presence here comforting. We get jostled, bumped, and smacked in the butt a few times as we weave through the throng, the smell of sweaty bodies and stale beer lingering in the musty air.

Or it is stale bodies and sweaty beer?

Same thing.

"This way." Cecelia nods toward Matthew's tall form, visible in the back corner where we left them twenty minutes ago—yes, it took us twenty minutes to go pee.

It's déjà vu over and over again—this crowd of people, in this place. Same faces. Same music. Same crappy lighting. Same sticky floors. Same, same, same.

The only difference is *he* wasn't here when I walked away to use the bathroom, and now…he is.

Six days. One hundred forty-four hours. Eight thousand, six hundred and forty minutes.

But who's counting?

Caleb

"Dude, incoming!" Blaze announces at the top of his voice, hands cupped around his mouth to create a megaphone. "Girlfriend rapidly approaching," he says to Matthew. "And she's got Walk of Shame hot on her heels, bro."

Stephan bumps me with his hip. "Showtime, your lover looks like she's about to puke her guts out. What'd you do to her, man?"

As if he didn't already know.

"Hey!" Matthew's sharp voice cuts in, stopping Stephan from continuing. "Guys, *enough*. If Cecelia hears you talking shit about those two, she's going to take it personally, and I'm the one who's going to hear about it when we get home. I didn't drive all the way here to get my damn ass chewed out at the end of the night."

Everyone looks at him, trying to determine if he's serious.

"Did I stutter?" he asks, holding his empty cup out. "Someone top me off."

"Man, you sure turned into an ass when you went pro," Miles mutters, grabbing the beer pitcher off a nearby table and tipping it over Matthew's outstretched beer cup to fill it.

Matthew Wakefield raises his eyebrows sardonically. "Since when does *not* wanting my girlfriend to be upset make me an ass? Grow up." His arm goes around Cecelia when the girls join us, and he plants a kiss on her temple as they turn toward me, giving me my first real look at Abby's best friend.

Wakefield's girlfriend is really good-looking, but not at all what I expected the girlfriend of a professional athlete to look like. For one thing, she looks normal, low maintenance. She's in well-worn jeans and a threadbare gray Blackhawks sweatshirt, its sleeves pushed up to her elbows and neckline slouching across her shoulders. Her long hair is pulled back in a messy ponytail, and sparkly studs adorn her ears.

Cecelia extends a delicate hand toward me, the silver bangles on her wrist jingling. "Hi. I don't think we've met. I'm Cece." Her pretty green eyes assess me, but not in an overly critical way, and my shoulders sag from relief, knowing I'm not about to get the third degree…at least I hope not.

Not surprisingly, Abby stands timidly behind Matthew Wakefield's imposing form, using him as a shield and eluding my gaze.

Alrighty, then.

I clasp Cecelia's fingers, pumping them up and down once before she releases my hand. She looks me in the eyes, unblinking, when I introduce myself. "Caleb."

I'm expecting her to respond with a snarky quip like, *Yeah, I know all about who* you *are,* or *Oh, Caleb the Liar?* Or even something catty like, *Trust me, she's told me* all *about you,* as I imagine most best friends of a slighted girl would—but she doesn't.

Instead, she shocks the shit out of me by smiling, her bright white teeth bending into a sincere curve. "It's good to finally meet you."

"How you been, man?" Wakefield asks. "Your stats are ri-motherfucking-diculous. Any teams trying to get you into bed yet?"

I look down into my beer cup at the white foam drifting on its surface, then glance up, shrugging. "A few, but…"

Wakefield cocks his head. "But what? What's the hesitation?"

The *hesitation* is the decision I've never voiced out loud to any of them: that I have no plans to enter the NHL draft after graduation. That ultimately, I intend to get my law degree and become chief council for a mergers and acquisitions firm, a lofty position defending small companies that won't have me standing in a courtroom.

That's the plan, anyway.

Clearing my throat uncomfortably, I look around at the curious, watchful stares of my teammates. Everyone seems riveted, waiting for my response, and I reach my hand up to readjust my ball cap self-consciously. "I, uh…"

As if sensing my distress, Cecelia removes her intuitive gaze slowly from mine and gives her boyfriend's meaty bicep a squeeze, leaning in to whisper in his ear. His eyes widen and shoot to mine, and he gives her a stiff, jerky nod. "Okay, okay, I'll change the subject. Sorry," he mumbles, both of them pasting on fake smiles.

Wakefield surges on. "So, what else is going on? How's everyone behaving in that hockey house of yours?"

I glance behind them to catch a glimpse of Abby, her teeth biting down on the plastic rim of her cup as she tries to fade into the background and become unnoticeable. She's avoiding my stare, and the hopes I'd been harvesting for the past few days that she and I would get the opportunity to talk tonight begin to rapidly fade before bursting into flames.

I pry my eyes away. "I'm sorry?"

Matthew Wakefield raises his eyebrow and repeats the question, glaring at me impatiently like I'm dumb as a box of rocks. "I asked how everyone is behaving at the hockey house."

"Good."

His dark eyebrows go higher into his hairline as he waits for me to elaborate.

I don't.

Curling his lip, he addresses Cecelia, who is still sidled up next to him. "Wow," he adds flatly. "I can see what the appeal is for Abby. What a deep conversationalist."

Heat rises from my neck, and I can feel my cheeks warming considerably. Shit, just what I need—I'm fucking blushing.

"Babe, would you do me a favor and grab me a water from the bar?" Cecelia cuts in, stroking his triceps with lazy fingers. He looks down at her hand then up into her face, the scowl on his face replaced by a relaxed, easy grin.

He leans in and kisses her on the nose. "Sure. Want

lemon, too?"

"Um, sure. And take Abby with you." Cecelia gives me a wink.

"One water with lemon coming right up," Wakefield says, grabbing Abby by the elbow and dragging her through the crowd to the bar. I track their movement as the crowd parts to let them through.

Cecelia is on me like flies on shit.

"Okay, we only have a few minutes, so listen up." She gets in my personal space, rises to her tiptoes, and talks close to my ear, conspiratorily. "What's your plan?"

"Uh..."

She throws her arms up in frustration, and I can hear her exasperated groan over the blaring music. "Ugh! This is the problem with you two. You're both so awkward."

Words fail me, but I manage to respond with, "Uh, yeah."

Cecelia glances over her shoulder. "Shit, they're already being served. Look, I know you didn't keep the ring on purpose, *Abby* knows you didn't keep the ring on purpose, and all this crap with your friends being rude isn't anything I didn't experience myself. I mean, Matthew's friends are—ugh! Awful."

She's babbling, but I'm hanging on her every word.

"So the way I see it, you're just going to have to suck it up and take one for the team. She obviously blew this whole thing out of proportion—and don't you dare tell her I said that or I'll kill you—but there's no way she's going to admit it. She's way, way too embarrassed to approach you. So, you have to be the one to make things right. I see no other way around it."

Abby's best friend grips both my shoulders, bears down, and gives them a firm shake. "Are you listening to what I'm saying? Blink once if you're getting this."

I blink once, afraid she'll whack me if I don't, and add a curt nod for good measure.

Cecelia smacks my right arm anyway then releases me, smoothing down the rumpled sleeve of my long-sleeved t-shirt. "Good. That's what I wanted to hear." And just when I think she's done with me, Abby's best friend levels a finger in my face, her pointed fingernail hovering dangerously close to the tip of my nose. "You better not disappoint me, Caleb Lockhart. I *know* where you live."

Shit, she's kind of scary.

Abby

I wish I could tell you that before leaving Lone Rangers tonight, Caleb and I had the courage to talk.

That I had the courage apologize.

That I had the courage to look at him.

But I didn't.

Caleb

I stand in the dark, surrounded by thick, overgrown hedges that rise to my waist, and study the window before me. Flashlight app illuminated on my phone, I shine it directly on the eyelevel casement window.

Somehow, before I can swing it open, I'll have to lift the pane until it's off the lock. Only then will I have access to the dark room inside.

I dig into the pocket of my track pants for my pocketknife, flip open the bottle opener, and wedge it securely into a crack at the base of the pane, giving the knife a firm tug.

Only the echo of splintered wood and rustling bushes fill the quiet void in this space of yard I occupy.

Ignoring the recognizable cracking sound, I make a mental note to come back and caulk it, my deft fingers grab hold of the window base and I push up. The pane gives a loud creak, then a moan, and I hear the telltale give of the lock coming undone before the crank moves the window forward.

Grunting, I pull, and the window eases opens. It's a tad too accessible for my comfort level, but I'll have to deal with that later.

Once I have the glass all the way open, I close the pocketknife and stuff it back in my pocket along with my phone and crack my knuckles. Bracing both hands on either side of the window, I stiffen my arms and upper torso, then bounce on my heels, warming up my body and preparing to hoist myself five feet off the ground and up into the window from a stand.

The curtains inside billow and wrap around my face when my waist is jackknifed over the side, half in, half out. I grunt, pulling myself forward, and fall into the dark room, bringing the curtains, curtain rod, and tiebacks crashing down with me in the process.

"What the fuck!" A loud screech comes from the dark recesses, followed by fumbling, banging, and a light being thrown on.

"What the *fuck* are you doing?" A voice that is most certainly not Abby's shouts down at me from my position on the ground, and I stiffen as angry footsteps approach from the other side of the room.

Did I mention it's a room that is most certainly not Abby's?

Shit, fuck, shit.

"Caleb?"

I look up into Jenna's shocked face.

"Um, yeah?"

"What the hell are you doing? God, you're such a jackass." She throws her arm out and reaches for my hand. "Get up, you idiot."

"Sorry." I take her hand and she helps pull me up, but I stumble, my ankles wrapped in a heap of twisted curtains. "Shit, sorry." Bending, I push down the gauzy purple fabric, yanking it from under my feet and stepping out of the tangled chaos.

"You're so lucky I didn't *shoot* your sorry ass." Jenna props her foot out, and my eyes flicker up and down her body; she's only wearing thong underwear and a tight, sheer half tank. *Fuck.*

"You have a *gun?*" I spit out in a near screech, incredulously, averting my eyes.

"I have a Taser. It's hot pink and I've been *dying* to shoot someone with it. Bummer that's it's only you."

"Sorry."

"Yeah, so you keep saying." Throwing on a short leopard-print robe that reaches her thighs, she ties the belt into a knot and turns to face me, arms crossed. "You really, seriously suck at this relationship crap, do you know that?"

Like I needed a reminder.

She continues. "Honestly, I've never seen such a bumbling mess."

"Thanks." Because really, what else is there to say?

"But it's actually kind of sweet."

My ears perk up.

"Even if you're a little old to be so clueless."

My shoulders sag.

"It's a good thing we're dealing with Abby here and

not someone more sophisticated. She eats this shit up."

Right. Okay, then. "Do you want me to help you with this?" I turn, bending to grab some of the curtains from the carpet.

"Dear god, no. Just go. Get the hell out of here."

I gesture back and forth from the door to the window uncertainly. "Do you think I should...?"

Jenna rolls her eyes skyward. "Yes, go back out the window. If you knock on her door from the hallway it won't be as romantic. Trust me." She walks over and grabs the curtains out of my hands. "But take that stupid hat and hoodie off. She's going to think she's about to be raped."

"Thanks for the tip."

"Um, excuse me, was that *sarcasm*?" Jenna narrows her eyes. "You want me to Taser your ass?"

Panicking, my hands go up in surrender. "No! I'm going. Jesus, stop trying to find an excuse to Taser me. I'm going."

***

Abby: *I THINK THERE'S SOMEONE OUTSIDE MY WINDOW!*

Cecelia: *Do you want us to come over?????!!! Call 9-1-1*

Abby: *This is FREAKING ME THE F OUT.*

Abby: *Know what? I'm just going to yell for Jenna. She just bought that Taser gun from some guy in an alley downtown.*

Cecelia: *Oh great. It's probably a black market Taser that shoots STUN darts.*

Cecelia: *Um... I was just talking to Matthew and he says to wait on calling the cops....*

Abby: *Why would he tell me not to call the cops????*

Cecelia: *Remember that time he pretended to be a creeper at MY door in the middle of the night? Thought he was being romantic in a Shakespearean kind of way but really just scared the ever-loving SHIT out of me?*

32

I hear the familiar grunt again, accompanied by the sound of metal being scraped along the side of my window-pane.

"Go. In. God. Dammit," the voice curses gruffly in a huff, doing God only knows what to my window, a dim light flickering through my curtains, aimed at the bottom right-hand corner of my window.

I bite my lip and pull the blanket up to my chin, debating.

I would know that voice anywhere.

Throwing back my blankets, I smooth down the shirt I'm wearing—Caleb's shirt, the one I was wearing the last time I was with him, um, intimately. My legs are bare, but I move across the room toward the window, my heart beating so wildly in my chest that I pause and press a hand to my breast to steady it.

The action does little to soothe me.

Pulling back the curtains, I unlatch the lock and crank open the window.

Crouching, I speak through the screen. "Caleb."

"Holy shit, Jesus Christ! Abby, you scared the piss out of me."

I ignore his startled litany of profanity and bring a hand to cover my mouth, chuckling. It feels good to laugh.

"*I* scared *you*? *You're* the one trying to break into my room."

"Yup." His low, grumbly voice rises out of the dark, but he sounds oddly pleased with himself. "Wanna help me up?"

It only takes me a few seconds to decide my next course of action. Reaching down, I pop the screen out of its frame then stand back as Caleb counts out a few bounces on his heels, and, like a gymnast, hoists himself up using only the strength from his upper torso.

Drool.

He hangs over the window frame, grunting, before falling to my carpet in a heap inside my bedroom.

I walk backward in the dark and sit on the edge of my bed as he steadies himself and rises to his feet. Kicking off his shoes, he neatly arranges them next to the closet door.

The uncertainty of the situation while he busies himself is killing me, so I adjust my position on the bed restlessly, pressing my palms to my flaming-hot face.

"What are you doing here?" I ask nervously when he stands at his full height, his tall frame silhouetted by the full moon hanging high in the night sky.

He hesitates. "Isn't it obvious?"

Oh, yes, when you put it that way…

I groan inwardly.

"Do you have a small light we can turn on?" he asks, crossing the room. "Not the overhead light. I just want… I have to see your face."

"Yes, m-my desk light, maybe?" I stand, careful to avoid contact with him. I feel my way through the dark to the little white light clamped to my IKEA desk and click the switch. A dim light casts a pallor over the room.

I turn to face Caleb, whose imposing figure swallows up all the space in the room, and I nervously flop down on the edge of my bed.

He approaches slowly then sinks to his knees in front of me.

Caleb

I sink to my knees in front of her, needing her to see me, and place my palms on her smooth, bare knees. It doesn't occur to me to ask permission, but when she doesn't pull away, my heart encourages me to power forward.

"God, Abby, I'm so sorry." I risk a glance at her face, and she's staring at me slack-jawed. "I'm such an ass."

Her head tilts to the side as she silently watches me.

"Right after you climbed out that window, when you stormed away, that's when I found your ring. It was shining in the sun, and I went to your cousin's. He would have given it to you, but"—I run a hand under my hat nervously before I continue—"I wanted to see you again, so I kept it.

"At first, I had it in my pocket, you know, just in case

I ran into you. Then, when I finally did see you out, either I was with Blaze, or my friends, or I was just ashamed to admit I had it. That day you stormed out of the yard and I walked you home, all I could think about was being in that moment with you."

As I babble on, Abby's lips part on a sigh when I run my large hands aimlessly up and down her bare thighs, stroking them gently.

"It didn't even occur to me after that. Well, okay, maybe it did a few times. Then when you were in my *room*, and well…clearly I did not handle that well." I clear my throat. "When you're around, I become… God, I don't know. Not that the ring wasn't important—that isn't it at all. The truth is you're literally all I can think about. I forget everything else—I fucking *adore* you. I want to make this work.

"Abby?" Pausing, I let out a deep breath, wishing she'd say something. "Abby? Is this making any sense or am I fucking this up, too?"

Abby

He says my name in a tortured whisper, and I watch, spellbound, as his big, strong hands caress my legs.

I'm so stunned I don't even know what to say. Everything I know about boys does *not* add up to this moment.

"Abby? Is this making any sense or am I fucking this up, too?"

Bravely, I raise my eyes and look into his face—his serious, broody, *sweet* face—peering up at me from under the brim of his ball cap. I take in his five o'clock shadow and the downturned curve of his full lips.

It's just barely a pout.

I don't know what to say, so I don't say anything.

I show him.

Reaching forward, I remove his baseball hat and throw it into the dark pit of my bedroom. It lands with a soft thud on the carpet as I lift my arms and run all ten fingers through his thick, shaggy black hair.

He shudders, closing his chocolate-brown eyes and tilting his cheek toward my palm as he nuzzles with an audible groan. "Abby, don't be mad at me anymore," he whispers again. "It was an accident."

I know his intention isn't to be funny, but a giggle escapes my lips as I finger the loose locks of his silky hair when he drops his head into my lap. "Oh, Caleb," I whisper back. "What am I supposed to do with you?"

"Whatever you do, just don't stop touching me," he moans. "God, I missed you."

Those four words are the most romantic thing anyone has ever said to me—it's sad, but true. "But we've only known each other for what, three or four weeks?"

He stops caressing my legs and lifts his head, those dark eyes boring deep down into my soul. "Does a timeline really have anything to do with how you feel about me?"

"N-no," I stutter, and then I take a steadying breath. "*No.* You're right, of course it doesn't. I don't know why I even said that."

His fingers trace circles on my thighs, and I fight back a shiver.

"Because you're scared."

"Yes."

His mouth hitches at the corner and his hooded eyes sparkle. "Not as scared as I am." He lowers his head and plants kisses on both my knees, one at a time. "I almost threw up in the bushes outside."

"What!" I laugh quietly. "You did not."

"I said *almost*, but yeah, I was so nervous I almost hurled my guts out."

"Poor baby." I take his head in my hands and pull him forward, between my parted legs, resting my lips on his forehead. His arms slide around my waist and his hands immediately begin stroking my back, painstakingly gently.

"Abby?"

"Yes?"

"I have a confession to make: I accidentally climbed into Jenna's room first." His muffled laughter quivers against my chest, doing funny things to my girl parts.

I shove him away in shock. "What?" I practically shout. "Are you serious? How—what did she do?"

"Well," he responds slowly, a huge grin spreading across his face. "You know how Jenna is—she threatened to shoot me."

"Oh my god, that girl is crazy! You could have been *shot* with an actual Taser gun!"

He makes a casual *pfft* sound, like getting shot with a stun gun is no big deal. "Yeah, but it would have totally been worth it."

My hand flies to my chest, covering my heart as it flutters. "You would... you would get *Tasered* for me?" I take back what I said before—*this* is by far the most romantic thing anyone has ever said to me.

He shrugs. "Course I would."

"Awww! Caleb, that is so…so awkwardly sweet."

He shrugs again like it's no big deal, like he contemplates a good Tasering on a daily basis and finds the process tediously boring.

God, he's adorable.

I lovingly stroke the side of his face and he leans in again, nuzzling the valley between my breasts with his nose.

"I noticed you're wearing my shirt." His muffled voice is barely audible, but I detect a pleased lilt to it.

I smile into his hair, against the top of his head. "It's *my* shirt now, remember?"

He leans back on his taut haunches, calloused fingers stroking my shoulders, down my arms, fiddling with the hem of our shirt and watching my face the entire time. I lean back, bracing myself with my arms, and look down as his big hands run slowly along the cotton trim then disappear underneath.

My breath hitches when those same hands linger over my belly button, drawing lazy loops around it. "I love your belly button," he murmurs. "It's so damn sexy."

He leans in and licks it, his tongue trailing its way up my stomach. Deftly, my t-shirt gets pushed up, and Caleb is sliding his hands up my abs, over my breasts, and pulling the shirt off in one swift motion.

"Caleb."

"Mmmm?"

"I just wanted to say that…oh, that feels good…I just wanted to say that…*mnnnuuh*…c-climbing…uhh…maybe you should s-stop doing that so I can s-say what I need to say." I get the words out as he's yanking his own shirt over his head, and my hands snake up his bare chest.

What was it I wanted to say?

"What did you want to say, baby? I'm listening."

Oh, Jesus. Who can think straight with these capable fingers stroking so perilously close to a person's, um, lace-covered crotch.

I struggle to string my sentence together.

"Climbing out that"—I gasp—"window at the Kappa house was the…single best decision I've ever made." My head tips back and his lips find the beating pulse on my neck. "B-besides coming to this university, with that house, and that window." I say it quietly in a slurred, drunken whisper before I lose my courage.

I feel him smile against my neck, and he nips my shoulder with his teeth as his hands caress the soft skin of my naked breasts. "I'm one lucky bastard."

I giggle. "I sure am glad it wasn't Cubby standing outside the day I climbed out that window."

Caleb pulls his mouth off my neck. "That's not even funny." He pouts and nudges me onto my back.

"Oh!" I gasp again as he climbs on top of the bed, on top of my pristine, virginal white duvet.

He leans down, rubbing his stubble along my jawline. "Did you miss me, Abby?"

"Yes. So much."

"What an awkward pair we make."

"Would you stop talking and kiss me?"

"Whoa, someone's gotten bossy in the six days I've been gone."

I groan in frustration and roll my eyes. "Stop teasing."

"You want a kiss?" He plants a chaste kiss on my cheek, a wet smacking sound resonating in the room. "Like that?"

No, not like that. My brows furrow, but I'm not yet forward enough to make sexual demands. I don't know if I'll ever be.

"Or like this." Another kiss, this one on my temple. "Or like...this." His firm, beautiful lips kiss one corner of my mouth, then the other.

"That feels...kind of okay," I joke, getting into the spirit.

"*Kind of okay*, she says." Caleb's mouth hovers a whisper above mine. "Kind of—"

"Would you. Stop. Talking already? Kiss me like you mean it." Even in the dark, I can see his eyes blazing with arousal as he stares down at me, shaggy, unkempt hair falling in his eyes. "Kiss me like you haven't kissed me in six days. Kiss me like...like *this*."

I pull his head down and our mouths reconnect, a reunion one week in the making, the delicious taste of him on my tongue assaulting my senses in the best possible way.

Pressing our lips together, we make out, unhurriedly. Recklessly. Moaning. Sighing. Wet. Tongues, lips, and teeth.

It's perfect.

"Shit, that's sexy. If I thought—"

"Shhhh!"

I pull him down again, my palms running lightly over his bent shoulders, memorizing every smooth contour of this boy's sinewy muscles—this shy boy who kisses me so sweetly that my heart could actually burst from the joy of it all. This shy and cautious boy who makes me feel beautiful. Wanted.

Confident.

Like I steal his breath away.

The way he steals mine.

Preview: Things Liars Say

Prologue

Greyson

The lie started off innocently enough, and obviously I never meant to get caught up in it— but then again, isn't that what everyone says when they lie?

Wait! No. Don't answer that.

Flipping my laptop open, I hit the power button and wait for it to boot, the soft familiar humming of the fan, CD drive, and modem stirring my computer to life, and shuffle the papers stacked in front of me.

I take a bite of the apple on my food tray, chewing slowly as I scan the meeting agenda on the table in front of me and my friends look on.

We're gathered in the university's dining hall for a quick lunch meeting on campus— the only time this week I could get my committee together in one spot at a time that worked for everyone.

"Rachel," I say across the cafeteria table. "Did you remember to call the catering company?"

My sorority sister gives me a victorious smile. "Yup. They have us booked for the third, and we have a tasting on the twenty-ninth at four thirty. It should have updated your calendar in Outlook."

I click open my Outlook and scroll through the calendar to the dates Rachel mentioned. "Excellent. There it is." I cross *catering* off my list and chew on the end of my BIC pen. "Jemma, are we all set with the silent auction donations?"

"Roger that, Greyson. I have ten alumnae lined up for baskets, and another thirteen parents who donated cash, totaling eight hundred dollars. We should be all set once we get everything purchased to put the baskets together."

"What other things do you have left for those?"

"You know, clear cello bags for the baskets, the wicker baskets themselves, labels... Those sorts of things."

"Who's going to be running the auction?" My pen hovers above the blank *auctioneer* spot on my agenda.

"You, Beth, and I can pull the silent-auction sheets at the end of the night."

I nod, crossing both *auction* and *donations* off my list.

"Ariel? Entertainment?"

Ariel, a tall brunette with a serious expression, pulls out an Excel spreadsheet and drums on it with her forefinger. "It looks like Cara put the deposit down for the DJ last week. He's scheduled to arrive a full hour before we start setting up the room so he can get all his equipment in the building without interruptions. I sent him a list of requested songs last night, so we should be good to go."

"As long as Vanessa doesn't request any of those group dances." Jemma snorts.

"Ugh. I hate 'The Electric Slide.'" Ariel laughs. "Should I add that to the do-not-play list?"

"Nah. Because you and I both know if the DJ plays it, you're going to run out onto the dance floor…"

Ariel sighs. "Probably."

I look down at my list and tap a pen to my chin. "So all we have to talk about yet is ticket sales. And getting everyone to sign the guest release waivers for liability."

I pull the form out of a file folder and slide it across the table to Catherine, one of three sisters in the sorority who are pre-law. She scans it with narrowed, articulate eyes and gives a curt nod when she reaches the last paragraph. "Looks great. Solid." Her lips curve into a smirk. "I like the addendum about recovering losses if property damage to the venue occurs by a guest. Good thinking."

Jemma snorts. "Remember what happened last year with Amanda Q's date? He ripped out an entire fern from the foyer of the hotel then threw up in the pot." We all laugh. "To add insult to injury, she snuck him out and then lied about it. Like there weren't security cameras everywhere."

Catherine gives a rueful shake of the head, disappointed we weren't able to charge anyone damages, and says, "Right. But since he hadn't signed a waiver, we couldn't charge him for the damage

"Thank God it was just a few bags of potting soil…"

"But still. She shouldn't have left us hanging."

"Yeah, that was shitty."

Rachel turns to me with raised eyebrows. "Speaking of dates… Inquiring minds want to know: who is Greyson Keller bringing to the Philanthropy Gala this year?"

I shake my head. "I don't have time to worry about a date, you guys. I've been up to my eyeballs in Gala preparations."

"Don't you have to bring a date?" Jemma asks. "As the Philanthropy Chairwoman, you're the hostess this year."

I fiddle with my laptop's power cord and avoid her eyes. "What's your point?"

"Oh, come on, what's his name?" Rachel waves a limp French fry in my face from her lunch tray to get my attention. "Focus here; this stuff is important."

I finally look up, giving my blonde head a shake. "Who says there has to be a guy?"

"Please, there's *always* a guy…" Rachel's voice trails off.

"Just tell us who it is." Catherine prods quietly. Cajoling.

"Spit it out. We're going to find out eventually."

No, you're really not.

Jemma looks me dead in the eyes. "Yes. We are."

What the… Okay, that was freaky. And it occurs to me that they're acting like a gang of unruly hyenas and aren't going to let the subject die until I give them a reason to.

"I-I'd rather not say," I stutter. "We, uh, just started dating. It's only been one date. Besides, he's hardly Gala material."

"What the heck does that even mean?" Jemma scoffs. "Hardly Gala material? If he has a pulse, he's Gala material."

"One date?" Ariel drops her pen on the table. "Why did you feel that wasn't worth mentioning? Why haven't we at least heard about this guy before?"

"I don't want to jinx it?"

"Are you asking us or telling us?" Catherine's eagle eyes are unnerving, and I look away.

"Are you bringing him to the Gala?"

I take another bite of apple and respond with a mouthful. "I don't know yet. He might have... a... game?"

"Game?" Jemma's eyes get wide and excited. "Ooh, what is he, an athlete? Which sport?"

Great question, Jemma. I'll let you know when I figure it out myself. Everyone leans in closer for my answer, and I resist the urge to roll my eyes.

"He, uh... He's..." *Honestly, people. Why do you care so much?* Of course, I don't actually say this out loud.

"Oh, come on, Greyson. Don't get all secretive on us. It's not like we're going to stalk him on social media."

A few of them exchange telling, stealthy glances. What a bunch of freaking liars. The first thing they'll do when they leave this meeting is look for him on Facebook. Twitter. Bumble app... wherever— my point is, they would absolutely social media stalk him. I mean, if he existed.

I lie again.

"Fine. His name is..." I look around the room, my hazel eyes scanning the room, the food posters and the advertising signs adorning the walls. One for fresh, cold Farm

Fresh California Milk jumps out at me. California. For some reason, it sticks out at me.

California. Cal.

"His name is uh, Cal, um… Cal."

"Cal?"

"That's right," I lie. "Yup. Cal."

"Cal? Cal what? What's his last name?"

Jesus, Rachel. Let it go!

I look at her dumbly. Crap. "His last name?" "Grey, you're being really weird about this."

Again, my eyes scan the dining hall, landing on a girl who just happens to be in my economics class— and I just happened to have borrowed notes from her. Brianna Thompson.

Thompson it is.

"Sorry, I just zoned out for a second. His last name is, um, Thompson?"

"Asking or telling?"

"Telling." I give my head a firm nod. "Yup. Thompson. His last name is Thompson."

Cal Thompson. I roll the name around in my mind, deciding that I like it. Sounds believable.

Legit.

The lie works, because eventually they leave me alone and we go back to our meeting agenda, finish our committee work, and finish our lunch.

An apprehensive knot forms in the pit of my stomach as I swallow the last bite of my spinach chicken wrap.

Little do I know, the lies that so easily rolled off my tongue today will soon become entirely too real.

Find Sara Online

Facebook: https://www.facebook.com/saraneyauthor/
Reader Group: https://www.facebook.com/
groups/1065756456778840/
Twitter: @SaraNey
IG: saraneyauthor
Email: saraneyauthor@yahoo.com

Other Books by Sara Ney

Kiss and Make Up:
Kissing in Cars
He Kissed me first
A kiss like this
One Last Kiss (Early 2018)

Three Little Lies
Things Liars Say
Things Liars Hide
Things Liars Fake

How to Date a Douchebag:
The Studying Hours
The Failing Hours
The Learning Hours (Fall 2017)

With Author M.E.Carter:
FriendTrip
WeddedBliss
Kissmas Eve